KV-039-374

# The Exiled

## a sequel to
## The Croppy Boy

## Declan G. Quaile

Copyright © 2021, Declan G. Quaile
All rights reserved. No part of this publication may be reproduced, stored in a
retrieval system, transmitted in any form, or by any means, electronic,
mechanical, photocopying, recording or otherwise, without the prior
permission of the copyright holder.

ISBN: 978-1-913275-37-2


This book was published in cooperation with
Choice Publishing, Drogheda, Co. Louth,
Republic of Ireland.
www.choicepublishing.ie

**Dedication:**

This book is dedicated to those, gone before, who inspired me with their words of a long ago time and place.

*Cover illustration by Anthony Corrigan (dbdlouth@gmail.com)*

While some of the incidents and characters in The Exiled are based on historical figures and events, the novel is entirely a work of fiction.

# Late Summer 1798

*"I understand you are inclined to hold the Insurrection cheap. Rely upon it; there never was in any country so formidable an effort on the part of the people."* Lord Castlereagh (Chief Secretary for Ireland) in a letter to his predecessor Thomas Pelham; written after the rebellion.

# Chapter One
## Slane

The rebels knew they were soon for the gallows! The young lieutenant could see the resignation in their eyes, as they were led brusquely from the village courthouse. A small but expectant crowd had gathered outside and they began to jeer and heckle them as they were led off in single file, tied together by lengths of rope. Whatever faint hope they might have had of receiving the lighter sentence of transportation, had been swiftly extinguished by the judge's pronouncement of the sentence of death by hanging.

The lieutenant and his troop had waited patiently outside in the square to receive the convicts. Alongside the yeomanry unit, a squad of militiamen surrounded the batch of doomed men. On the lieutenant's command the escort led them down through the village, on their way to the place selected for their execution. They stretched out in a ragged line, out the road from Slane to Navan, with the road to Kells before them, veering off on their right. Beside the lieutenant was another officer; both men leading the troops who were securing the column of shuffling men towards their place of sentence.

In the early afternoon, Slane and its hinterland were quiet. Some villagers, hearing of the court-martial and its aftermath, had gathered on the outskirts to watch as the condemned men passed by. Most remained silent through the proceedings, some secretly feeling pity but knowing there was nothing that could be done for them. A few among those present tossed spittle at the condemned; others harangued and cursed them for daring to bring rebellion and death to this now quelled part of Meath. One of the officers, Lieutenant Barton, noting the lack of pace from those walking, turned to the cavalryman behind

1

him.

'Is there a way we can get these men to move at a faster pace? It is enough that they are been jeered at by their own countrymen, never mind that their final destination is drawing near. We need to get this dealt with expediently.'

The corporal acknowledged the request and in turn, ordered the guards to infuse a little more pace into the proceedings. Despite the warmth of the day, the other lieutenant, Thomas Gettings, felt a certain foreboding inside him, on what was his first assignment in discharging the execution of convicted rebels.

Withdrawing his sabre from its scabbard, he waved the villagers away, not wanting them to interrupt or impede their progress, difficult enough as it was. Glancing behind him to establish if the tempo had increased, he noted the prisoners' heads were down, almost on their chests, each man following the bare feet of the one tethered by rope in front of him. Their worn, defeated faces anticipated their imminent fate.

The increase in pace was kept up by the guards, forcing the convicted men to shuffle along on their toes in an ungainly manner. Gettings had heard that they had not been given any food for a few days and by the look of them it was evident that hunger was gnawing insistently at their empty bellies.

'No point in wasting good food on dead men,' Gustavus Barton advised rather too cheerfully. Gettings gleaned little amusement from his jocular tone and didn't reply. At the Kells Road junction, Barton, with a section of guards, peeled away with half a dozen rebels separated out and prodded to follow them.

'As per our orders,' he shouted back to Gettings, 'I'm off to Tankardstown Hill to dispatch this lot. Let's make an example of them, eh? We will discuss the value of this exercise later, on our return to Slane.'

He saluted Gettings briskly and cantered off in front of his section towards their destination. Gettings, in charge of the remaining rebels, watched the group disappear out the Kells Road, his heart sinking at the Lieutenant Barton's callous and dismissive utterings.

How he could be so glib about eliminating lives, he could not fathom. Yet soon, he too would have to carry out similar instructions.

*

With Barton's group headeding north, Gettings made steady progress out the Navan Road, away from the village. They passed the walled demesne and turreted castle gates of Baron Conyngham's on their left with the afternoon sun beating down relentlessly on them from high above, with little cloud cover to offer shelter. The lieutenant spurred his horse on and he heard the rattle of flintlocks and boots of his rear-guard trying to keep up, their military tattoo jarring in the quietness of the pastoral surroundings.

Ahead of them, their destination, Carrickdexter Hill, loomed ominously large. Further along the road, to his right, he saw the gap in the hedge made for them and swung his horse through. He, his troop and their six prisoners, began the slow climb up the grassy slope of Carrickdexter. He could see some men above him on the hill, maybe a third of the way up, busily finishing the erection of a stout wooden construction on top of timber supports. Hemp ropes had been uncoiled and made ready to throw across the hanging beam. The chill of what he was about to enact surfaced in him again and he flinched uncomfortably at the onerous task put upon him. Up ahead, the gallows, which the court-martial had commanded be erected that very morning, was ready and waiting for him to carry out its instructions.

Reaching the execution site, he pulled his horse up and waited patiently for the prisoners and escort to catch up. Gettings acknowledged the workmen, who had gathered their tools and were departing quickly away from the site. The prisoners drew near and, witnessing the preparations, knew their fate was now sealed and that this was where their end would be. Gettings ordered his men to draw the convicted rebels out in a line, facing the gallows. Then, drawing a deep breath, he withdrew a prepared scroll from his inner pocket and began to read out their sentences presented by the magistrates at Slane.

'On this day,' he called out, hoping his voice wouldn't show his discomfort, 'the 18th of July, in the 38th year of the reign of His Majesty, King George III, a general court-martial, held in Slane village under General Meyrick, determined that you, standing before me, were found guilty of waging war against the King and his peaceable subjects in the counties of Kildare and Meath. It is the court's solemn verdict that you be taken from the court of trial and be put to death in a nearby place of execution, as a warning to those inhabitants and passers-by of the consequences of treason.'

He paused then added his own addendum.

'Likewise, Lieutenant Barton has, this very day, has escorted six rebels up to Tankardstown Hill, where they will also be dealt with under the judgement of the court.'

He moved his horse closer to the men, all of whom looked at the ground, not willing to glance at the instrument of death before them. Gettings regarded them with no little amount of pity but was frustrated that their misguided activities were leading to their demise on this otherwise pleasant hill. Undoubtedly, they understood little if any of his words he was obliged to read out to them. In truth, the only thing they would really understand, he acknowledged unhappily, was the tightening of a noose around their necks.

He motioned to the guards to bring forward the first batch of three men. One of his men approached him and asked, 'Are these men for drawing and quartering also, sir? I see no implements to carry it out.' Gettings shook his head severely.

'There will be no disembowelling of these men, only hanging' he answered quietly, secretly relieved that strangulation was the only penalty to be meted out this day.

They picked out three men at random and promptly forced them up onto the makeshift wooden platform, a couple of planks balanced on top of two cut pieces of tree trunks. Overhead, a roughly-hewn branch lay on two end supports, with just enough length to accommodate three ropes thrown across. The workmen assured him that the timber would take their combined weights and that there should be no mishaps.

4

Gettings watched the proceedings unfold with a muted sense of dread. And if he was feeling that deep-seated aversion to his orders, how must the convicted men be feeling? He was quite taken by their quiet stoicism, in what would be their final moments. None of them cried out. None of them begged for any leniency. They knew they had participated in rebellious deeds, he reasoned, and thus they understood the consequences of defying the authority of the King.

Although these were not the first executions he had participated in since the recent rebellious events in Meath, they were, he found, becoming increasingly uncomfortable and unpleasant to stomach. He had led a section of the yeomanry forces who had routed the rebels army over in a bog outside Wilkinstown and, in the days following that engagement, he had been placed on patrol out in the surrounding countryside, supporting Captain Rothwell's Kells Yeomanry and Speaker Foster's units from Collon, in their hunt for any Wexford remnants who had attempted to hide in the countryside between Kells and Slane. There had indeed been much distasteful scenes of insurgent killings when, following the battle, they had tried to conceal themselves in cornfields, ditches and woodland in the area. Once discovered or apprehended, the yeos orders were to dispatch them without mercy and discard their bodies where they fell, strewn like bundles of rags in the fields and roadsides, effigies of men in ignominious defeat.

It was with much reluctance and no pleasure, that Thomas Gettings partook in the gruesome task of hunting these wretches, yet, he was inclined to leave it to his more enthusiastic subordinates to complete the final coup de grace, unable to bring himself to put men away in such an arbitrary and callous manner. And each evening, on his return to his quarters in Slane, weary and somewhat dispirited, he would sit and read some relevant sections of the Bible, trying to rationalise his actions; that the ones he was taking were the correct ones. And in the mornings, when he awoke, knowing another day of bloodletting would soon be at hand, a sudden, strange urge would well up in him, a desire to be away from this vengeful work, perhaps curiously, even to resign from his position altogether and to seek out more peaceful pursuits.

He pulled back from these daydreams and forced himself to concentrate on the grim task at hand. Only yesterday, following a week of wanton bloodletting, the local magistrates had eventually insisted that judicial examples be made of some of the rebels and from then on, rather than summarily killed, they were to be apprehended, and offered up for court-martial. Thus, those captured in the intervening period around Slane and Collon had not been dispatched out of hand but had been temporarily incarcerated, awaiting trial. To Thomas Gettings, it gave a certain degree of propriety to the ghastly business and meant that these young men would get a trial at least, and that his heart could rest a little easier, for the time being.

*

His men stood up on the bench and placed nooses around the necks of the batch of three men. Then pulling and tightening the ends around the branch, they forced the men into lifting their heads. The rope ends were knotted securely and, with little enthusiasm, Gettings ordered one of his officers on horseback to proceed with the task of execution. The ropes were pulled hard around their necks, jacking their heads up further and forcing them to balance precariously on their toes. One of the men, shorter than the others, was already off balance and swinging from the rope, struggling for his life.

The lieutenant averted his gaze from their despairing death-throes; his thoughts drifting again to their rash rebellious actions that brought them to this unpleasant juncture. Was life so intolerable for them that their only recourse was to rise against the King? He found it hard to countenance such scheming. Then, from nowhere, a notion came to him. What if he were to talk to some of them and discover *their* thoughts; and find out why these unremarkable men, most just simple labourers and tillers of the soil, would come from the faraway county of Wexford and end up fighting against vastly superior government forces in a bog in north Meath? It was inconceivable that they were ever going to triumph; surely they would have known that. He had heard that their home county was all but destroyed and many of their comrades lay dead in fields and ditches across Leinster.

He shook his head gloomily at this folly of his. It must be a form of induced mania that these men possessed and mainly instigated, he had heard, by various Papist clergy and a few disillusioned Protestant gentlemen, who had enticed them to march through several counties to their inevitable deaths. Ultimately he felt more than a pang of sympathy for them, in spite the punishment he had been required to mete out.

One of his men, standing at the side of the wooden bench, was waiting patiently for instructions, but Gettings' eyes were suddenly diverted to a figure on horseback, galloping rapidly up the hill from the road. The condemned men on the scaffold were oblivious to the new arrival but the other three standing, waiting their turn, raised their eyes expectantly at the approaching sound of the horseman. Gettings became agitated. Was this some last minute offer of reprieve coming from General Meyrick, he wondered, or even some correspondence from Speaker Foster of Collon, perhaps granting the convicted men the reduced penalty of transportation to Van Diemens Land, where a lucky few at court this morning had been sentenced to?

Nonplussed at arriving at such an inopportune time, the messenger stalled uncomfortably on his horse, until he was ushered over by the lieutenant.

'Could this not have waited until later, officer?' Gettings suggested brusquely. 'As you can see, we are performing a rather irksome task here?'

The messenger reported timidly, 'I was ordered to present this note to all yeomanry officers as soon as possible, sir and the sight of it verbally acknowledged before I report back.'

Gettings reluctantly ordered him forward with the missive. Waiting their turn on the ground, the convicted men glanced at each other with anticipation, the faintest of hopes flickering in their eyes.

However those on the frame were still struggling forlornly, oblivious to the conversation being conducted beneath them. The lieutenant took cognisance of the letter directed from the rider. It concerned an urgent meeting to be held at Speaker Foster's house in Collon on the following Friday evening. All officers from the various yeomanry corps in north Meath and south Louth were being instructed to attend. But, such an inappropriate time to have been presented with the note! Gettings, noting the contents, advised the rider he had read the script and returned it, dismissing him. The messenger wheeled away back down the hill before the lieutenant turned and ordered his officer at the platform to proceed with the three men. With a quick salute the militiaman immediately pulled away the timber that the men were balanced on. Two men dropped into air, joining the shorter one, whose life was already over.

Inevitably, the lives of those on the frame ebbed away in convulsions of pitiable preservation, until finally their exertions yielded, leaving a line of gently swaying corpses in the breeze. The three rebels beneath the structure, knowing they were next, stood mesmerised and horrified, yet unable to avert their eyes. One of them, who appeared younger than the others, whimpered quietly as he lost control and soiled his pants. But his comrades neither noticed nor cared; they were too immersed in their own final torment.

The yeos waited until life had ceased on the scaffold, before loosening the ropes, lifting the bodies off the frame and dropping them onto the ground, ragged and lifeless. Gettings nodded to the officer, who proceeded to force the remaining three up onto the replaced plank. Averting his eyes, he was anxious to get this finished with, to be on his way to other business. He had arranged to meet with his fiancée, Emma, that very evening, if he could rise above the day's events. Reaching into his breast pocket he withdrew a small locket she had given him as a token of their betrothal. Silver and hinged, the soft edges were comforting and familiar. He hoped to be married within the year. Her father was a coastguard on the River Boyne and he was trying to put a word in for him, for when the next surveyor's position arose, if and when he resigned his position as yeomanry officer. He must speak to him again about that.

8

But now was not the time to think of such things. He replaced the locket and looked at the dismal scene before him. Again the nooses around the men's necks were being placed and pulled tight, stretching their heads to the heavens. On his instruction the standing plank was again kicked away, leaving the three remaining croppies turning and twisting in their dance of death. The grisly task was soon complete and leaving the six bodies, the lieutenant raised his arm to order his men away from the place, leaving a small squad of four to preserve the area temporarily, in case the locals tried to cut down the bodies, as some were accustomed to do.

His orders, to carry out the executions and establish that the bodies remained visible to all those who travelled on the Slane to Navan road, were now completed. Yet, he couldn't quite rid himself of a fundamental feeling of wrongdoing and a form of guilt now coursed through his brain. It had been a horrendous week of hunting and retribution, all told; as if the yeos had been chasing and eliminating a pack of dogs - not fellow humans! He knew what they had been ordered to accomplish was an unsavoury evil, yet if there was another way to deal with the seditious nature of these young rebels, he could not think of it.

But one thing stood abundantly clear; he knew now that this way of life was not his calling; most assuredly, it was not. He determined that he would ride over to Queensborough the very next day and gain some much needed convalescence with Emma, even perhaps reveal his reluctance to participate in his military life. It was a decision that he had finally decided on, irrespective of the consequences.

# Chapter Two
## Lobinstown

From deep within himself he knew that his mother was no longer alive. In the depths of the fever and pain of his injury, Laurence Moore heard his father talk about it, as if from a great distance. But despite his discomfort and the knowledge of her death seeping through him, he had eventually risen from his sick bed, with the only meaningful thought in his mind of going to visit her grave and that of his younger siblings in nearby Killary graveyard.

Along with young William Geraghty, who was laid up with yeo-inflicted injuries, Laurence had occupied the same corner of a room with him for a number of days. His arm was bandaged and bound from the injury he received and his lungs felt constricted from inhaling smoke after their cottage was torched by the yeos last week, but his wounds were not as severe as William's, who was still drifting in and out of consciousness in a straw cot at the rear of the room. Laurence's false well-being lasted only briefly as he just made it to a stool with sweat flowing from him. His father, in from helping George, disapproved of his newly found mobility, but Laurence insisted on going to the graveyard by himself, something his father disapproved of.

'Look at the cut of ye, gossoon,' Henry said. 'You're in no fit state to be travelling the roads,' He eyed Laurence's bindings and his pale face. 'And what about the cut of your hair? You still have the look of a croppy about you. If you are going out, put a hat on your head. Do you want the redcoats to come after us again?'

Laurence, his mind still grappling with reality, would not hear tell of remaining indoors. 'They're lying in their graves father and I have yet to be near them. I must be over there now and pay my respects.'

Henry shook his head, knowing that he couldn't keep Laurence from going.

'And how often have *you* called to their graves, father?'

'Didn't I help dig the holes for them, me and George here, and also my cousin John? And we scraped out two more pits for them young croppies behind George's shed the week before, after the yeos were finished with them. If you were in fine fettle, you wouldn't be throwing insults like that at me. And put a hat on ye, for God's sake, will ye and don't be going off to fight with any more rebels. Do you hear me now?'

Laurence, floundering about in frustration, grabbed a stick and his father's hat from behind the door and left the cabin. Hobbling away down the lane, with his head reeling, he made tentative progress at first, stopping periodically to draw breath and listen out for any militia or yeos about the place. He walked slowly up the path to Lobinstown and turned west, out towards the graveyard. Emotions flowed through him at the scene that awaited him as walked up the gentle hill to the entrance gate.

A stone wall draped the edges of the burial ground, enclosing a scattering of small marker stones where families had loved ones buried, and would be cognisant of their own burial stone. Around the ruined church walls, more ornate stones belonging to the middlemen and big farmers of the parish dotted the consecrated ground. Close to the broken remnant of an ancient high-cross he saw the mound of freshly heaped soil above the ground. He drew near, hardly daring to breathe. Bar his solitary presence the cemetery was empty and forlorn. Some crows and jackdaws cawed away in a nearby yew tree, perhaps building nests; otherwise silence enveloped the place, an eerie silence. His father had told him that the bodies of some croppies, killed in the recent fighting, had been secretly buried in the graveyard and over in a corner he observed more fresh mounds of earth.

Almost reluctantly, his gaze returned to the family plot, the one he had come to visit. He knelt down cautiously beside it, using his stick for leverage, favouring his wounded side. Placing some loose earth back on top of the heap, he looked blankly at the small heap of brown earth. His mind was void and as he stared dumbly at the site, he was unable to comprehend the gravity of who lay in the covered pit. Nothing came to him, no thoughts, no memories …. nothing! It was as if he was waiting for some kind of divine intervention to aid him in his grief. But nothing came. The earth remained just that and not a place of mourning.

After a while he stood up and cautiously walked around the enclosed graveyard, looking vacantly at other recent burials, before coming to the mass graves of the buried croppies in the corner. Standing there he wondered was the body of his friend Pat Sheils amongst those in the large grave? He stood awhile and his mind began to hark back a number of weeks before, when he and his cousin James had hidden Pat Sheils, who had been returning from the battle at Tara in late May. While recuperating, Pat had told them of the United Irishmen and their fight against the Crown and the reasons why he had joined their cause. A few days later a yeo search party had arrived at the house and, only for Pat had been aware of their approach and made his escape through a shed window and across a nearby field, he would have been killed there and then. But alas, his destiny was to be cruelly denied as he was later apprehended by a yeo patrol south of Killary and after being tortured was swiftly executed.

Laurence looked at the hastily dug croppies grave again. His father and George Geraghty had said many more of these unfortunates had been buried where they died; at the edge of fields and hedges around the countryside. Indeed hadn't he lately helped with the burial of two such croppies at the back of George's haggard, as his father had only just reminded him? Thinking back now, he realised Pat's escape from the shed was so reminiscent of his own recent near brush with death. And, superstitiously, he wondered, did that mean that his time was nearly up too and would soon be joining them in this burial ground or some field about the place?

He wandered back to his mother's grave and stood at it silently, beginning to think wistfully of her now, a vision of her finally welling up inside him. His last impression of her was in their kitchen one morning, only a few days after his cousin James, had returned him home, injured, from Mountainstown. Groggy and only partially healed, he had woken to the distraught sounds of his younger brother Jack screaming at him to get up, that redcoat cavalry were coming for them. Moments later shots were fired and shouting emanated from the yard. Rising up on his knees he saw fire in the thatch above taking hold. His mother stood beneath, her face resolute, shielding his two young brothers, as clumps of burning straw began to fall into the kitchen. He knew his father was out in the fields and his sister Kate was away fetching water, both of them a good distance from the house; they were safe but could not help them.

The yeos had quickly set the cottage alight as they yelled aloud, shouting for him to come out, that they knew he was in there. They had come after him as his cousin James had forewarned. But Jack had grabbed Laurence and hefting him up from his straw, forcibly shoved him out through the dairy window at the back of the cabin. Then Jack, poor hot-headed Jack, went back into the developing inferno to help the others. Laurence had staggered away from the house and threw himself into a nearby pond and covered himself in clumps of mud and reeds, weeping quietly at the destruction taking place around him, all because of what he and James, had done.

His memories flooding over him, he knelt down at the family grave again, his feelings finally overflowed on his mother's demise and of Jack's final heroic actions in saving his life but losing his own. And the two younger ones, either side of ten winters old, taken from them too, now gone before their time. Unexpectedly, tears came to Laurence and, though he wiped his eyes repeatedly, the tragic loss finally registered and he, at last, wept openly for them all.

Only much later, did he gather himself together and, almost ashamed at having let his emotions run away from him, he skulked away from the graveyard and returned to his temporary residence. But, through the midst of his grief and the aches in his body, he had come to something of a revelation in himself. It was akin to a hardening of the heart around the actions that had been perpetrated on them and a

13

resolution had formed that, with all the recent deaths, he made a vow to do whatever he could to avenge those taken from him. And as he finally drew close to Geraghys and saw George repairing his thatch with Henry assisting, a recollection came to him of a promise that was made as he lay injured in front of his house, when James had returned him to Killary a week ago. In a defiant gesture of his new found determination, he pulled the cloth bandage away from his shoulder and, though his arm still throbbed with the injury, threw it into the ditch.

*

After his son had departed for the cemetery, Henry Moore shuffled out through George Geraghty's cabin door and into the morning sun. Shielding his face from the low rays, he looked around the yard, his eyes still raw from several days of mourning. Seeing George sitting by the gable end, he walked round the dunghill and sat down beside him on a bockety stool. Following a night of rain, a blanket of mist, which had enveloped the fields around, was evaporating rapidly, with the rising sun drying out the earth. Henry's terrier came running from the side of the cottage and sat beside him, waiting for a crust.

Remaining silent, Henry and George gazed at the tranquil surroundings; the little sound there was, came from feeding birds and nearby animals in the fields. It was as quiet and peaceful a morning as most days in Killary, despite all the recent troubles!

Henry lifted his head and scanned the sky. He noticed a leaden bank of clouds moving gradually towards them from the west and what looked like a repeat of the previous day's weather; a bright warm morning followed by an overcast and wet afternoon. He was minded to repeat the words he had said to George over the past couple of days, as if it were part of their morning salutations.

'It will be hard indeed to get the grain harvested, with all this rain,' he mused to his neighbour. George followed his gaze and he too noticed the rain-bearing clouds approach. His heart sank, not for the first time.

'Ah sure 'tis not weather at all, Henry,' he repeated, 'and after the fine weeks of May and June we were blessed with.'

George had his eyes cast on nearby pastures and pointed with a crooked finger to one of his neighbours.

'I see Patsy Dillon is out early. See him beyond at the headland, trying to make hay out of rushes and bulterrins.'

'More the fool he!' said Henry easily. 'He should have cut when the sun was out. It will hardly be tossed and lapped before the rain lands on him.'

Henry considered the ongoing repairs on George's thatched roof. They had gathered a few bundles of surplus straw from the barn and had made a start on the job yesterday but had to stop on account of the wet evening that came in. Henry nodded to George, eyeing the bare hazel scollops. George grunted. 'It'll wait for a turn. There's still some more dampness needed in the straw.'

He left his stool and disappeared into his house, returning a short time later with his clay pipe kindled with a cinder from the fire. Sitting down he fitted it to his lips and began his morning ritual of lighting up and drawing the first tobacco of the day. Henry had made himself busy by whittling away at a newly cut blackthorn stick with his pocket-knife. Though gnarled with age, his fingers were active to the task, holding the stick with a claw-like left hand while paring the knotty wood with his right. When sculpted he would give it to Laurence to replace the crooked one he had. It helped keep his mind occupied, warding off thoughts, even temporarily, of the recent events that overtook his family.

''Tis good neighbours to have in days like these,' Henry said, eyeing critically a slight curvature in the stick.

'At times like this, 'tis all we have,' acknowledged George and added, 'Aye, and some neighbours are a lot better than others. Didn't I see neighbour Pat Brennan's young lad Bryan away off with his redcoat friends yesterday morning. A troop of them passed by here at cockcrow; all away somewhere on their fancy horses, looking for trouble, no doubt. So you and Laurence should stay out of sight for the time being.

15

He has death on his hands, that lad.'

There was silence as Henry inspected his handiwork and declared himself happy with it. He leaned on the stick, testing its strength. Then Ellen and the children's deaths sprung in his mind again.

'Tá gach rud caillte againn, George,' he said, spitting out some tobacco beyond his brogues. 'We're bet indeed. And they'll keep our noses in the ground until we're fit to get up no more.'

'Buíchos le Dia gur seanfhir muid,' added George. 'Too old we are to have to make a decision but 'tis dreadful for our young ones and their future.'

'If only Laurence and James hadn't stood up to the authorities,' Henry continued ruefully, 'I'd still have my family now. My eldest son Laurence and my brother's son James, it was their youthful bravado that has us where we are today. Ellen's been taken, and Jack and the young ones. They're gone and nothing will bring them back.'

His words caught in his throat, thoughts of the recent attack by the yeomanry on his house, its burning and the deaths of most of his family, seared like a hot iron into his memory.

'Aye, and our William still poorly from his wounds,' added George, 'and at every crossroads around Rathkenny and Wilkinstown, and as far as Slane and Ardee, they have strung up Wexfordmen and anyone else found helping them. I fear that Speaker Foster of Collon and the magistrates around the area will not stop until there is none of the young ones left to help save the harvest.'

They both nodded miserably as they contemplated their personal losses in the recent reprisals; at the sheer waste of the young men and above all, at the wanton savagery of the authorities on those perceived to have offered opposition to them. From the silence, George began a lament, one hand to his ear as he softly carried the words of loss and betrayal before him. Henry knew the ballad too. It was generations old. He caught some of the words but could not carry it like George. He reckoned they wouldn't have to wait long before there would be songs aplenty about the current trouble.

With George concluding the final verse, Henry heard footsteps coming from the house and turned to see his daughter Kate rushing towards him, tears in her eyes. 'What is it, a stór? What's happened to you?'

She hugged him tightly. 'I just can't believe their gone, father... forever. What is to become of us? I have no mother and no home.'

George turned away to offer them some privacy as Henry tried to console her.

'Tá mo chroí briste freisin, Kate. But, I'm still with you and our neighbours are good to us. Hasn't George and his wife, with their own loss, been good enough to put us up these last few days?'

She nodded but continued to sob against his shoulder. The, wiping her eyes she turned silently away and retreated back into the cabin. His eyes misted at her distress but he held his own sorrow tight to his heart, not wanting her to see his emotions in play and there was still so much grieving to do.

When the two men had finished their early morning rites they drew the old patched-up wooden ladder round to the front of the house and began final repairs to the thatch roof on the cabin. George mounted the steps while Henry passed up forkfuls of dampened straw that had been saved from last year's harvest. The two worked away on the task, quietly and efficiently, years of roofing repairs and restoration of their respective homes, coming easily to their experienced hands.

Inside, Kate helped George's wife, Elizabeth, with the household chores and child-minding. Elizabeth did her best to keep her from being idle but Kate, briefly bereft of tears, cared little for being busy. She also could not do what Laurence had done that morning, and visit the family grave. She had attended the funeral mass and burial and had accepted the solace of the priest, Fr Connell, the parishioners and her father and Laurence, but her happy, contented life was now all asunder and nothing could knit it together again.

Carrying a pot of dirty water out to throw it into the channel in the yard, she saw Laurence return from the graveyard. He was still using a stick for a crutch but there was a forceful gait to his stride and a determined look in his eye. He didn't disturb the men on the roof but came near his sister and they both entered the house together.

'Where is the bandage for your arm?' she asked him.

'I'm done with bandages and lying up.' He stood, uncomfortable in the porch, holding his arm. 'I am feeling there's business to attend to.'

She eyed him quizzically, a look of concern on her face, her hands outstretched. She leaned close and whispered.

'What more can you do, Laurence? She shook her head, exasperated with the recklessness of it all. 'You did more than enough and are blessed to be alive.'

'And you sound like my poor dead mother when she used to berate me.' Immediately, tears welled up in Kate's eyes and she turned away from her brother.

'Please don't say that, Laurence. She's gone and I can't be her, though father expects me to be. What are we to do?'

He pulled her back towards him, looking into her tearful eyes.

'The Geraghty's have been good to us, he said, 'and have taken us in, despite suffering their own misfortune. But father expects we will go and stay with his cousin John Moore, who lives the other side of Killary. He says he call to him shortly.'

Kate looked up at him. 'But you have something else on your mind,' she said. 'I can see it in your eyes.'

He regarded her steadily. His sister knew him well, but he was afraid to divulge his innermost feelings, ones which harboured dark notions of making amends and retribution. He gripped her shoulders.

'Hear this, Kate. There is much work to be done after these events, some of it with father. But on our mother's grave and on our brothers' graves, I will not rest until I bring some justice back to this family. Because we spared a man from been hung outside Collon and had killing to do to save him, the authorities have deemed our families lives forfeit. They have killed Uncle Barney and his family at Smarmore and ours here at Killary and destroyed our houses. And our cousin James, despite him bringing me home from the battle, is probably now dead along with the other rebels, after he left here. So I am the only one they now seek. I am the one the yeos want and they will keep looking for me, keep burning people out of house and home until they capture me or kill me. But I will not go down without a fight, Kate, I will not. I have nothing left to lose anymore. They have murdered us and scattered our families, but they havn't put me away. I will bide my time, take my chances and see where it leads.'

He stopped suddenly, aware of the look of concern in her eyes. He let her arms go, emotion still flooding his face. Kate was struck silent by his outburst, not knowing what to say, hardly comprehending it. Behind them, Mrs Geraghty entered the room and made herself busy cleaning around the open hearth. Wondering had she heard his belligerent words, Laurence hurriedly turned away from the two women, grabbed his stick and limped out of the house to see could he help the men with the thatching.

# Chapter Three
## Glenmalure

A low stone wall shielded James Moore from the worst of the driving rain. Yet he and the others in the hunting party were already soaked through, as they crouched, shivering in the evening gloom. The enemy patrol marched below them, on the main path through the valley, slowly, methodically, their heads swivelling left and right, watching for movement, any movement in the surrounding foothills.

The foraging party had spotted the redcoat column coming up the valley shortly after they captured the sheep; their first meat in days for the camp. Before they had a chance to butcher it they had sought temporary refuge behind a low stone wall. Lying in the wet heather, Daniel Hoare, their leader, glared at his men to not make a sound, while he himself struggled to control the frantic movements of the captured sheep.

They had spent the afternoon on the trail of the sheep. The animal had been spotted in the heights above Carrawaystick waterfall the previous evening by some of Michael Dwyer's men. There had been no meat eaten by the men for some days now and the camp deemed it essential that a raiding party go into the hills, to find and seize the animal, possibly the last of its kind not captured and eaten by the rebels hiding out in the mountains. Five of them had left the other side of the valley earlier in the day. There was little food to be had anywhere in Glenmalure and with the redcoats constantly scouting along the mountain tracks it was becoming increasingly difficult to hunt across the hills without encountering some military presence.

Some hours into their endeavour, one of the men had pointed to movement further up hill. As they climbed through the rocks and scree either side of the waterfall, James stopped momentarily to look at the powerful rush of water through the stones and channels it had formed over aeons as it cascaded down the hill. He was awestruck by the natural phenomenon before him and of the sheer wilderness all around him, compared to the gentle hills around his home in the county of Louth. The men with him had said that the falls had nearly dried up during the dry days of early summer but with the recent rains it now sluiced down the mountain, immersing them in spray as they passed on its windward side. Despite their already bedraggled condition the additional spray on them just added to the overall miserable conditions.

'Use your eyes, An fear Lú, watch where your prey is going or you'll be wanting for supper this evening.' The group leader, Daniel Hoare, pointed over to the left.

'Look, see where she goes, through those rocks.'

Though his eye still smarted occasionally from his recent encounter with a redcoat cavalryman, James followed the direction of the animal. He was almost used to being called 'An fear Lú' now, the only man from Louth in the ranks of the Wicklow and Wexford men hiding out in the mountains. As the particular animal continued to elude them James was beginning to think it was a wild goat they were chasing rather than the docile ruminant that was a sheep. A war of attrition ensued as they endeavoured to corral the animal between various rocky outcrops. The sheep had bolted to safety on them more than once before they finally caught her through sheer perseverance.

Now the five men lay cowering behind the stone wall, a two man section of the redcoat patrol hardly a hundred paces from them. Daniel Hoare wrestled doggedly with the captured sheep. Her eyes were wild with fear and only for he had one hand clamped tightly around her muzzle, her bleating would have no doubt alerted the enemy party below. Nevertheless she continued to struggle wildly, snorting through her nostrils, kicking her four spindly legs out in all directions, with clumps of her unshorn fleece tearing off in the struggle. James was nearest Hoare who hissed at him to draw near. The other three were close by, frozen with the fear of being discovered.

'Take the knife from the pocket,' Daniel urged. James reached over. 'No, no, this pocket, here. Here!' He intimated the small satchel which hung from his waist. James drew near and extracted a short narrow scian from the bag.

'Lad, I am doing all I can to hold her,' Hoare grunted, 'but I'm telling you now, she will surely escape us with her kicking and lepping.' He struggled to secure his hand around her jaw.

'I will keep a tight grip and lift up her neck, but you must draw the knife sharply across her throat. Do you understand?'

James nodded dumbly. He looked around to see if some of the others were going to assist him, but they all lay tightly up against the shelter of the wall, oblivious to the request, rapt in their own terror. A random shout rose up from below them; it was an officer berating his men.

Yet, they were drawing ever closer.

Hoare ushered James as close as possible and with a supreme effort pulled the sheep's head up further, offering the taut skin up to him. James' hand shook as he lowered the blade to the animal's throat. Almost sensing what was about to happen, the sheep made a final lunge to escape. But Hoare held on grimly, silently begging James to do the deed.

With his eyes wet and hands slippery in the rain, he placed the scian to the side of the animal's throat and with Hoare's frantic nod he drew it decisively across her neck. At first nothing happened and James raised the blade to repeat the process, then the taut neck skin separated and bright red blood seeped and then spurted from the wound. James' hands were soon covered in a red torrent and, as it mixed with the rain, the liquid ran in a bright pinkish flow down his britches and onto the wet ground. Hoare held on to the dying animal, his fingers still clasping her mouth, her final movements becoming feeble, until she finally came to settle in his arms.

James could not watch her final death throes. He laid the knife on the ground and leaned over to spew hot bile into the heather. The others watched silently as the sheep bled out in Hoare's arms, its final spasms fading. Below them, the enemy patrol had drawn close to the wall. No one moved. All were hunkered down, chill sheets of mountain rain beating on their faces. Only Hoare carried a flintlock pistol and the scian, the other men's only form of protection were blackthorn sticks. Soon, it would either be surrender or a savage fight to the death. Then a distant voice shouted from further down the hill.

'Privates Sinclair and Adams, get back down here now! You will see nothing from up there in the mist. We must be moving on.'

The rustle of uniform and boots stopped momentarily then edged gradually away from the wall. A short time later, five desperate breaths were released simultaneously.

The enemy patrol was long gone before the party eventually departed their hiding place. Skulking their way across the heath and down the valley and up the opposite side to the hidden encampment, they were immersed in cloud and incessant rain, which cloaked their movements. Two men carried the sheep's carcass. Hoare and James, as they walked, tried to wipe off some of the blood from their jackets and pants. James was stationed at the rear, checking that they were not being followed. His clothes were soaked through but only his britches held evidence of the recent slaughter and as the rain soaked through the material he scrubbed at it repeatedly.

*

An unexpectedly busy camp awaited them on their return. Something was afoot, James could tell. Captain Dwyer's lieutenants were running hither and thither, ordering the packing of bundles, loading horse bags and gathering arms together. As James and the others rested following their exertions on the hillside, word had spread that the captain was calling a meeting that evening and all his men were ordered to attend. James lay down, too tired to be enthused by the latest rumours. He still had residual aches from the retreat with the Wexfordmen and his eye socket remained tender. In the days after reaching the camp, he had been billeted with Dwyer's men and had

23

immediately joined them in reconnaissance missions and the search for food. Many of them, older and hardier than he, had unofficially adopted him as their lucky talisman; this young lad who had escaped the clutches of the enemy more than once in his short life. It was they who had begun calling him 'An fear Lú', the 'Louthman'. In particular two of Dwyer's trusted men, Dan Hoare and Dominic O'Farrell, had befriended him and give him their hospitality during the weeks he was there.

While their quarry was taken away to be carved up and augment their paltry supplies, James relaxed under a temporary canopy with a few other men but despite being exhausted and hungry his mind couldn't settle. Only when he was busy up in the hills or completing duties in the camp did his mind wander from his worries. He had been like this for the fortnight he was there. He wondered vaguely how long he could be of use up in these deserted unwelcome hills. He and some of Dwyer's men had taken turns sleeping in a rudimentary cavern just above the main camp or, if it was dry, he lay out under the stars about the campsite. Even though water was plentiful, food rations were scant and their days consisted of hunting for animals, big or small and avoiding the regular patrols.

But in the quiet interludes he wished desperately for home, home in the county of Louth with his family; that is if any of them remained. Sometimes he tried desperately to remove them from his head, because when he dwelled upon their predicament, it brought tears to his eyes. He knew his father was gone, murdered by yeomen outside his own house at White Mountain, but just before his killing, his father, in one of his last acts, and with the cabin surrounded by cavalry, had helped secret the family out beyond the rear of the house.

After that, James had fled the scene, not knowing their subsequent fate. The following days had been a blur of flight and battles, death and chaos. He considered Timothy Whelan, the brave Wexfordman who, when the leaders had fled from Mountainstown, took control of the remnants and led them back across the Boyne and to their final engagement at Ballyboughill. In these rare moments of solitude,

24

his mind returned to, and ached for, all those he had fought with and left behind.

His time in the camp had passed rapidly. Fending of hunger and avoiding enemy patrols had seen to that. On arrival at the hideout, another of the commanders there, Miles Byrne of Wexford, had requested to see him in person. James had captivated him and his aides with his tale of the death throes of the Wexford army in Meath. He told him about the Byrnes from Monaseed, who had departed from the main column and made a break in the direction of Ardee. Even General Holt and Michael Dwyer, intrigued by his tales, had attended the briefings. They could do nothing but shake their heads at the brave futility of the march into Meath and the inevitability of their final decimation in Dublin.

Shortly after he had brought them up to date on the events in Meath, Miles Byrne's brother, Hugh, had made his way into the camp at Glenmalure along with three Finn brothers and a few other stragglers. Miles had just returned from a scouting expedition when his party spied the small group of men making their way furtively along the valley floor. Even it was damp and the cloud cover was so low that they were in a perpetual fog, Byrne had spotted his brother's unmistakeable gait and silhouette through the mist. Welcomed heartily into the camp, they celebrated by cooking some rabbit and potatoes, with a reserve of poitín coming out later. At least some more survivors had made it back.

But at night, before a fitful sleep, James still keened and quietly sung laments over the loss of his immediate family, his cousin Laurence, and recent ally, John Mathews. How many now lay dead he did not know, but he had set his mind to return to Ardee in due course and determine their fate.

*

James was shaken from his reverie by a man beside him and he rose swiftly and walked the short distance to the centre of Dwyer's camp, where he and his few dozen men had set up camp. Despite the fear of being spotted, a small communal fire was lit and his men had gathered around it. Miles Byrne and General Holt had been invited and stood beside Dwyer. Without much preamble Dwyer addressed his men.

'Men, I'll spake quick and true to ye, for we have little time to spare. Listen well now to what I have to say.' He looked around at those assembled, moving his strong gaze along them, steadfastly meeting their curious eyes.

'I have already informed General Holt, Captain Byrne and my two lieutenants of the plans I present to you now. Most of you will have already seen the hasty work been done here in the camp this last day or two. What it amounts to is, although we are here but a month, we must now cross the mountains and make for the Glen of Imaal... and we must make for it...tonight!'

Those not privy to the plan drew audible intakes of breath. Men looked at each other, fearful and on edge.

'The group that was out today,' he continued, 'those that brought back the sheep, they were fortunate to avoid a militia patrol coming through the other side of the valley. And the groups that were out in the last week, all reported many troops moving up and down the glen. Then two days ago my cousin Vesty Byrne, received credible information that the English were building up their forces, starting at the northern end of the glen, and making a full sweep of the area to the southern opening. We are in the middle ground here boys and, as I stand before ye, the enemy have already started out on their journey.'

The men were hanging on his every word and were coming to the realisation that this would be their last night at the camp. That was what all the packing had been about. Both Holt and Byrne fidgeted beside Dwyer; silently brooding and considering their own options, because the imminent disappearance of Dwyer's men would reduce their own capacity to defend the area. They also had to decide quickly how to avoid the military stranglehold that was about to be unleashed in Glenmalure.

'Like I said, we move to the west, to Imaal, this very night. Many of us have family and friends there. We will be safer there.

General Holt and Captain Byrne have decided that they and their men will remain in this area and take their chances against the enemy here. I admire them for that. But from tomorrow our fight will be at Gleann Uí Mháil. We leave within the hour.'

He turned and shook hands with Holt and Byrne then left for his tent. Throughout the camp there was silence. No one spoke. James was dumbfounded. His aim was of returning to Louth, not heading further into the fastness of Wicklow. Panic spread in him as his comrades began to move away and prepare for their departure. He stood stock still, unsure of his next move but he really only had one option, when all was said and done. He was determined that he talk to Captain Dwyer before they left, for he knew in his heart he could not go with them.

\*

Dwyer's tent was no more than a long sheet of heavy canvas thrown over two upright posts and a cross-beam, all tied down with a couple of ropes pulled tight around some nearby trees. And as James edged through the entrance he noted that Dwyer's broad shoulders were nearly the width of his temporary abode. Puddles of rain lay on the floor, pooling from trickles running down the interior. More drops came in from the apex above his head and there was a damp smell pervading the space. Dwyer was bent over, gathering his belongings together, when he heard James enter. He rose up, his head lifting close to the high point of the tent.

'Come in, An fear Lú, that's the name they've given you, isn't it?'

James nodded, not sure whether to address him unless asked to do so. One of Dwyer's men entered the tent behind James to see if he was required to help. Dwyer waved him away.

'I travel light, as you can see, lad. Whatever will go across my back, that's all that I bring. Well, what is it you want, young Moore?'

James began to talk before fully formulating his request. The words stumbled from his mouth, as if he had an ailment.

27

The captain raised a hand. 'You cannot travel with us, Louthman. Is that what you want to say?' James was flummoxed. How would he have known?

'You have worked hard with my men since you came here, lad. You have taken orders and there has been no dissent. But my men told me that the few words you uttered were of returning home; that you wanted to get back to the Boyne. Am I right?'

James nodded nervously

'I want to go home too, young Moore, as do many of my men. That is one of the reasons we depart from here tonight.'

'Yes sir. That is right sir. When I arrived here, you and your men helped me with food and shelter and with my injuries. I am indebted to you for that. But I arrived here with a shadow hanging over me. My father had been killed by the yeos some days before and the rest of my family were dispersed. I must go back and find them, captain. I must be the man of the house now. To be honest, I don't even know if they are still alive.' He paused, looking down at his bare feet. If nothing else his request had finally sounded plausible.

'So, do you know your way home from here?' Dwyer asked.

James shrugged. He hadn't had the time to think that far ahead. His journey to the mountains had been mainly by horse and he and a few others had made it the rest of the way by walking at night-time, because one of them had known the way. Dwyer knew by the lack of a response that James would be lost and would find it hard to leave the mountains, never mind return to his home. As James shook his head Dwyer considered the young lad's predicament.

'And you don't want to remain with General Holt and his men, I take it?'

'I want to try and get home, sir,' James repeated simply.

Michael Dwyer nodded and turned back to his bags. James stood still, wondering whether he had been dismissed. A moment later the captain turned to face him again.

'Well, I suppose you could go back by way of Dublin or Kildare. The commanders in Kildare, Aylmer and Fitzgerald and their forces, have surrendered but both counties are filled with yeos and militia. With some luck you might be able to scheme your way back into Meath unobserved.'

He stood quietly and considered if there were any other options.

'I'm thinking, there may be yet another way.'

He ruminated for a bit. James waited patiently, trying to avoid the raindrops coming through the canvas.

'I think I know what we can do for you, James Moore. One of my lieutenants, Dominic O'Farrell, is originally from Arklow, down on the coast. You know from the camp. He was a fisherman from that town but after the battle there in June he and some of his men came up into the mountains and joined us here in our redoubt. He will know someone who might take you back up along the coast by boat to your territory. 'Tis probably the safest way to go, if you were to take that direction.'

He went to the entrance and called out for O'Farrell, who appeared almost immediately, puffing and out of breath. Dwyer outlined his plan and the lieutenant pondered on it, gently stroking his chin before turning to face James.

'You need to leave here as soon as possible, get to Arklow and look for a fisherman there called Tyrell, Andrew Tyrell.'

'How will I know this Andrew Tyrell, sir?' James asked.

'You will have to enquire around. But, hear me now! Make for a place in the town called The Fishery, where all the fisher-folk live. He keeps a boat there. He will be known there.'

Then he remembered something and fished around in his pocket before withdrawing an object, wrapped tightly in a small piece of cloth.

'If you find him, show him this. When he sees it he will know it was me who gave it to you. You just might be able to grind a favour out of him.'

James took the package and placed it carefully in his coat pocket. O'Farrell gave him directions out of the glen and the road to Arklow before bidding him a safe journey. James thanked O'Farrell, who hastily withdrew from the tent to finish his own preparations. James turned to face Dwyer.

29

'Captain, thank you again for your help. Maybe 'tis a good idea you have. Better to travel home by boat than to chance a return journey around Dublin again.'

James reached out to shake his hand. Dwyer shook it strongly and patted him on the shoulder.

'Away with you, lad! And be sure to be off these mountains by morning before the redcoats arrive, or it will be a prison boat that you'll be sailing on.'

# Chapter Four
## Collon

'I must be on my way now, father - immediately,' Thomas urged. 'I'm already leaving late for this journey to Collon.'

Alwyn Gettings, brushed some bits of dust from his son's shoulders, muttering, 'Heir yw pob aros.'

'Away with ye and the Welsh proverbs from the old country, father! It is bad enough that I've retained the lilt and the mockery I receive for it. Anyway, not one of us understands your sayings, apart from Emma's father.'

Alwyn took the rebuff in good humour. Thomas stood in front of the hall mirror, adjusting the hair around his neck collar and with fingers full of spittle he tried to dampen down the unkempt curls of his fringe. Moderately satisfied with his efforts, he belted his scabbard to his waist and tightened the strap of his Tarleton helmet securely on his head. Being slim and of medium stature, he conformed well to his uniform, his jacket accentuating his waist, the shoulder epaulettes enhancing his shoulders. He had shaved and, though he would soon be on horseback, he had the maid press his shirt and jacket for the meeting. Alwyn lingered at the door, stoking his pipe and quietly assessing his handsome son.

'Thomas, this young lady that you're walking out with, she would be impressed with your appearance this very evening. I am sure of it!'

Thomas turned to face him, a bashful look on his face.

'Well father, perhaps I shall invite her here some evening and she can get the measure of you also!'

Alwyn dearly wished his wife was alive to see how her son had

31

grown into a fine young man and how impressive he was bedecked in such fine military attire.

He gave his uniform a final dusting before folding two sheets of paper notes into his breast pocket and was finally ready to travel to Speaker Foster's house in Collon.

'Be careful how you go son. You may have forgotten, but hardly two weeks ago, that group of rebel scoundrels, everyone is still talking about, had the audacity to ride through Slane. If only I had been ready with my firelock...'

Shaking his head at his father's belligerent words, Thomas said a final goodbye to him and left for the stables. He met his old adjutant, Felimy Quinn outside his lodgings on the hill above the bridge and from there they walked round to the outhouses where their horses had been made ready by one of the stable-hands. Mounting their steeds they proceeded at pace up through the village then further up the hill of Slane and the road leading north.

It was a glorious summer's evening, with a clear sky overhead and a languid balmy heaviness in the air that suggested harvest-time was near, ready produce its bourgeoning crop in the surrounding fields. As his horse pounded the ascent up through the village, Thomas knew his mind would soon be considering, once again, his ongoing preoccupation. As Felimy was not prone to idle conversation and was soon turning off on his own journey to Grangegeeth,

Thomas' thoughts were his own for the rest of the journey and yet again they were dominated by this innate sense of decency he possessed, which was throwing him into so much turmoil at present. He could not understand why there was such a pacifist sentiment in his nature? His yeo training included inhibiting whatever inner emotions one might have and to behave like the officer he was supposed to be; tutored to keep the peace and be prepared for any hostile intentions, whether they emanate from the local area or from an external invasion. The militia and yeomanry had been established recently in defence of just such a threat. Yet did mercy extend to men who brought rebellion to this peaceful place, men who took their American and French ideals of liberty to such a kingdom as this one, and which invariably led to war, strife and bloodshed? His conscience couldn't condone the rebel actions but the chasing down and killing of these men in the aftermath of battle, twisted heavily in his heart. Maybe it was a human reaction which all men in combat encountered, he wasn't sure. However for all that, his recent experience of marching men to their place of death at Carrickdexter, and having them strung up and pivot wildly in their dance of death, drove him to a place akin to despair. His gut told him that he was not up to that kind of task.

Riding along on the quiet evening road, he knew he did not lean towards cowardice either. In the first serious military engagement of his life, a week ago against the Wexford rebels, he had acquitted himself well enough in leading his cavalry troop in harrying and chasing the insurgent army up through Stackallen, Wilkinstown and onto the final confrontation in the bog at Mountainstown.

Reminiscing on the events of the year so far, he had spent the earlier months seconded from the Slane Yeomanry to Captain Rothwell's group at Kells, learning the art of horseback musketry, swordsmanship and military drill manoeuvrings. Yet, despite his honing as a military officer, his innate revulsion to the rebel executions on Carrickdexter Hill the other day disturbed him greatly. Granted it had been his first time in charge of such a harrowing event, but his abhorrence at what he had to undertake only bolstered his view that his instructions were nothing more than an act of callous retaliation and vengeance. There were no lessons to be learned by the rebel Irish peasant other than the authorities providing swift retribution; which would be the inevitable result of any infringement of the common laws of the kingdom.

What would his father think of his reticence in carrying out his duties? His father Alwyn and mother Ann had originally come to Ireland from north Wales to work for Baron Conyngham when Thomas was a boy. That was over twenty years ago and now his mother lay in the cemetery in Slane, dying a year or two after settling in Meath. He didn't remember her but his father, still talked of her as if she was still part of his life, and on some nights when he was a lot younger, he would hear him speak to her in the stillness of the evening, as if she were present in the room, next to him. He still lived with his father in their modest house and grounds in Slane. Of minor Welsh aristocracy, Alwyn had once been a successful merchant but had returned to north Wales following his wife's death, aged only thirty. Thomas spent a decade at school there before he and his father came back to Ireland and bought a house and land close to where they had previously lived in Slane, close to the Conyngham estate.

So, with Thomas joining the yeos as a self-financed officer, the local hierarchy, after a little pondering, had determined that his father's lineage contained just enough blue blood to warrant his inclusion into the yeomanry ranks.

Recently, Thomas was even tempted to discuss with his father, his feelings on the slaughter, but ultimately he thought better of it. Alwyn was of older basic Welsh stock with a deep-rooted sense of rectitude, of forbearance... and venerable Welsh sayings! His reticence hardly emanated from him, a God-fearing Christian, who was seldom parted from a bible in his hand and seldom espoused the New Testament tenets such as mercy and charity for his fellow man. His father's philosophy was that of the Old Testament; a fear of the Lord and justified retribution for breaking God's laws; Thomas had heard him use the 'eye for an eye' expression on more than one occasion. Vengeance of the just would be his maxim in any discussion regarding rebellion in the kingdom.

At an early age Thomas' father had taught him the rudiments of horse-riding and swordsmanship. The recent cavalry training in Kells had been interesting but was not without its hazards, chief among them being Captain Edward Rothwell himself. Thomas Gettings felt he was encountering the man too often for the good of his health. The last of the secondments had been at Easter, and following that week of instruction under the tutelage of Rothwell's bullying nature, he swore that to never cross his path again would be too soon. He found him to be a harsh taskmaster; a martinet with his own men, never mind other officers, including Gettings, who were transferred in for training. And to see him at morning inspection; mounted, ramrod straight on his black hunter, his Tarleton helmet with white plume atop, striding along the ranks, striking an imperious aura in the saddle. His criticism of the trainees was unrelenting and Thomas, at times, felt he was regressing in his exercises rather than improving in his performance.

Gradually, he grew to hate the harsh training schedule, which culminated one day, as they practiced with swords, in an incident that singled out Thomas for special treatment from Rothwell thereafter. Rothwell and Ogle had paired off with two trainees, one of whom was Thomas. Thomas' rudimentary but adequate training in swordsmanship from his father had stood him in good stead but he had declined to reveal the fact of his prior coaching to Rothwell.

Over the course of a few days and amid various forms of training, Rothwell had pushed Gettings ever harder in the art of sword-fighting, in which he allowed the captain to lead the way. However on the final session, Rothwell had insisted on an actual duel, claiming Thomas should have acquired enough basic knowledge to be able to defend himself against an opponent. Following a bout of parrying and mock attacks, Rothwell suddenly lunged in, as if to strike his trainee, only for Thomas to instinctively side-step and nick Rothwell with a subtle side swipe of his sword. Rothwell stepped back in horror, looking down at his bloodied shirt before the pain of the cut manifested itself. The other pair stopped sparring and looked on incredulously. Despite Thomas' profuse apologies, Rothwell retreated silently to his quarters, holding his side, and sought medical attention. There was to be no more training for Thomas. Rothwell's lieutenant, Nathaniel Ogle, ordered Thomas and other Slane trainee home that evening.

Weeks later, in the wake of the battle at Tara at the end of May, the Slane Yeomanry had sent cavalry units into the countryside north of Navan, hunting for the United Irish rebels that had been dispersed and, sure enough, Gettings stumbled upon Rothwell and his troop around Wilkinstown as they too swept the general vicinity. His cursory dismissal of Gettings and his men during the introduction that day was also replicated after the encounter with the rebels at Mountainstown. Rothwell had harangued Gettings for not covering his flank as they chased the Wexford group into the bog. In the flurry of battle, Thomas determined that silence was the better virtue but felt that his own actions and that of his men were at the very least commendable in the heat of that encounter.

Letting his horse take her own speed towards Collon, he shrugged resignedly at the idea of meeting his adversary again this evening, so soon after the previous encounter. Approaching Collon village, the darker hue of evening had crept across the heavens as late summer twilight descended. Gettings crossed the Mattock river bridge and into the county of Louth. His mare trotted ably up the ascent towards the crossroads and at a distance above him he could see some horses and carriages arriving at John Foster's imposing house on the corner of the broad junction. Drawing near, he spied Lieutenant Barton, from Bellevue House, step down from his brake and be greeted warmly at Foster's door. There was limited space at the front of the Speaker's house, where a surplus of carriages had congregated, so many of those arriving were being ushered around to a side entrance. He trotted under a stone arch and into a yard of outhouses, one of which gable-ended an imposing greenhouse, off to one side.

While he dismounted and passed his horse over to one of Foster's men to tether, a twin-horse curricle came at pace through the archway, its right wheel clipping the jostle stone at the entrance, the chaise briefly lifting up in the air. Two men were aboard, and Gettings could overhear the passenger berating the driver for taking the corner so sharply. As the carriage came to a halt, he groaned and sighed deeply, for it was Edward Rothwell ready to disembark, accompanied by one of his lieutenants, Nathaniel Ogle. The lieutenant hopped out and took the rig over to have the horses tied and given water. In the meantime Rothwell strode towards the entrance door, walking close to Thomas as he did. Tall, straight and spare, Rothwell suddenly swivelled his frame and faced him.

'Ah ha! If it is not Lieutenant Gettings, the hero of our late

36

confrontation with the rebels.'

Rothwell's salutation came with his usual twist of sarcasm. Without forethought, Thomas advanced his hand towards Rothwell in greeting, but it was immediately rebuffed.

'I would like to have a word with you later, lieutenant, after this meeting is over.'

Thomas' eyebrows rose, taken by surprise at the request. Rothwell leaned in towards him, his height intimidating him somewhat.

'Yes, some of my men have been telling me rumours that, out in the countryside, you have been hunting these wastrels with a light touch. Apparently, if any are caught, you get your men to administer the coup de grace, rather than yourself. It appears you might be afraid of a little rebel blood on your hands? Hmm?'

His accusations were interrupted by one of Foster's servants coming to the door, calling on all those to present themselves in Mr Foster's library without further delay. As Rothwell strode briskly away, Gettings was left standing, perplexed. He was pointed to the entrance and regaining his composure he removed his helmet and placing it under his arm he proceeded through the entrance door and was pointed towards the library. Several rows of ornate chairs were laid out, facing towards a large mahogany desk. He secured a seat on the left of the room, beneath an array of painted family portraits hanging above a panelled wall. Pushing his helmet under the chair he withdrew his notes. Muted conversations trailed around the room with handshakes being offered in introduction to some who had not met for some time. Thomas took a moment to inspect the gathered officers. Some of them he knew but many were unfamiliar. He noted Rothwell and Ogle had procured seats up near the front.

Then, off to the left, a door swept open and the conversation of those in the room tapered noticeably as John Foster, Speaker of the Irish House of Commons, made his entrance. The dozen or so officers in attendance stood up to acknowledge his presence, before he settled into a large chair behind his desk. He gave a small bow and encouraged everyone to be seated. He made eye contact with some officers near him, briefly nodding as he recognised the faces. Settling some papers he stood up and began to speak. He was a short man, though of imposing presence and from his red jowls emanated a deep voice which carried a clear, precise delivery throughout the room.

'Gentlemen, gentlemen, you are all most welcome to my house on this pleasant evening. I am indebted to you all for intruding on your valuable time. After our discussion concludes, we will have some delicacies and imbibe a little wine to toast the success of your good work over the past few weeks. Let me begin by saying that General Meyrick sends his apologies for not being able to be present this evening, due to urgent matters he must attend to. But I am indeed glad to witness this fine gathering here of officers from all relevant areas in the counties of Louth and Meath who have had to deal with the late state of insurgency in the area.'

Foster reached for his glasses and placed them on his nose to check the details of those present in the room.

'I will now confirm the attendance of the following representatives of yeomanry units in the district and they are; Ralph Smyth and George Tandy, esquires, from Drogheda; Lieutenants Manning and Caldwell from this village, Captain William Ruxton and Lieutenant Logan from Ardee, Captain Edward Rothwell and Lieutenant Nathaniel Ogle from Kells and Lieutenants Thomas Gettings and Gustavus Barton, both from the Slane troop and lastly, Captain Samuel Croucher from the Rathkenny district. This evening we are also privileged to have Major-General Wemyss in attendance from Drogheda, who will shortly give his own account of the late actions in dispersing the rebels from north Meath.'

John Foster paused for a few seconds to further check his notes and then proceeded with his introduction of the Major-General.

'Gentlemen, before we attend to the accounts from the yeomen's districts, let us first hear from the Major-General, who will give a brief first-hand account of what transpired during the late incursion of the Wexford rebels into our locality.'

He nodded towards Wemyss and gave way for the general to

stand at the desk and face the audience. The general cleared his throat roughly. He too was a sturdy man and wide but not of excess weight and in possession of a swarthy facial complexion, which was expressive as he began to speak. Thomas leaned forward in his seat, trying to interpret the words of the general's strong Scottish accent. It required a good ear to follow his narrative.

'Firstly, forgive me if I speak with some haste, fellow officers,' Wemyss began. 'As I explained earlier to our host, Speaker Foster, I must return to Navan town by the close of this day, so I will not dally before you, save to give this short account of the recent military happenings in which we were able to successfully extinguish the potential of the Wexford rebel group to make mischief in these counties.

As was reported, various commanders in Kildare and Meath first noted the presence of a large group of rebels, who emerged from an area known as the Bog of Allen in the county of Kildare and who had begun to make progress in a general northerly direction, raiding villages and houses as they went. Lord Lieutenant Cornwallis was advised of the potential danger they posed and hurriedly issued instructions to generals in the pertinent areas to contain their dangerous foray. Hence, myself and General's Myers and Meyrick were requested to proceed with our forces from Navan and Drogheda and engage with the enemy in order to suppress their movements. Initially we adopted a policy of harassment, not allowing them to settle or recover from setbacks. Yet, I grant that, in hindsight, they were a wily bunch for a week or so. And their ringleaders, who some say, were a papist priest and a Protestant gentlemen, led them gamely and seemed to be able to keep one step ahead of us as they advanced north. By the time we became fully engaged with their itinerary they had crossed the Boyne to the west of the village of Slane. They then embarked on an erratic trajectory through the countryside north-west of that area, until they finally were stopped and were forced to offer battle at a bog in the wilderness, north of Navan and west of Collon,'

Wemyss looked down briefly to check his notes and clear his throat again. 'Yes, I have it here, a place known as Mountainstown Bog or sometimes called Knightstown Bog.'

A brief murmurous swell carried through the room as most of those present vividly recalled the details of the bloody encounter. Though only a week ago, Thomas' images of the engagement were ones of turmoil and confusion, a melee of charging horses, bloodied militia and rebels, all immersed in a thick morass of clinging wet bog.

'And seeking shelter in a dry part of the bog' Wemyss continued, 'this rebel force offered stiff resistance for a period, with their pikes and the desperation of the doomed. Our cavalry units became bogged down in the mire, so to speak, and had to withdraw, before infantry and militia troops were advanced to do battle. This skirmishing was inconclusive but of necessity as we awaited the arrival of a couple of field cannons to dislodge the foe. Our forces were then withdrawn sufficiently to allow us space with which to launch a series of grapeshot barrages into their midst.'

Weymss looked up from his notes and added boldly. 'And, I dare say, the feel of the grape certainly moved them along fairly sprightly.' His words brought a round of whoops and handclaps from the officers, including Foster, who then asked for silence to allow the General Wemyss conclude his talk.

'In conclusion, gentlemen, the army and dragoons, with the able assistance of the local militia and yeomanry, initially contained the threat these insurgents posed to the localities they passed through. They were then harried all the way on their trek, brought to battle and eventually wiped them out as a coherent group, apart that is for a remnant to escaped , across the Boyne but who were finally caught and dispatched in north county Dublin; thus bringing an end to their final fruitless efforts. And that, gentlemen, brought our task of putting down the rebellion of the United Irishmen in this kingdom to a successful conclusion.'

A brief moment of silence was followed by a round of applause as the Scottish general folded his notes, said his goodbyes and was ushered out of the room by one of Foster's aides. When everyone had settled down Foster brought forward a representative from each of the yeomanry districts and asked them to make a brief report on the relevant action that occurred in their area. With Drogheda's George Tandy beginning the session by outlining the recent preparations made by them and assisting with deployment north of the Boyne, Gettings perused his notes as Lieutenant Barton had asked him to give the report on the Slane unit's intervention.

The next half hour was taken up by accounts from the various districts with follow up comments and queries by other officers and indeed Speaker Foster himself. He took a keen interest in the machinations of the yeomanry and militia units in Louth and Meath; taking some notes and interrupting with a few pointed questions.

When it came to his turn, Thomas rose, acknowledged those in the room and read aloud from his papers, the details of his unit's participation in the events over the last ten days; noting their involvement at Mountainstown and the follow-up actions in searching for any remnants of the rebels in the area. No queries arose from his account and he retook his seat, quietly satisfied of his contribution.

Last to be called was Edward Rothwell. Thomas noted a certain aura he exuded in the room as he stood up; an added quality of austerity he courted as he accounted for the actions of his yeomanry troop, its involvement in the Tara battle and its aftermath. He listed numbers of rebels killed by his men after that battle, the interim period in June when they followed up on search missions and then their response to the threat posed by the advent of the rebel army from Wexford. Foster interrupted him at one point asking if his Kells troop had any casualties of its own during the campaigns. Rothwell paused briefly then mentioned the two militiamen he lost outside Collon. Foster looked up and responded.

'Yes, yes, captain, that is the incident I wished you to elaborate on, seeing as it occurred just out the road from here at Mount Oriel. Were you able to apprehend the perpetrators of that heinous deed?' Rothwell nodded.

'I am happy to inform you, sir, that in response to their action, we fired the houses of the two miscreants who committed the evil act and can only assume that they were consumed by the conflagrations. I attended the first mission personally, over at Smarmore and saw no survivors from the torched cabin. Four of my men carried out the second mission in Killary some days later and again they reported no survivors at the scene. It would seem both of the culprits were cousins.'

A hand went up from the body of the room. Foster nodded for the officer to speak.

'Lieutenant Manning, sir, of the Collon yeos in this area. I beg to intrude, sirs, but an informant revealed to me only the other day and which I am only at liberty to report now, that at least one of those Moore cousins you speak of, may have assisted some of the Wexford rebels from Mountainstown escape back across the Boyne before heading south. So therefore, one of them may still be alive.'

Rothwell gaze was frosty at this news, which he had not been privy to, but he remained stone-faced, holding his neutral expression and hiding his annoyance of not being aware of this. Foster thanked Manning for the supplementary information.

'Let us be forthright... even candid here, gentlemen' the Speaker said. 'It is a just thing that our regular troops, yeos and militia have delivered the harshest of lessons to those inclined to act in a seditious manner and that, in future, there will be always be an example made of those rebelling against the King and his loyal subjects.'

He paused, refocussing on Rothwell. 'Incidentally, may I also ask, Captain, what led you and your men to be outside your normal confines of Kells and surrounding district on the day your yeomanry were murdered?'

'Well sir,' Rothwell said, 'if you recall, it was the day of Boylan's hanging at the Tholsel and some of my unit had been sent to Drogheda as part of a security detachment. It was I who headed that detachment. As you are well aware, sir, Boylan was the leader of the United Irishmen in the southern part of Louth. At the Tholsel, a known member of that proscribed organisation was spotted in the crowd and reported to me by a new recruit, Corporal Brennan. I decided to follow the suspect as he left the precincts of the town. On stopping him on the hill known as Mount Oriel, outside this village, and ascertaining that it was indeed a person known to us as John Matthews, a United man from Ardee, I arranged for him to be hung from the nearest tree. After he was bound and trussed up, I left two men to carry out my orders, but sadly they were killed by associates of Mr Mathews, who apparently were lurking nearby. I later discovered that the two assassins were these Moore cousins and whose habitations, as I have outlined, were subsequently destroyed under my instructions.'

'Well, indeed, that is a story, Captain,' Foster mused. 'Note it well, all you fellow officers here this evening. Though you may be committed to defend your own area, if circumstances pertain, do not shirk your responsibility to pursue these agitators beyond your own boundaries, if it means your pursuit ends in their capture or demise. Thank you again, Captain Rothwell for your contribution.'

He nodded and Rothwell sat down, somewhat satisfied with his explanation.

As the officers were speaking, Thomas had been mulling over whether to ask a rather innocuous question that had been nagging at him. He decided it was time to hear from those present, even Speaker Foster, what they thought had brought on this sudden sortie by rebellious men from so far away? He put his hand up tentatively and Foster noticed him.

'Yes lieutenant? What is it you wish to contribute to this discussion?' Thomas stood up and directed his query to Foster.

'Yes, thank you Mr. Foster. I would like to put the following question to the floor. What scheming, do you think, had these men from Wexford travel so far away from their home in what, to all intents and purposes, was a hopeless quest?'

Silence flowed through the room. Gettings was left standing, retaining the floor, satisfied at least, that he had asked a valid question. He noticed the heat in the room, the lack of air. Feeling stuffy, he hoped someone would open a window soon. Foster stood up from behind his desk and looked around to see if anyone would respond. Seeing none, he grunted briefly before offering his own reply.

'It's an interesting question, Lieutenant Gettings; one that I'm sure, a few in this room may have pondered since the unfortunate events transpired. My opinion is that they were fleeing from our forces, having being pursued all the way, from when they left the fastness of Wicklow. They were little more than a band of brigands who were determined to keep moving. They would not disperse or even take the clemency that was being offered by Lord Cornwallis - a folly of the highest order.'

Foster pursed his lips and looked round for more contributors. Edward Rothwell requested to speak. He stood up and addressed the room, his arms spread out.

'With respect, sir, we are not here to try and interpret the motives of these croppy rebels, or what drives them to the lengths they went to.' He paused before turning to the officers around him.

'Indeed, I am at a loss as to why the question was even asked of us. Our duty is to the Crown and our vigilance is to the loyal people of the Kingdom and not on what a priest-ridden, peasant mob are prepared to do to bring our peaceable way of life down.'

Then he pointed an accusatory finger at Gettings.

'You, sir, should concentrate more on apprehending and punishing these mischief-makers rather than proposing pedantic questions over their disloyalty.'

Gettings reddened and stood up to challenge Rothwell's slight.

'My reasons for asking...,' he began heatedly, but Foster interrupted him.

'Now, now, gentlemen! There'll be no fractious debates in these chambers, not on this evening. We are all here to celebrate the happy outcome of the late insurrection and our local success.'

He was reluctant to allow rancour develop and sour what should be an evening of rejoicing and good cheer.

'As it appears that all matters have been attended to, let us bring this meeting to a close and we shall retire shortly to the dining-room for refreshment.'

Thomas sat down, fuming quietly. He reached into his pocket for the trinket Emma had given him. Somehow it comforted him, a link

44

to the more pleasant things in his life. He waited until the room slowly cleared, then, grabbing his Tarleton, he made to leave, wanting no part of mingling in the same room as the Kells captain.

Drawing close to the door, from of the corner of his eye, he saw a figure advancing towards him. It was Edward Rothwell! Still seething at the effrontery of the Kells officer, he pulled himself together and turned to face him, his features outwardly calm.

'Captain Rothwell, we meet again…and so soon too!' The captain drew close to him.

'Gettings, why did you drag the tone of the meeting down by asking such an immature question about the rebels' intentions? You are now the laughing stock of your peers.'

Gettings bristled with indignation.

'After the military proceedings we have dealt with' he answered, 'I have every right to query the event itself, as have you.'

He breathed in, trying to hold his temper.

'And tell me this, Captain Rothwell. Why do you insist on haranguing and humiliating me at every opportunity? I resent it and you should withdraw your insinuations now regarding my behaviour in the field.'

Rothwell's eyes narrowed at Gettings' riposte.

'I will not stand for insults from any man but especially from you,' he responded, poking Gettings in the shoulder. 'I'll have you know, I have been a yeomanry officer for many years now, with experience against Defender and United Irish activities over most of this decade. As for you, during that time, you were but a lad romping around the Slane meadows. And now it would seem that you are inclined to do the same romping around, while your men work at flushing out those in hiding.'

Gettings was incensed at the slur, roughly pushing Rothwell's hand away.

'Don't slight me, sir, I warn you! I too am an officer and your behaviour towards me, as an officer, is contemptible. I'm inclined to think it warrants me reporting your behaviour to your seniors in Kells?'

Rothwell stared at him incredulously, his gloved hand hovering close to his scabbard.

'You are the lower rank, Gettings, so you would do well to withdraw your threat. If you don't, my superiors will side with me and you will also bring down my anger on you. Trust me, you would not want to be a witness to that!'

With that warning, he strutted swiftly out the door to his waiting horse and carriage. Thomas' eyes followed him, still shaking with unreleased rage. He went outside for air, feeling that for a variety of unrelated reasons that he had yet to quantify, he had now made an implacable enemy of the Kells captain.

From the stables, one of Foster's stablemen appeared and stepped up beside him, asking if he should fetch his horses. Gettings nodded distractedly, his mind fully preoccupied, not only with the butchery he was obliged to be part of, but also Rothwell's mounting vendetta against him.

# Chapter Five

## Smarmore

George Geraghty harnessed his small black and white cob horse and brought her round to the front of his cabin. Henry and Laurence Moore were waiting patiently for him. Henry had decided that, notwithstanding the danger involved, this was the day they would travel over to Smarmore and see for themselves the devastation visited on Henry's brother, Barney, and his family. George handed over the reins to Henry and both he and Laurence mounted the cart. George declared his anxiety at their dangerous journey.

'Are you sure you're doing the right thing, Henry? What if you meet a troop of yeos on your way? A couple of caps pulled down over yer heads may not be enough to save ye.'

'We have to take that chance, George. I'm obligated to make sure Barney got some kind of burial and to find out what happened his family, one way or another.'

George shrugged and briefly explained the horse commands.

'Call her by her name Ginny, to whoa and stop her. Click your tongue and then pull her to the left and right to turn. Give her the odd clip of the rein on her back and she'll move along quicker. She's fed and watered and good for the day, but stop at a stream or trough if you see one.'

Laurence secured his peillic of water between his feet and mounted the cart, using the walking stick his father had pared for him earlier. Elizabeth and Kate came to the door to see them off. Laurence noted Kate standing to one side, morose and tearful; looking what remained of her family heading off on the cart. Henry nodded down at George.

'You know where we're going George and I'm thankful to you for providing the means of transport. We should be back before nightfall, all being well.'

George waved them away and returned to his cabin. Henry clipped the reins and Ginny pulled away out into the lane. Laurence gently castigated his father.

'"All being well", father! I don't think there will be much that will be 'well' where we're going. Do you not think, it'll be more freshly dug mounds in graveyards and burnt cabins?'

'I don't doubt that, son. I don't doubt that at all.'

He flicked the reins again and the cob picked up a little speed. The morning was grey and overcast but Laurence was imbued with a little more resilience now that more time had passed in his recovery. He had spent the last few days helping with the final repairs to George's cabin and sheds, following their damage in the raid. And each evening he had rambled across the fields, to build up his strength and stamina. His resolve to do something had not wavered; in fact his solitary walks had only enhanced his desire to fight back and avenge the family deaths. He smiled sadly, realising that these were the rebellious inclinations that his brother, poor Jack, used to have too. Jack's temper would ignite more quickly than Laurence's and it was a sight to see as he flew off the handle at the first sign of persecution or slight. It was all Laurence or his father could do to calm him and quench that burning flame of resentment he possessed.

But now, following his death, Laurence felt those same emotions that Jack had found so hard to control. It was as if the flame of rebellion had been passed to him. Yet he knew he was powerless to do anything for the present; powerless against the likes of Captain Rothwell and his troops and powerless against the massed ranks of the redcoats that had chased them all the way from the Boyne to the bog at Mountainstown. Indeed wasn't he lucky to have escaped from there at all? Only for the help of his cousin James Moore, he too would be lying beneath a mound of earth.

He wondered about James and what might have happened him.

He had last seen him in his yard at the head of the Wexford men, men who had no idea where they were, leading what was left of them back to the river Boyne, in search of an escape from the ever tightening trap that the Crown forces had thrown around the place. Had he made good his escape, he wondered? His circumstances had played on his mind repeatedly since they had parted on that fateful day.

From a vague recollection of the events, he heard the leaders of the rebels, Fr Kearns and Colonel Perry, had somehow escaped from the slaughter in the bog and it was left to one of their lieutenants, Timothy Whelan, to organise an attempt to break out and head for home. But it was James, when he got injured, who rescued him and got him home safely. So this journey to Smarmore today would only be small way recompense to James for saving his life! James had told him his father Barney had been killed and the rest of the family dispersed and his house burnt down. At least then, even if his cousin had succumbed in the retreat from Mountainstown, he and Henry would try and establish if any of them were still alive. His father might be trying to find his brother, but *he* was doing it for Laurence. It was the least he could do.

He hadn't been concentrating on the road when his reflections were interrupted by his father talking at his side.

'… was right. He warned Ellen, the day he took you back to us, that the yeos were out to get you and him. I should have left the house, took us all away to safety, but there was hay to be cut, drills of praties and turnips to be weeded. I just didn't think…didn't think they would come after us like they did.'

His father cleared his eyes wistfully, assuming Laurence had been listening to his meditations. Laurence nodded as if he had been heeding him all along.

'Your mother had told me…,' Henry continued, 'she told me what young James had cautioned that day, the day he left you back. He said the redcoats would be coming for us next, after destroying Barney and his family. I should have heeded the warning. I should have… Christ, but what would father and mother say if they saw my family and Barney's family now.'

He drifted into silence, lost in his own memories and moot deliberations.

The road moved along beneath them, with Ginny trotting along at a useful pace, the whip of the reins seldom used. Laurence tried to tease out his next move, to formulate some kind of future plan. It would be futile to try and take action by himself and he knew that, but what about the local United Irishmen? Had they disbanded? Did he know any of them who might still be active, still eager to strike a blow for freedom? And what of that turncoat neighbour of theirs, Bryan Brennan? He, who had joined the yeos and had brought misery to their peaceful townlands. He despised that kind of people with a passion. Besdie him, his father nudged him out of his reverie.

'The road is very quiet today, thank God. No sign of any patrols - so far!'

He was making small talk, trying to shorten the journey. Laurence proposed a question. 'What will you do, father?'

Henry looked at him and shook his head, not understanding.

'What will you do with the house, the fields, all the animals?'

'It's too early to consider those things, a mhic.' Laurence persevered with his question.

'But we can't stay for long at Geraghty's, or even John Moore's, if it comes to that. You've helped George repair his home, so can we do the same for ours?'

Henry grunted uncomfortably, unused to having to argue his case, except perhaps occasionally, when Ellen voiced her strong opinion!

'The thatch was set afire and collapsed into the house. 'Tis all destroyed.'

'But surely we can rebuild it, father, put a new roof on. George will help us.'

Henry shook his head sadly. The high spirits of youth, he thought ruefully. They will build houses today but have the redcoats at your door tomorrow. He turned to look at Laurence.

'A mhic, if you must know, 'tis all I can do at this stage to rise in the mornings. But for the good nature of George Geraghty we would be living in one of our sheds now, and perhaps we might have to go back there yet. What will happen if the yeos come round again and see our house under repair? They will surely see fit to destroy it again. We must be careful now in these hours and days of mourning. From what Barney's son said, 'tis him and you the redcoats are after, for the yeos deaths outside Collon. 'Tis hard for me to say, but it was a wrong thing to do.' He shook his head sadly.

'Anyway, my life is done now. Your mother is gone. You cannot stay here for they will be vigilant in their pursuit of you. I only have Kate now and she will have to look after her father.'

Smiling ruefully, he flipped the reins on Ginny who give an extra spurt to her trot.

Laurence mulled on his father's words. Was he now casting his son adrift from what was left of the family? That he was too dangerous to have around? Not long after, he noted their approach to a junction in the road. His father clicked his tongue loudly and pulled the left rein and the cob dutifully obliged by swinging to the left and trotted gently downhill.

'This is Smarmore,' Henry revealed, pulling gently on the reins for Ginny to slow down a little. 'We've made it.'

'What are we looking for?' Laurence asked, the cart bucking gently under him. They crossed a small water course in the rough gravel road. Henry pulled up and let the cob take some water. She slurped greedily.

'I suppose we'll know when we get there,' Henry said finally. Barney's cabin lay to the west of White Mountain. We're close to there now.'

Laurence noticed the rising domed hills all around, mostly furze-covered, yet lower down lush in pasture, more than adequate grazing for the animals dotted throughout. The afternoon breezes drove the late summer heat around the surrounding hills and channelled its warm layers through the low-lying valley pastures, filling the area with myriads of buzzing flies and swooping birds, all bathed in shafts of sun flickering through the trees and hedges. It heralded a promise of harvest and bounty and longed for sated appetites, but usually only for those in the big houses and the middlemen who serviced them. Henry remembered the times during the last few summers when his brother Barney was obliged to seek assistance from him; even sending his son James over to him to labour through the summer months for Henry; all to bring home a few shillings to help pay Barney's rent to Taaffes at Smarmore. There was seldom a bountiful harvest for Barney, nor indeed for Henry, who himself had worked hard for many years, just to meet the needs of his own tenancy and just a little left over to help keep his family alive.

Henry was first to spot a disturbed area beside the gripe on the road. He pointed to it and Laurence could see evidence of a dug out channel, or what looked to him like the remains of a grave. As they drew closer, it appeared to be a haphazard pile of earth and grass. He pulled the horse to a standstill and both dismounted to examine the site. Laurence stood at one end while his father knelt and sifted through the disturbed soil. He noticed the shallow form of the broken ground, like a hollow, as if something had been removed from it. There also seemed to be tracks, cart tracks, going up onto the grass. Laurence echoed his observations.

'Did somebody come with a cart and remove who was buried here? If there was a body buried, they're not there now. Look at how the earth has been dragged aside.'

Henry agreed silently, standing up slowly and walking to the other end to where Laurence stood. They both stood, looking into the shallow pit with heads slightly bowed, as if they were two mourners at a graveside.

'It does indeed look like an empty grave,' Henry mused, removing his cap and scratching his head. 'Could it have been Barney's? His house is only down the road a little way. Anyway, there are no remains here now. We'll go further and see if anyone knows what happened.'

Regaining the cart, Ginny gently took them further down the

desolate road. There were no cabins on this stretch of the road; the first one they would meet would be the ruin that was Barney Moore's. Henry stared into the distance, becoming increasingly tense as he neared the scene of his brother's demise. Laurence remembered it from the night he had slept there, less than a month before, after he and James had fled with John Mathews from the yeo killings at Mount Oriel.

Rounding a slight curve in the road, they saw the mud cabin on the left, situated just off the road, now roofless and gutted. Henry eased the horse to a stop and let her eat some grass on the mearing. Laurence grabbed his stick and followed his father around the ruin. The lingering smell of smoke pervaded the air. Only the four mud walls remained upright and even then, the gable ends had partially collapsed in on themselves, leaving stone and lumps of caked muck spread around in disorderly piles. When the burning thatch had fallen into the interior, it had blackened the walls and destroyed everything. In the debris of ash, neither of them could find a single item that might be salvageable or even identifiable. It was utter destruction, the imprint of the family who had lived there wiped out forever.

Henry stood in the centre of the ruin with his hands on his hips, shaking his head sadly, the enormity of what had happened only hitting him now; his sadness now amplified by the deaths in his own family and with both families now utterly ruined. Outside, Laurence walked around the perimeter, surveying the rear, the few blackthorn trees that stood behind the cabin were badly scorched from the flames. Even the small turf pile Barney kept was still smouldering from the heat and the smell of burnt sods strongly permeated the air. Beyond the trees, the furze bushes had survived and he ambled his way through them, wondering had anyone from the cabin escaped? He noted the few small fields beyond the shelter belt, neat lines of recently built lap-cocks in them. Barney had been busy out there until recently, getting the hay cut, Laurence mused ruefully.

Stroking the stick through the furze and other undergrowth, a small streak of colour caught his attention, a shred of red cloth caught in tangle of furze. He used his stick to pry open the bush and reached in, tugging the fabric away and into his hand. He looked at it carefully, turned it over, smelt it. Was it clothing from one of the family or maybe Uncle Barney's wife Mary, or perhaps one of the children? He walked round to where Henry stood and showed him what he found.

'It was caught in furze around the back,' Laurence said. 'Could it be one of them tearing it and they trying to escape?'

Henry examined it critically. 'It could also be from one of the yeos red coats. It's their colour. They could have gone round the back to make sure no one got away.'

Laurence's brief optimism faded. Henry pocketed the scrap and returned to the cart.

'An empty grave,' Laurence said, 'a ruined house, nothing to show that anyone was ever here. Maybe no one was ever put in the grave, father. Maybe it was dug to bury someone but they were scared away... or something like that.'

'Who knows what happened, a mhic? Who knows?'

Henry untied Ginny and was about to board the cart when a stranger appeared from behind a field hedge next to the burnt house. Henry and Laurence both stopped in their tracks. The man emerged through a gap and, looking up and down the road, drew closer to them. Small of stature and stooped, he held a cattle stick in his right hand and he beat the ground with it rhythmically as he came up to them.

'And who might ye be?' he asked quietly, his eyes lowered furtively, a suspicious menace in his voice.

'We're looking for the family who lived in that cabin,' Henry explained, nodding back at Barney's, but standing his ground. Laurence drew up close to his father, providing a united front. The man's stoop meant he hooked his neck to look at them sideways, looking through trails of greasy hair plastered down one side of his head.

'The yeos were here not so long ago,' he reported cryptically, nodding over at the blackened remains.

'So I see,' said Henry.' Did any of the family get away?' The man squinted at them and spat into the ground, unwilling to answer any questions.

'What would I know?' He grunted. 'Sure, you could be in league with Foster and his yeos, for all I know.'

He made to turn away. Henry was stung by his abruptness but Laurence shouted after him.

'Wait! Wait! We are relations. We are kin to Barney Moore, who lived here. All we want is to know what happened to him and his family?'

The man stopped and turned back. A brief smile flitted across his mouth as he looked at them again.

'What way are ye related?' he asked.

'Barney was my brother,' Henry said. 'This is my son Laurence.' The man leaned closer to inspect them.

'Aye, now that I see you, I can see the resemblance to Barney. Why have I not seen either of you around these parts though?'

'We live in Lobinstown and seldom got over to Smarmore. Barney would send his son, James, to us in Lobinstown, this past few summers.'

The man beat his stick on the ground some more, thinking, before he relented. 'I'm a newcomer to here meself. John McQuillan is me name. We just moved to here from Hurlestone. Taaffes wanted someone up here and we were told to move a couple of months ago. I'm just round the corner there, next to poor Barney. Fine neighbours they were too, him and Mary and the children.'

'Do you know what might have happened to them?' Henry asked, relieved that he might be getting somewhere at last. John McQuillan twisted his face towards them again, his eyes lowered.

'Well, you can see his cabin or what's left of it, so that'll tell you something. But 'tis not safe to talk of these things out in the open. Come back to my cabin and I'll tell ye as much as I know about all this.'

He turned and headed down the road. Henry followed him while Laurence retrieved the horse and cart and followed the two men.

*

55

They sat around the unlit fire of John McQuillan's dilapidated cabin. His wife lingered quietly in the dim background but he didn't introduce her. From the top of a bare dresser, he took down a dark green bottle and uncorked it.

'Sure you'll have a drop of the oul craytur,' he said, offering them a sup. Henry sipped quietly and smiled when Laurence gasped at the fierce kick from the mouthful of poitín. John raised the bottle in the air.

'To Barney and his family,' he whispered, 'and cursed be all those redcoat bastards that done them down.' He put the bottle on the floor and they waited for him to speak.

'I was only here a wet week when Barney helped me plant me pratie crop and when done I did the same for him. Then I saw him little after that. He seemed to be coming and going a lot.'

John took another sip and handed the bottle to Henry. Laurence was getting restless. They had been in this man's company for a considerable time and he had yet to give them any substantial information. He considered a question to ask him, to progress their enquiries.

'Did you go to the United Irish assembly at Michael Boylan's farm with Barney?'

The bottle was back with John and he was in mid-sup when Laurence asked the question. Some of the fiery liquid went down the wrong way, causing him to splutter and cough uncontrollably. He choked for a few seconds, hawking gobs of spittle and phlegm towards the floor.

'What would I know about things like that?' he said defensively, still gasping.

'You were neighbours. You must have talked about the United Irishmen,' Laurence suggested. Silence ensued, save the sound of John McQuillan clearing his throat. Henry eyed Laurence, intimating that they leave, that they would get no more from him. They went to stand up. McQuillan rose with them and seemed to gather his thoughts, then stammered, 'Wait…wait! I've more to tell ye. Can't ye see I'm nervous...afraid? Sit down for a bit, will ye?'

With that, he began to talk in a disjointed way. His eyes hardly left the dirt floor as he spoke and he fidgeted constantly with the stick in his hand. He related that Barney had called to him one evening after planting tubers in his pratie field.

'He wanted me to go with him to go to Ballapuste that evening, to a meeting, he said. I had heard others talk about these United Irishmen gatherings and their secret oaths, but I'm not a man for things like that. Anyway, but doesn't he persuade me easy enough? And off we go to Thomas Markey's house, beyond the crossroads. Do you know of him?' Henry didn't recognise the name and shook his head, willing him to go on.

'Agin my will, I took the secret oath, as did others there that night and a man called Kelly, from Ardee... Dan Kelly, he told us there was going to be a rising agin the government and that all right-thinking men should rise up and join the rebellion. He said there would be thousands of us, and we'd all have pikes and guns.'

He let out a half-hearted laugh, as if somehow amused at his own actions. 'But Barney was more up for it and me and he went to Blakestown on the night of the rising... and I didn't. I couldn't trust myself. Anyway, didn't I meet him a few days later and he was a poorer man for the trouble they all went to. He had built his hopes on this rising and its success... and then nothing. The Louthmen failed to march and the men from Meath were beaten at Tara. And they say, many of the men involved were caught and strung up at every crossroads between here and Kells.'

He passed the near empty bottle around but Henry and Laurence refused the offer. John finished it himself and spluttered as the last drops trickled down his throat. He swallowed hard then continued.

'Me and Barney kept our heads down after that. We stayed busy, got some hay cut and then one day he tells me his eldest son was in some kind of fight outside Collon and killed a couple of yeos.' Laurence looked at Henry, but neither said a word.

'He was afraid then. He told me so. He knew they would be

57

after his son, maybe come after all of them. He had a man staying with him too, somebody hiding from the magistrates, but would say nothing about him. Then, that morning… that morning…!' In the dimness of the cabin interior, he shook his head silently. Laurence held his breath.

'That morning, the morning that the yeos rode up the lane, I'll never forget it, as long as I live. I heard them coming from far away, from near Ballapuste itself. Christ, but the thunder of horses' hooves in the early morning, it was like a nightmare. Me and herself, we covered ourselves under the straw for the pig; hoping they were not coming for us…and thank Christ, they wern't. But, all along the road, the people were afraid of the same thing. What if they stopped at their home? But it was at poor Barney's they stopped at, so it was. And those that saw what happened there will take it to their grave. It is said that the stranger staying at Barney's, took off on his horse and cart while Barney led the family out the back. And those that witnessed it say, he came back and stood with his back to his cabin, facing the redcoat cavalry. He fought them off at his door with his pike… brave Barney Moore. Why didn't he run away with the family? Why? And then what did they do but shoot him dead, no quarter given. And they left his body on the ground while they burnt his home.'

John shook his head at the ending of his story, sweat beading on his wrinkled brow. His eyes look up at them at last, a feverish sheen to them. Henry and Laurence remained silent, caught up in the drama of the tale.

'What became of Barney's body?' Henry had to ask. 'Did someone give him a burial at least?' John's rheumy eyes focussed on him.

'Well, here's the quare thing about it all,' he reflected. 'Nobody but the foolhardy put their noses beyond their doors, long after the yeos left the place. Didn't I tell you, Barney's killing and the burning of his house was early in the morning and none of the neighbours came out till noon for fear of yeos still being round? A few began to walk up and down the road, about their business, passing the smouldering house - and his remains. They all walked by Barney, averting their eyes and blessing themselves, but no one would move him or lift him in case spies were about or the yeos returned. Bad cess to them! Some said there was another body further up the road, towards Leabby Cross. Perhaps it was Barney's lodger. But who knows? But it was a shocking day for all of us around these parts.'

'Anyway, that evening another yeo patrol made their way down the road. They called to no one, but up and down the road they went, some of them even taking their horses through the fields. Everyone stayed in. Declare to God, but there was little work done that day. So, anyway, darkness finally came and Andrew Malone of the next house down from me, knocked on my door and told me Barney's body was gone! Both of us went up to his cabin and sure enough, all that was left was the patch of blood around where he lay. We were convinced the yeos came and took it, as a warning but a few days later Andrew heard where Barney's body was taken.'

He got up and, tapping his stick on the floor, left Henry and Laurence and headed for the door, gesturing for them to follow him outside. He pointed to the road leading north from his cabin.

'We will go on a little journey now,' he said, adjusting his stick, 'for I want to show you something. You will need your cart but 'tis not that far from here.'

The two men claimed the cart bench, with Laurence clambering onto the back and holding on to the corners with both hands. Where were they going now, he wondered? This man, John McQuillan, had spent all afternoon talking and they had learned little about Barney, other than he had been killed; and nothing of the whereabouts of his family.

There was little talk among them as Ginny took them down towards White Mountain crossroads, where McQuillan pointed his stick to take a right turn. They travelled down a small twisty boreen, with a few straggling cabins strewn along either side. As they crossed a small humped bridge, John gesticulated with his blackthorn stick.

'That bridge that we're crossing is known as the Hogs Hill Bridge. It goes over the Keeran River, which, around here, divides the county of Louth from that of Meath… and 'tis Meath we're in now.'

Henry remained silent, unappreciative of the information; more concerned with where this journey was taking them. In the rear, Laurence was thinking likewise, now wary of this cross-country passage, of who might see them, or if they were unlucky and come up against a government patrol, although they had done a lot of travel that day and had ne'er seen one redcoat.

Early evening was settling across the countryside and the sun began to hide behind the tight hedge on the roadside. Further down the lane, John waved his stick, again to the right, for Henry to wheel in that direction. Neither of the Moores had an inkling of where they were! They travelled on unhindered, the single track undulating but quiet, until John urged Henry to slow down and pull into an entrance on the right. They ventured up a short way until John motioned, 'That'll do. We'll walk from here.'

After tying up the cob, they walked through a gap and along the edge of a field full of nearly ripe corn, the stalks waving gently in the evening breeze, their heads already heavy. In the distance a cacophony of crows circled the trees surrounding Smarmore Castle, before disappearing through the branches to their nests. Laurence, growing ever more concerned, was about to ask what this errand was about, when John guided them through a stone wall and into a small secluded cemetery. He turned to face them.

'This graveyard… this is Smarmore graveyard. This is where Barney Moore and, supposedly, his lodger, are buried.'

John led them to a corner where a newly dug grave lay nestled under a large yew tree.

'How do you know this?' Laurence asked, not for the first time, looking at a recently excavated burial site.

'I told you already, me neighbour, Andrew Malone, recounted it to me. He was up here the other evening, digging out a small plot for an infant he lost, when, as he made to go home through the trees, a horse and cart with a driver, pulled in under cover of dusk. He could see two bodies stretched out on the cart and the man proceeded to dig a grave for them, here against this wall. The stranger heard Andrew in the trees and called out. He made himself known and the man explained what he was doing; that he was burying the two men killed that morning at White Mountain. Andrew had remembered the man mentioning the Moore surname but he had not heard a name for the other body.'

'Barney Moore and John Mathews', whispered Laurence,' it must be them.' Names and events were now beginning to slip into place. 'Barney's son, James, he told me the yeos killed both men that morning, during the attack on the house.'

Henry removed his hat and knelt on one knee. Laurence joined him with the aid of his stick. Staring down at the grave, his mind was blank, still unsure whether this was indeed his brother's final resting place, yet wishing to acknowledge that, perhaps it was, Henry looked over at John and asked him.

'But who was this man who buried them? It couldn't have been any of his family.'

John McQuillan scratched his head and tapped his stick gently on the turned soil.

'That, I don't know, sir. That... I don't know.'

# Chapter Six
## Wicklow

Like a tossed grey ribbon on the stony slope, the track down the mountain meandered out before him. His bare feet treaded carefully on the wet shale-covered path, as he eked out the circuitous path from the Glenmalure valley towards the south-east. The earthen mearings topped by furze bushes, heavy with raindrops, bordered him on each side and on every turn. Rivulets of excess water ran onto the path, but fortunately the early rain had cleared away and the morning sun now glared into his eyes. He hadn't seen a soul since he left the camp before daybreak; not even a wild animal had crossed his path on the way down from the rebels' redoubt.

The route eventually levelled off and he began to hear the sound of birdsong all around, something he had missed up in the mountain wilderness. He continued along the path, searching for the small river, the Avonbeg, which Dominic O'Farrell had told him to look out for. He would notice it, he was advised, as the track merged with the Rathdrum to Aughrim road. From there he was to follow the river's course until he reached the village of Avoca. It would be a long journey, he was told. Walking briskly, he tried to think of little, just concentrate on each stride, one step at a time. His calloused soles bore the brunt of the stony ground. They were well used to the soft ground of White Mountain and Smarmore in his native county, not this hard unforgiving rock of Wicklow.

He tried to count his footsteps, a h-aon, a- dó, a trí. A h-aon, a-dó, a trí. He remembered some of the numbers in the Gaelic, from a hedge-school he had attended briefly years before. But that was all the numbers he knew and his mind soon wandered back to the present, to a vision of the bare hills and empty pitted stone-walled fields all around and this journey he had commenced to get back to search for his family. It left him feeling debilitated, to the point of almost deciding to curl up under a tree and go no further.

Then he spied the river off to the left, through some trees, a small gurgling stream flowing along the hedges and undergrowth. His spirits were raised a little and, hoping this was the correct course to follow, he set off along its banks. Its soft burbling meander, together with the softer ground underfoot, gave him some comfort, something to concentrate on, as he strode onwards, hopefully towards the village of Avoca.

Yet a curious fear gnawed at him, a fear of the unknown that shook him at every turn. Fear of being an exile in this land of his birth but not his rearing, he had a fear of having no family left to return to. This morning, on the track towards the coast, had been the first real chance that he had to think of his circumstances and of what had come to pass during the last number of weeks.

He had found himself in the midst of battle and bloodshed, deprivation and strife, only escaping with the few horsemen from Meath by the narrowest of margins. That final skirmish, when they stood to the last man in a field somewhere north of Dublin, the injuries he suffered when a yeoman rode his horse over him and then to have the luck to survive and be able to walk away; eventually joining up with some other survivors and making it to the Wicklow Mountains. But it had been like a long unending horrifying dream. And yet, here he was, still scarred but alive, weeks after witnessing the brutal series of retaliations by the authorities. He had concluded that the only escape was to survive the violence was to make his way home, find his family and run their tenancy. He was finished with all the running and hiding and violence.

He ventured a bit off the path and sat down, making a nest in a glade of ferns. Putting his hands behind his back he sought a moment to further consider his options.

He awoke later with a start, the shrill sound of crows cawing incessantly in trees close by, dragging him to his senses. Sitting up, he quickly realised he had fallen fast asleep, unknown to himself. At some stage he must have lain down to take a brief rest, but now, looking at the position of the sun, he determined with a shock that the sun had travelled half ways across the sky and that this day was well into the afternoon. He must be weaker than he thought, he conceded, his body forcing him to rest up like this. He rose to his feet, found the path and began to walk again. Still feeling a little unsteady he left the path to find the stream he had been following. Pushing through some vegetation he scoured the place, then stopped still and cocked his ear. He could not hear the sound of flowing water! He listened intently before moving around in the rough undergrowth, but the only noise was of distant animals and birdsong. He had lost the stream and lost his way!

He remained standing where he was, disorientated, trying to remember when he had last been near the river, the river that would bring him to Avoca. He walked back to the path and stood there, wondering whether to go forward or retrace his tracks. For no good reason he decided to go back the way he had come but stay on the path this time. But the way also looked unfamiliar, no features looked the same or stood out and there was no sound of water. He concluded that he didn't know where he was and was now totally astray!

Squatting down for a few minutes to gather his thoughts together and draw breath, he brooded over his predicament and figured out that his only option was to keep walking until he came across someone, who could put him back on the right path. With that, he travelled back the way he had come, retracing his steps for the second time but there was still no sight of the Avonbeg!

The sun was well over in the sky, occasionally hiding behind fast moving clouds. It was bright, windy and he reasoned it was heading towards evening. He trudged on, still meeting no one on the trail, only some animals in the near pastures and the chatter of birds all around. It was almost idyllic, yet in the midst of the quietness and tranquillity, he had become disorientated and could be heading in any direction, for all he knew. He tried to remain calm, so he hummed some tunes he knew and tentatively tried to whistle them - without much success!

Sometime later the rambling track brought him to a junction with a wide path stretching off to the left and right. He stood for a while, mulling over which direction he should take. But before deciding, he heard a sound, like an animal scuffling in the undergrowth. He tried to identify the noise. As he turned to his right he caught sight of a small figure struggling off the track, beyond the mearing. Relief and concern flooded through him in equal measure. A human at last, yet it was one who needed help. He could only see his face and arm reaching up from the ditch. It seemed to be a man beyond youthful years. James ran over and reached in to help him up, but he was splayed out on his back and badly winded. James clutched his arm and tried to lift him.

'Easy, a mhic, easy, or you'll have me arm off.'

The man attempted to sit up but collapsed back on himself.

'No, I cannot get up. My accursed horse threw me in here and ran off. I tried to get out before and couldn't. My mind is clouded. You'll have to leave me be.'

James stood back and considered what he should do. There was little sense in abandoning the man in the ditch, leaving him to an uncertain fate.

'No, I'll stay with you sir. 'Tis no bother to me.'

A rivulet ran at the bottom of the mearing where the man had fallen and James splashed into it, gathered some water in his cap and offered him a sup.

'A mhic, see that cloth bag on the stick over there,' he said, directing James. 'Fetch it here, there's a good lad. There is a little food in it, no more than a crust or two.'

James did so and eventually, still feeling sorry for himself, the man eased himself up in a sitting position and with the use of James' arm for help, got up unsteadily onto his feet. Briars and nettles pulled at him and he groaned loudly with aches and pains. James helped him out bit by bit onto the track. He was small of stature, with a face full of whiskers and grey unkempt hair beneath a floppy caipín.

'The beast of a pony threw me,' he protested again, 'and me

feeding and watering her every day.'

He reached for his walking stick in the dirt and checked the contents of cloth bag attached to its crook. He wore a dark, crumpled frieze coat that was much too big for him, the coarse wool tattered and worn throughout. But it had saved him from more damage when he had tumbled off the horse. It covered him up to his neck and went way below his knees! He held his head in his hands, shaking it wearily.

'Are you all right now, sir? Will you be able to be on your way?'

'God bless you lad. I was struggling there. I could not get up off me back. But my head is still spinning. I cannot get my bearings at all.'

He brushed himself down as best as he could, flicking nettle leaves off his coat then gathered his few possessions and prepared to be off. James reckoned it was time to seek some information from him.

'I'm trying to get to a place called Avoca, sir, but I don't know where I am.'

The traveller regarded curiously, looked him over, as if satisfying himself that he posed no threat. Then he laughed. He laughed liberally, holding his belly and then his head, opening his mouth and guffawing out loud. James saw the man's eyes water with mirth. He was in danger of smiling himself at the man's response. 'You're lost, a mhic,' the old man said, drawing a painful breath. 'You're lost. But if truth be told, I'm lost meself. Sure wasn't I dozing when the pony upended me, so now I've no idea where I am either.' He looked around, scratching his head.

'Now isn't that a happy collision of fate, for me and you, to be standing here and neither of us knowing where we are.'

He continued chuckling to himself and made to walk on, passing around James in the fork.

'If you're going this way, maybe I can travel with you?' James stepped up to walk beside him. The little man turned and looked at him again.

'And bedad, why not, a mhic? Sure the two of us might as well be going the wrong way at the same time.'

He giggled to himself at the absurdity. James liked him. There was some humour to him and he seemed inoffensive. But he still didn't know the way to Avoca.

They walked together, the man regularly chuckling away to himself, ignoring James but not excluding him either. James was wondering was the man a bit simple, was just wandering around, that maybe the idea of following him might not be the right one at all.

'I'm looking out for a river,' James mused,' the Avonbeg it's called. I'm hoping it will lead me to the town of Avoca.'

The fellow traveller turned and cackled at him.

'Well that bet all. So am I, a mhic. I'm looking for it too. What takes you there?' He winked conspiratorially at him, 'I'm wagering 'tis a cailín. Am I right?' James felt himself blushing.

''Tis then so. 'Tis a cailín.'

''Tis not sir. I know no one from here. I'm not from here at all. Can you not tell by my brogue?'

'Sure, 'tis a strange accent to my ears, but 'tis not for me to find fault in a lad's way of talking.' He smiled a toothy, crooked smile. James decided he should introduce himself.

'My name is James Moore. I'm from the county of Louth. I'm trying to get home to that place.'

The man nodded silently, chewing his mouth, his eyes blinking hard. He offered a gnarled, blackened hand to James.

'The county of Louth, is it? Aye, that would be the land of the Brown Bull... and Cuchulainn. I am acquainted with those stories. Well, let me tell you then, I am Sylvester Kavanagh, otherwise known as Sylvie.' He blew air from his lips and laughed at his feeble effort.

'Sylvester Aloysius Kavanagh is my full name. My dear father always thought I had been given too many high-falutin names, so he just called me Sylvie. Some even call me the King of Wicklow, because I know everyone in it.'

His chest almost swelled out of his big coat with pride. James reached out and shook his hand, smiling wondrously at the wee man who would be king. They continued on their way, still not knowing where they were going.

'I'm a storyteller, a mhic,' he explained. 'We were what used to be called bards by the old people. I travel round to some of the big houses and meet the important people there, to persuade them how important they are…even if they're of little or no importance!'

He cackled again. 'There's a few of us still left who carry on the tradition. There's a man from Galway, let me think… O'Kelly. Patrick O'Kelly. He visits this way now and again, as well as up your way too. Yes, there's still a few of us travelling bards left.'

James noticed he had but a few teeth left and his laugh came out like a wheeze, whistling through the gaps. Sylvie carried on.

'I tell these big people how good they are and they feed me and let me stay for a few nights. As I told you, there are a number of us and we have an itinerary mapped out, so we try to avoid each other. You don't want two of us arriving at the same town… or house, do we?'

They were walking through lowlands now and the land was better and the air smelled fresher. They hadn't met anyone else yet and James was anxious to do so. They could easily be walking away from his destination and not towards it. Sylvie was walking along, hardly caring whether he was going the wrong way or not, content in the telling of his stories. The only think that calmed James was that the sun, when it showed, was getting lower in the west, over his shoulder, so it meant they were travelling in an easterly direction, the right way, if not the right path.

'Do you not know if we're on the right track, Mr Kavanagh?' But he kept walking, his mobility recovering. He looked like one of the little people James had heard about.

'Truth be told, a mhic, I'm off to make myself another fortune,' he said, not answering. He pulled his crooked smile at James' puzzled expression.

'Another fortune?' James replied, sceptical.

'You don't believe me? Then, let me weave a story for you, young James, as we seem to have a long road ahead, one that ought to set your mind racing. I was passing through Avoca many years ago, which is the place I hope we are heading for.' He laughed to himself for a minute.

'Anyway, I was calling to some of the big farmers around that very place, casting their family history and extolling their virtues. Some will grant you their time and give generously of their food and lodgings, whereas others will run you down the road after a while, with their dogs chasing your heels. I was staying with a family in Woodenbridge, the other side of Avoca, and was entertaining them, when I happened to meet the local teacher of a hedge-school. He was a man I had met a few times before and we enjoyed each other's knowledge and insight. And, in the midst of our dalliance, didn't he go on to tell me a story about the local river, the Aughatinavought it is called. His name was Donoghue and he told he would take me to the stream the very next morning. I imagined he was going to catch for me the salmon of knowledge, no less! But no, when we got there, he rolled up his britches and walked into the water, wanting me to follow him. I told him I couldn't because I'd drown all the fleas on me! But he hauled me in all the same, up to me shins I was, and made me hunker down in the stream. I said to him, nearly half-drowned, "Wading must be what you teach in the hedge-school." But he silenced me and then he did a strange thing. With his hands cupped he began to scoop up water from the river and let it sift through his fingers. He did this a few times and encouraged me to do the same. '"Are we trying to catch fish for our breakfast,"' I asked him foolishly. But he drew me near and cupped his wet hands together. "Not a fish," he said, "...but gold! Look at it glow in the palms of my hand." And I looked closely and there he had cupped what looked like a little pile of wet yellow grains. Yet how it sparkled and glittered in the morning sun. He moved his hands around for the sun to capture its reflection.

He revealed to me that he lived close to the river and some of the old men told him of the glittering silt they would see in it. He investigated and had determined through trial and error where the best places were, to locate the gold flakes.'

James listened to the story, intrigued. Kavanagh had told the tale so well that he had lost track of time and place and how far they had travelled. He glimpsed a few men out working in outlying fields along the way but the outcome of Kavanagh's yarn was all that concerned him now.

'Numerous visits I'd make to the site; sure I fancied that I was the reincarnation of King Midas for a season.' He laughed his infectious laugh at this. 'I ended up collecting a fistful of small nuggets and, on my visits to Dublin, sold them to a jeweller I knew. Out of the money he gave me, I gained enough that I could buy somewhere to live, maybe a farm, or even a wife.' He laughed crookedly at this, finding his own asides an amusing embellishment to his narrative.

'But instead, do you know what I got with the selling of the gold? No, not land or cattle…or a woman! I got made for myself a few small ingots and rings. Do you know what an ingot is?' James shook his head, bewildered at the extraordinary tale.

'It's a small, round or square shaped piece of gold, the size of a farthing, maybe. I'm thinking, would you like to see one?'

James nodded dumbly, thinking this was some trick being foisted on him. But Sylvie reached for the sack at the end of his stick and rooted around before withdrawing his hand. He made a fist, then slowly opened it to reveal a few small yellow coins, like fancy buttons off a jacket, though much prettier than buttons, James concluded in awe. There were also a couple of bands of gold; narrow rings that looked delicate and brittle.

'See the lustre from them, James Moore. See how the sunlight dances on them.' He tilted his hand left and right to allow the sun play on the surfaces. 'I arranged with the jeweller in Dublin to make these for me. And now I'm off to the river again to see if there is more gold in the water. What do you think of that story now?'

'Do many people know about this magic river?' James asked, his eyes still locked on the contents in Kavanagh's hand.

'Aye, plenty went to the river in later years, it was like a little town along its banks. But earlier, when only a few knew, me and the teacher sat in the river, with our pans and sieves, filling our pockets with the river's generosity. I spun the tale of discovery into my stories and many great men in great houses sought my allegiance to hear about... as you say, this magical stream. However, with the recent troubles, the Wicklow militia have the valley sealed off and the last time I was up here, much of the timberwork and workings had fallen into ruin. Yet they say it's quiet there now, and if you know your way in, you can slip by the guards and get to the site. I'm going to try my luck again. Every time I pass through the area I like to see how my luck is faring out.' He finished with a self-satisfied little chortle.

They walked along in easy silence, James contemplating Sylvie's story, until he saw a river come into view to their left as they walked along the track. It was much larger than the one he had followed initially, its width and volume of water reminding him of his recent visit to the River Boyne. Yet, no matter how often he asked, his fellow traveller would not say where they were. But James went along with him anyway. What other option had he?

With dusk settling across the sky, they reached the outskirts of a small village, a few meagre cabins sitting on each side. James still had no idea where he was, but Sylvie Kavanagh walked purposefully down the street, crossed a bridge over the river and headed for a cottage sitting at the edge of the habitation, on the road leading away from it. James trotted up beside him and forced him to a stop, outside the house.

'Mr Kavanagh, where are we?' he asked slowly, deliberately. 'Tell me. I want to know.' Kavanagh smiled at him, exposing his few extant teeth in the evening dimness.

'You've followed me on the road this far. Do you still think we're lost? I was having fun with you, a mhic. I knew the way all along. I was a bit winded mind you, but I just fancied some company along the way. And you have kept me such good company, that you have boy, that you have.'

James stood looking at him, startled.
'So where are we, Mr Kavanagh, in Avoca?'
'Yes, we're in Avoca, your destination.'

71

James looked around him, at the bridge and the row of small lime-washed cabins beyond. Kavanagh rapped on the door of the cottage. James could see dim candlelight through one of the small square windows.

'You and I will stay with these kind folks tonight.'

'Do they know of our arrival? They will hardly have room for the two of us.' Kavanagh shushed him and waited at the door.

When it opened, a woman peered out and quickly recognised the old man. She whispered a word of welcome and guided the two travellers into the house. James stood aside, bashful, before the woman and her husband extended a welcome and positioned a black kettle on the hob. Later, as the talk picked up around the fireside, James sat on a stool by the back wall and, exhausted by the heat, nodded off. Later, still half-asleep, he was shown to a bed of straw in an outhouse, where he collapsed and drifted in a dream-filled sleep, replete with sheep, waterfalls, mountains and rivers of gold.

And it was only the next morning, after he departed on the journey on his own and was nearing the village of Woodenbridge, that he discovered some articles in his jacket pocket. He had departed Avoca early, after a generous breakfast of cheese, oaten bread and buttermilk. Sylvie had bid him farewell with a shake of his hand and a glint in his eye as they stood outside the cottage.

'I hope good luck follows you all the way back to the land of Cuchulainn,' he said, directing him onto the road to Woodenbridge and from there onto Arklow. It hadn't been a gruelling walk and he had made good headway, but well into the walk his stomach had rumbled and to partially sate his hunger, he dug into his pocket for a crust of bread he had saved.

It was then that he felt his fingers curl round some small round objects at the bottom. His curiosity aroused, he took them out and palmed them, seeing the midday sun sparkle off them. Immediately he knew it was Sylvie who put them there. He must have placed the gold coin and ring in his jacket the previous night or this morning at breakfast. He considered going back to return the gift; even to wait in

Woodenbridge for Kavanagh, who had mentioned that he too was going there, as the river of gold was outside that village. But, crossing the bridge over the Aughrim River, James continued out the Arklow road. Amazement seeped through him at the generous gift from Kavanagh for, he supposed, helping him out of the gripe and accompanying him on the walk. In fact, it was more than generous, yet in a way it was useless too. But on earth could he do with items of gold in his pocket? People would think he had stolen them. At that very moment he would have preferred if he was in possession of a package of bread, some cheese and a jug of buttermilk because all he wanted now was to fill his stomach and make his way back home.

*

He smelled the Fishery area of Arklow town before he came upon it. The tide was out and the area was overwhelmed with the powerful smell of fish, mud and water. The main street was busy and as he stopped and asked several people if they knew Andrew Tyrell, he was directed down to the far end of the town, where most of the fishermen lived. It was an area of congested alleys full of small mud cabins. Women and children were outside their houses, gutting fish and putting them in baskets with salt. Not used to a coastal village, James was overwhelmed with the reek and the clamour and bustle of the place. Very few men were around. When he enquired, he was told they were all out on their boats but would be back in the evening. He walked down to the riverbank and decided to bide his time until the men came back from their excursion on the sea. He found himself a dry spot on the bank and, apart from the distraction of the cloying smell wafting around him, he settled in for a long wait.

To him, it took ages for the boats to begin sailing slowly up the river and cast their weights over the side onto the mud. James watched with interest as baskets of fish were offloaded from the boats and taken away by the fisherwomen and children, who had come down to help their menfolk. Many boats had tied up and when the unloading was completed, some of the crews drifted off to their homes or the ale house. James resolved to ask for Andrew Tyrell as they headed off to their cabins. He stopped a crewman and enquired of him.

'I'm looking for a fisherman named Andrew Tyrell.'

The young man, unshaven, unkempt and with a coil of rope around his shoulder, didn't even stop. As he passed he looked hard at James before shrugging and continuing his journey. James stopped another fisherman, who was bow-legged and weather-beaten, a pipe in his mouth.

'Have you heard of a fisherman by the name of Tyrell, sir, Andrew Tyrell?' He did stop and looked at James suspiciously.

'And if I have?'

'I would just like to speak with him, that's all.' The man continued to stare, knowing from James' accent that he wasn't from any of the families around here.

'And what might ye want to talk to him about?'

James remained resolute. 'That would be between him and me, sir.' The fisherman took his pipe from his mouth and laughed.

'Aye, you won't get much help out of me with that tone of voice.' And he walked off towards the cabins.

Most of the men were gone from the boats by now, only a few still tying up for the evening and bringing their gear from the vessels. He approached three men from the same boat as they lugged netting up to drier ground.

'I hope you can tell me where I might be able to find Captain Tyrell?' They had been talking amongst themselves but stopped suddenly at the question. Drawing near him, they glanced at each other. One of them drew closer.

'Are you looking for work?'

'No sir. As I said, I just wish to speak with him.' The man continued to stare at James. 'Who sent you?' he asked sharply. James, reluctant to declare his intentions, shook his head, noncommittal.

'No one sir! I just wish to have a word with him.'

The man questioning James turned to the others, his eyes

expressing something to them, but then they walked away, leaving James to look after them as they disappeared up into the street. He turned away and found an empty lobster pot and sat down on it. All the boats were empty now, lying askew on the muddy side of the river. The sun was already slipping behind the town, its silhouette growing shadows of the buildings out towards him. He had spent the evening at the moorings and was no further on. He contemplated hiding out on one of the boats, but immediately dismissed the idea, as he didn't know when they would sail to next. He could be lying under a sail for days! Around and above him seagulls swooped and dived, some landing and forming into raucous groups, fighting over scraps of fish and offal left on the mud by the fishermen.

The evening drew in quickly but, without having a plan formed, he got up from the pot and turned towards the town. His feet squelched through the mud until he made it onto the drier street surface, where he was forced to jump over a channel where human and animal waste ran down towards the river channel. Despite the stench, he was hungry and he wondered would there be an eating-house open nearby. He had no money other than the value of Sylvie Kavanagh's gold coins but he couldn't very well throw them on a counter and hope to get change or food for it!

Feeling morose and somewhat home-sick, he walked back up to where the fishermen's mud cabins were huddled together. Dusk had settled quickly and a chilly breeze came down the street towards him. He could make out dim rush-light in some of the houses and a few women were shooing the last of the children in off the street. He decided he would ask the next person he met if there were any lodgings he might stay in. Yet he knew he may well have to sleep rough for the night. He was nearly used to sleeping in the open now.

Nearing a corner, where the street adjoined another row of houses stretching back to the left, he saw a man standing alone on the other side, looking down at his feet, fidgeting. He had reached a corner house junction, when another figure came up close to him from the left. He was about to ask about accommodation when, from out of nowhere, he received a punch to the jaw, knocking him senseless. As he landed heavily, a sack was pulled down over his shoulders and face. Someone else grabbed him around the legs, lifting him into the air, where he was roughly bundled off into the maze of back streets.

# Chapter Seven

## Bellevue House

A long row of glass-panelled lanterns, suspended from wooden poles above the driveway, helped illuminate the avenue leading up to Bellevue House. As darkness settled over the heavens on a wonderful balmy night, the evening ball by the River Boyne was due to commence at dusk and carriages and brakes, carrying those invited, made their way, as if a cavalcade, up to the house. Beside Thomas Gettings, in their two-wheeled, covered buggy, was his fiancée Emma Morgan who, captivated at how the Barton's drive had been lit up, squeezed Thomas' arm excitedly.

'Isn't it marvellous, Thomas? Look what they've done to light up the way to their house. It's like something out of a fairy-tale.'

'It is beautiful, really beautiful,' Thomas responded light-heartedly, clutching her hand. 'As *you* are, my dear,' he added, 'just beautiful.'

The artificial lights added a frivolous, magical touch for the arrival of those attending the soirée at the Barton estate. The glittering occasion, held every summer at Bellevue, drew invitees from all the titled and landed classes through the locality, and also included officers from local militia and yeomanry corps. To be in attendance following an invitation was a prerequisite; to be absent without good reason was considered perilously close to an insult.

Thomas was quietly impressed by the entrance decorations, though he continued to be distracted by the machinations of Captain Rothwell, and indeed whether he would be in attendance at this evening's festivities. And if he was, how he would avoid him in the expected crowd as he certainly did not a confrontation with him with

77

Emma by his side? He tried not to dwell too much on it.

Half way up the avenue they were waved through by a contingent of men on security detail. Thomas slowly guided the buggy around the last sweep of avenue, where the house and lawns opened up before them. Over a dozen large lanterns, hanging high from stakes in the ground around the outer wings of the building lit up the frontage like an amphitheatre. It was an impressive sight to behold! Their horse came to a halt before the house where Thomas assisted Emma in dismounting. After removing her travelling cape and leaving it on the seat, a steward took the reins and led the horse and trap away to the side. Several groups of people stood outside on the lawn, chatting animatedly. Placing her arm through Thomas', they both walked towards the main doors, where two doormen invited them inside. They were met by the gentle music of a chamber orchestra originating from the depths of the house.

Many guests were already there; groups of people, congregating, with glasses of wine in their hands; some were being announced, with ladies bowing gracefully on an introduction, extending their fingers to be kissed. Taking a glass each, Thomas and Emma advanced carefully through the entrance hall and into a large, already crowded, reception room. At the far end, French doors were swept open to allow egress onto the back lawns, which sloped gracefully down to the river. Emma glanced at Thomas and he could feel her tremble slightly at his side. Though beyond her debutante years, she would be unused to large social gatherings, such as this. Thomas had been to Bellevue the year before, on his own, and he too had found it a rather daunting experience. Emma observed the array of ladies in high-fashion apparel pass by. Most were in wide-hooped colourful gowns, displaying all the fashionable shades of white, pink and lavender, swaying along as if they were floating on air. Thomas looked down at her, noticing her reticence and clasped his hands in hers. He regretted their lack of romantic assignations recently, his active service with the Slane yeos since May precluding all but the briefest of liaisons with her.

'You will be fine,' he said soothingly. 'We will find some

people that you and I both know.'

Alongside him, she looked beguiling in her plain but elegant white cotton dress with a simple bonnet and patterned cashmere shoulder stole, lent to her by her fashionable aunt in Drogheda. Her hands were covered by fine lace gloves and her fair hair hung in stylish ringlets. Her cheeks were gently rouged and the interior lighting of the room embellished the natural green lustre of her eyes.

He smiled down protectively at her, but she had already sensed his somewhat subdued behaviour this evening. Up until recently he would appear for some of their meetings, resplendent in his military tunic, with a posy of picked flowers and a small gift for her. He would be ever attentive and sometimes she wished he would let her say more in their conversations. However their rendezvous two weeks ago, during a short furlough he had from yeomanry duties, and now again this evening, when he had seemed detached and not as focussed as usual, made her worry about their relationship. Was his fervour waning? Had something occurred to diminish his affections? Some issue or other had arisen that was troubling him and she determined this very evening to find out what it might be. His concerns were her concerns how, she felt.

He lent close to her and whispered affectionately into her ear. 'You are the belle of the ball tonight, Emma, he told her gently. 'I cannot afford to let you too far from my side.' She reached out to him and placed her arm gently around his waist.

'Oh, come now, Thomas! Your soft Welsh brogue will always be enough entice me, yet I am but small pickings in this sea of riches here, yet I fear I know very few. I have not laid eyes on one familiar face so far this night.'

But, out of the corner of his vision, Thomas just had! It was the face of Edward Rothwell, his nemesis, deep in conversation with Thomas' fellow officer in the Slane yeos, Gustavus Barton. He averted his eyes rapidly, just as Rothwell turned to scan the crowd. He was damned if he was going to be caught making eye contact with him!

Both he and Emma stood and surveyed the large reception room for some recognisable faces, though it was hard to concentrate with the noise and constant movement of the quests. Even the orchestra's music was being dampened by the voices of the crowd. 'Oh, look Thomas! I believe I see some young ladies I know from Drogheda, over there. Will you lead me over and introduce me, please?'

The pair made their way through the crowd and approached the small group. Welcome smiles prevailed in their congenial company as Emma presented Thomas to her female acquaintances. Some had met him before, a few now for the first time. He bowed briefly to them all, saying, 'Emma, you will have to introduce me to these ladies.'

Pleasantries abounded and Thomas remained at Emma's side for a reasonable period before whispering to her that he would move on and speak to her later. With a gentle squeeze of her waist, he slipped away. He looked back briefly and she had already launched into some anecdote and, satisfied that she had found kindred company, he sought out some of his own.

He had known Emma Morgan for almost a year now. They had been introduced by mutual acquaintances at a summer ball at Smyths of Greenhills in Drogheda, not unlike the one they were attending this night. She was the second daughter of Evan Morgan, a Welsh coastguard officer, stationed on the River Boyne at Queensborough, a hamlet to the east of Drogheda. After an initial period of chaperoning by her older sister, they had been walking out together for some months when they finally introduced their respective parents to each other. Despite the fact that the two fathers came from the opposite ends of Wales and of social class, both men quickly established a warm rapport and had become amiable friends. Emma's mother Margaret had become quite fond of Thomas and he quickly became a favourite on his visits to the Morgan household. Thomas and Emma had intended to pursue their designs for marriage this summer, but because of the rebellion and Thomas' extended duty with the yeomanry, following the battles at Tara and Mountainstown, plans for the nuptials had been put in abeyance and only recently were they brought into the open for discussion again.

But Thomas' preoccupation and concerns regarding the grim work he was impelled to do continued to play on his mind and he knew it was also beginning to impinge on his relationship with Emma. It was a concern that he would have to carry covertly within, because, like Edward Rothwell's verbal abuse the previous week, and from surprised looks of some of his men in the field, they would disparage what they might regard as a form of weakness in a man's character. So, he knew he would need to be careful in who knew about it.

A roving waiter offered him a glass of port and he stood, sipping it on his own, nodding briefly at guests as they walked by and listening distractedly to the chamber music, until he caught sight of the Slane yeo officer, Gustavus Barton, engaging a circle of men in conversation. Glancing round, Barton happened to notice him and ushered him to join them. Reluctantly, Thomas walked over and was announced by Gustavus as his fellow lieutenant in the Slanc yeomanry. Thomas bowed towards the men, already recognising some of the faces. Gustavus' father was opposite in the circle, Charles Barton, and beside him his wife, Frances. Also introduced to Thomas were three other titled individuals that he was only vaguely familiar with, one being Baron Conyngham of Slane Castle and two elderly gentlemen from Navan and Drogheda whose faces he didn't recognise.

Slightly unnerved at being drawn into this esteemed assembly, his voice was hardly heard in the general conversation. After the baron's wife slipped away to tend to other groups, Thomas spent much of the time discerning the traits and characteristics of the men around him. Charles Barton, the rotund host of the evening, was avuncular and spirited and poured forth on all matters of interest that came to the fore. Gustavus, tall and plain-looking and the only one Thomas knew well, had inherited a rather more dualistic mind-set. There was a certain cunning simplicity to him and he didn't dwell too much on preambles and obfuscation. It was his straightforward estimation that people were either good or bad and that the good were born into it!

Next to him, Baron Conyngham, in gilded jacket and puffed wig, exuded a self-satisfied yet jocular nature and was full of pleasant bonhomie. The two elderly gentlemen, to Thomas' surprise, each seemed to plead a conversational ignorance on many of the topics under discussion and remained largely mute. Thomas attempted a furtive glance in the general direction of Emma, who was still busily engaged with her friends, and barely heard the question directed at him.

'I say, young Gettings,' Charles had turned to him and was speaking, 'we have not heard from you yet. You and Gus here, you are the only men within hearing distance who are actually out in the field, on patrol, hunting these… what do they call them, yes, these croppies. Gus tells me that the more he and the Kells captain, Rothwell, can find and string up from the nearest gallows, the better. He says that we should be rid of them all soon. But what say you about these errant rascals?'

Thomas, having little to impart up to then, was taken aback at this problematic question. Yet, immediately he knew his response as a yeomanry officer would be critical to his standing amongst these eminent men, therefore his inner emotions must remain secret from them. Uncomfortably, he cleared his throat.

'We don't know why these men do what they do,' he volunteered. 'Since the final stages of the rebellion, Lieutenant Gustavus and myself, have been out in the countryside with our units, clearing it of the danger from remnants of these rebel groups, many from as far away as the county of Wexford. What has brought them all the way to the peaceful pastures of Meath, we cannot fathom. Perhaps the glory of battle drove them on, or perhaps it was their religious zealousness, for it would appear many remained in awe of their priests, who, you would imagine, should be preaching the virtues of peace and tolerance. Then again, many more were led by supposedly disgruntled Protestant landholders. To sum up, sirs, it is indeed a mystery to me.'

Silence briefly enveloped the group while the din of conversation encircled them. Baron Conyngham was the first to respond.

'That is interesting. You have provided a very pertinent and quite eloquent answer, young man, and you would appear to have been considering the wider spectrum of the late conflict.'

On the far side of the group, Gustavus chortled into his glass before exclaiming, 'Interestingly, the lieutenant posed just such a question at Speaker Foster's house last week and he now kindly has attempted to answer it. Meanwhile, as he has been meditating on the actions of the rebels, I've had the pleasure of hanging six of these croppies by the neck, up on Tankardstown Hill. That was the same day, you, Thomas, took your batch out to Carrickdexter and Captain Rothwell advises this very evening that he has dispatched simply dozens since the affair in the bog.'

Gustavus pointed at Thomas curtly. 'He might be thinking more about the wider implications, but as far as I was concerned, I was helping rid the land of those who wish to overthrow us. It is a simple but effective solution to our problems. We can write as many pamphlets as we want about it later.'

The two elderly gentlemen emitted a couple of brief hurrahs for his statement, but Baron Conyngham retorted. 'Yes, that is a strong sentiment too, Gustavus, but perhaps our retribution should be sated now. Don't you know we have a harvest in the coming weeks? May I be so bold as to suggest we should offer a form of magnanimity in our victory?' He offered his glass out to a waiter to be topped up and then continued.

'Soon some of these men will be needed to harvest our corn and later, to till out fields. And if not here, then back in their native county. You know, in England we are regarded as their breadbasket and even their larder betimes, and if their problems with France continue to deteriorate, they will seek more of our produce than ever before.'

Gustavus frowned into his drink, not unwilling to accept the Baron's reasoned argument. Thomas knew Barton as a brash young lieutenant in the same unit, patrolling their area around Slane and unafraid of showing bravado, such as at the executions last week, when he and Thomas had let the convicts to their deaths. Of equal rank to Thomas, being Charles' son offered Gustavus a sense of privilege within his rank and Thomas remained quietly circumspect when he became fond of issuing orders to him, and for an easy life, Thomas usually acquiesced. It was bad enough, having to deal with Rothwell's tirades, without drawing the ire of Charles Barton of Bellevue onto his head too, if it was seen that he defied some of his son's instructions! Meanwhile Gustavus was trying to defend his point of view.

'Still, despite the executions, we must be vigilant around these croppies,' he said, 'for some are still at large and no doubt plotting against us, even as we speak. Captain Rothwell says he and his men are still scouring the countryside for them, even ranging over into the county of Louth in pursuit.'

'Didn't he lose some men over there recently?' Thomas said. 'Perhaps he is still chasing those culprits.'

'I believe you are right, Lieutenant,' the Baron agreed. 'He is a tenacious one, that Captain Rothwell. I have heard it said that many crossroads around Kells have men dangling from gibbets, whether guilty or not.'

The two elderly men in their company had become tired of nodding in agreement at everything said, so drifted away to look for some savouries. The Baron was continuing his theme of looking towards the future, away from the recent unrest.

'Because of the uprising and the amount of imported English troops required to quell it, there is now talk emanating from London, that Ireland is to be reconstituted into the union with the English Crown, as if it were the bold child who needs to have manners put on it. I fear there will be much resistance to it though. And I hear Speaker Foster will not be in favour of such a move.'

Thomas was seeking a way to extricate himself from the political discussion and vowed to leave in search of Emma at the next suitable opportunity. The Baron was extolling to Charles, the virtues of being re-joined politically to the Kingdom of Great Britain.

'Events can occasionally overtake us, Charles, when we presume that the power we hold dear, here in Ireland, is in fact a nebulous thing and our ultimate masters across the sea will do as they will, whenever it is expedient for them...'

Just as he was building up the structure of his theory, Charles' wife, ever the attentive hostess, arrived with a waiter and invited everyone to replenish their drinks. Thomas eyed tables of supper buffet in the next room, made his excuses and took his leave with a full glass in his hand. It was uncomfortably warm, even in the spacious rooms and he needed to get some air. He went in search for Emma.

\*

Turning from the group Thomas glimpsed Rothwell staring in his direction, his eyes hooded with menace. Thomas took a circuitous route round the room to avoid any encounter with him and soon after he located Emma out on the back terrace, beyond the open doors of the conservatory. She was in conversation with the same young ladies she had been with earlier. When he approached they nodded politely and moved along. Some other couples were standing outside, listening to the music through the open windows and taking in the majestic view of arboreal elegance around them. Thomas placed his arm around Emma as both faced the panoramic view of the river, a section of it shining brightly in the moonlight below.

She looked up at him. 'What a beautiful evening, Thomas, a beautiful evening for a little talk, between you and me.'

Thomas could discern a certain anxiety in her. Perhaps now was the right time to confide his worries to her; he had no one else to confide with. If he was to make her his wife, then shouldn't he be able to talk about his worries? It was an indulgent thing to think, spill out your woes to another. His father had always encouraged him to act strong, to get over ones frailties, but his inner turmoil was something he found difficult to bottle up. Perhaps Emma would understand his disquiet about the work he was obliged to carry out.

'Shall we walk down to the river, Emma? There appears to be even more lanterns here to guide us down to the riverside.' She looked at him. 'Will you talk to me by the river then?'

A wooden rail with lights suspended on poles directed them down the slope to the lower lawns. He went in front and while she held the rail post, he helped her negotiate some slippery grass surfaces. Not many had trod this path, only a few shadowy figures melded against the tree-lined path down this far. Despite some further lanterns brightening up the periphery of the glade, Emma held on tight to Thomas for fear of losing her footing. They were silent as they walked gently on towards the riverbank, the soft gurgling of the Boyne, adding a luxuriant backdrop to the sounds of the early August night. Gently, she removed her gloves from her hands, letting the evening air waft against her skin.

'Isn't this wonderful here,' she said, drawing close to him, taking his hands in hers. 'Yet you fret, Thomas. Something is bothering you. You would not have come down here with me if you did not want to talk about it, would you?'

She searched his eyes, trying to winkle him out. He paused, hesitated, words not coming easily. He had contemplated this moment before and now he hesitated. How could he explain his emotions to her, rationalise his fears and anxieties?

'I am so lucky to have you Emma, my love.' He squeezed her hands gently. 'Our talk should be of our wedding, where we would live, our future...' She encouraged him.

'Then let's talk about those things now. We have so much to talk about.' She drew close to him, kissed him gently on the lips, wanting him to open up to her. He eased back and held her bare arms; her cool, smooth skin drawing a yearning in him that caused him to choke.

'Truth be told Emma, but I have much on my mind,' he said finally. 'Matters of conscience haunt me; work I have to do that I am finding increasingly difficult to carry out.' He looked into her eyes, her soft blue eyes, eyes that he could look into forever.

'Tell me what work this is, Thomas, that is upsetting you? You know that whatever upsets you, upsets me.'

He shook his head and pulled away slightly, his feelings shrouding him in gloom. Why should he be upsetting her over this?

'Tell me,' she insisted, holding his arms tightly. He shrugged, a lump in his throat, vulnerable now having declared his intention to speak. Would she remain strong for him, when he opened his heart to her?

'Emma, to be truthful and to use language unaccustomed to your ears, my duties include…,' he paused, troubled by the darkness in his soul which he was releasing. '…the indiscriminate hanging of captured rebels from a gallows, whether summarily in the field or following court martial. I try to ensure that they meet their fate both quickly and efficiently. Yet I must stay and watch as my men pull the boards from under them and endure the spectacle of them swinging in the air before me. It is an uncommonly depressing sight, I admit, which never wanes in its horror and will remain with me to the end of my days.'

He shuddered inwardly as he spoke the words, reliving again the executions in his mind. Emma, taken aback at his blunt detailing of events, nevertheless, clung to him, offering him her support.

'I have come to the conclusion, Emma that I am just unable to participate in the killing of these rebels any longer.' His eyes cast down, unable to look directly at her.

'I hate what I have to do! It makes me sick to witness it and it is a grisly, revolting display of man's inhumanity to man. Yet, some will argue that it is what they deserve after agitating against the government and, in truth, I find it difficult to reason against that…'

He made as if to stop, feeling he had said more than enough, but Emma looked into his eyes, encouraging him on, to have it out.

'But this fault I have, this foible in me,' he continued, 'it flies in the face of everything I am, a lieutenant in the Slane Yeomanry. I am no coward Emma, and the duties of defending the area for law-abiding citizens, of putting down all forms of insurrection, of defending the peace, I carry out with vigour and zeal. Yet this defence of the realm is predicated on putting these rebels to heel, butchering them if it helps remove the problem and unfortunately the requirement to do that is prevalent now. But seeing men stabbed or shot to death in the fields or hung from trees, swinging on the gallows, kicking out the last vestige of their lives; that kind of suffering is beyond my resilience.

I believed that I could control my abhorrence of the deeds,

override it, become immune to it, but it has only gotten worse as the events of this summer continue.'

Emma was alarmed at having him expound his fears about his duties like this. Yes, she had heard him mention his nemesis Edward Rothwell of Kells on some occasions and that man's boorish attitude to Thomas, but he had never discussed his daily undertakings with her before. This affliction was something new in him. The shock of his words began to overwhelm her but nevertheless she drew him close.

'Thomas... Thomas... this is such sad news you bear. If it causes you so much grief, then you must be rid of it. If it 'tis forming like a cancer in you, you must cut it out. No man should be asked to do such work if it causes so much grief in him.'

Emotion swept over him as he had now let loose such a terrible secret. He hugged her tightly and searched for her lips, to salve his thirst on her love and understanding. She responded fiercely and they remained locked in a passionate embrace, whispering soft endearments to each other. Then, reluctantly, he eased away from her. He still felt a need to explain himself more fully.

'You must know this, but as soon as this present emergency is concluded, I shall resign my commission as officer and seek work in the coastguard. I have already spoken some words with your father about it.' Her eyes lit up at this news.

'And hopefully, you will be close to where we live,' she offered. 'That is should good news Thomas. Oh, that it will come to pass.'

'And another thing I wish to fulfil,' he carried on, finally glad to be shedding some of his burden, 'is a desire is to talk to some of these young rebel men and determine their attitude that drives them towards this rebellious madness in them, this trend of railing and rising against their government. If I could only learn and perhaps understand, we might be able to prevent such explosions of anarchy in the future. We might but try.'

He ceased talking, but still continued to wrestle with his conscience. The last of the guests had returned to the house and they were now on alone, close by the river, the nearest lanterns throwing only faint glimmers of light their way. Thomas held Emma's hand tightly as he turned and they both walked deeper through the trees towards the water. Here it was much quieter, the noise from the house barely audible as they drew up close to the riverbank. The moon flitted through passing cloud cover, illuminating the silvery flow of the water, its gentle rush quiet and soothing in the night. They stood side by side, hands grasped tightly, looking at the river flow by.

'It is indeed a beautiful night, Thomas.' She spoke quietly to him, almost whispering. 'Too beautiful, don't you think, to languish at this low point. Let us try and enjoy the rest of the night together. We'll go back to the house and indulge ourselves a little more and then we will talk about these things when we next meet. What do you say?'

'You are right, my darling Emma. We are here to enjoy this night, not to dwell on these problems. They will wait for another day.'

He was eager to agree to her idea, ready to place his dilemma behind him, wish it away temporarily, even for this evening. They turned round and faced the direction of the house. As he held her hand to make their way back, his ears picked up a faint noise. At first it was only the gentlest of sounds, but at close quarters, it came from somewhere quite close. He thought it might have come from the house and he turned around to listen from that direction. But no, it seemed to carry from the other bank of the river, the north side. He leaned close to Emma's ear.

'Do you hear that?' he whispered. She looked to where his arm was aiming, pointing across the water.

'Maybe I *can* hear something,' she speculated, 'but I don't know. What is it? Is it the river?'

It came to him again, like a soft murmuring, but not the river. The more he listened the more it resembled a group of people talking quietly, but he needed to be sure. The foliage spread thickly up along the river's edge on both sides and motioning for Emma to stay where she was, Thomas drew himself in through a section of it, making sure to make as little noise as possible. The ground gradually grew wet and soft and he stopped his advance and waited.

Perhaps thirty yards across the flowing waters, the vague silhouettes of a number of individuals were discernible in the moonlit reflection of the water. They appeared to be lying down, in deep undergrowth close to the bank; some were reclining on their elbows and a few were on their knees. A subdued discussion was in progress but he couldn't make out the words.

Thomas was perplexed and considered his next move. Perhaps they were some local peasants out hunting wildlife? But would five or six be out together? Or maybe they were locals with fishing lines in the river, illegally waiting on a catch? Or, and it hit him almost like a blow; could they be croppies lying low, trying to evade capture?

He grew alarmed and was in a quandary now. They were hardly considering an attack on the house and its guests, were they? How would they traverse the river? He was reluctant to make his presence known to them because they would simply run away. Perhaps he should keep this development to himself and investigate further on the following day.

Returning to a now impatient Emma, he shrugged nonchalantly. 'Well did you see anything?' she asked.

'No Emma, it was nothing, nothing at all. It must have been an animal close to the river. My ears were deceiving me, it would seem.'

He didn't want to alarm her further or indeed for her to mention it casually in conversation, but his mind was in confusion about his next course of action. Emma was feeling the gradual chill of the night and was impatient to get back to the house. She linked his arm and together they climbed the steep incline back to the party in Charles Barton's house.

# Chapter Eight
## White Mountain

Laurence's mood had turned subdued since their journey home from White Mountain some days ago. With only the basic knowledge of his uncle's grave and nothing at all on the whereabouts of Barney's family, the expedition had left him and his father more frustrated than ever. All they had seen was a burial mound and McQuillan had heard nothing of the others. Laurence had spent the next few days with his father, both of them helping George Geraghty finish off the repairs to the roof of his cabin, while inside, the ruinous result of the yeos attack was tidied up as best they could.

On one of the mornings, with his injuries healing well and feeling stronger each day, he had gone with Kate, his sister, to retrieve water from across the fields at Tobernagapple well. It brought memories back to Kate.

'Me and James were collecting water here, the morning we found Pat Sheils. He was hiding in the hedge the other side of it, just over there.'

Laurence nodded in a distracted fashion. 'Kate,' he said, 'I intend to return to Smarmore on my own. I must search for James' family, whoever is left. Nothing was gained from the first journey. He would want me to do it and I can't rest until I hear something of them.'

'Poor James,' said Kate. 'A good cousin he was too. Do you think... he's... dead, Laurence?'

He swished at a tall bulterrin with his stick. 'I don't know. I wish I knew, either way. The last we saw of him, he was racing off on his horse with Whelan and the rebels. Who knows what happened to them after that. I have a fear that they were all wiped out by the army. I saw what the military did to us in the bog. Those poor lads from Wexford stood little chance against them.'

Between them they filled the four pails with water and trudged back along the path to Killary, with Laurence hooking the buckets onto his stick and hobbling along. He warned Kate to say nothing about their conversation.

The following morning, the day he had decided to go back to Smarmore, the weather hung grey and overcast, with a blanket of fog lying along the roads and low fields as he started out on his journey. Laurence had thrown a few boiled praties and a pouch of buttermilk into a leather pouch and departed for Smarmore as the cock crowed in George's yard. Only Kate knew he was going but she didn't disturb him. The dense morning mist gave him plenty of cover as he began walking along the road to Lobinstown and, apart from the appearance of a horse and cart with its driver, where he hid in the ditch, he met no one else along this early part of his journey. At least, he thought, there would be little yeo activity on a morning like this.

Drawing close to what would be the crossroads to the east of Lobinstown, which intersected with the Drumconrath-Slane road, the morning fog had grown increasingly dense and his progress slowed to a shuffle as he kept to the grass in the middle of the path. It was as if he was walking through a cloud and he could almost lick the dampness on his lips as he breathed in and out. The quietness of the morning became eerie in the half-light. There were no birds singing, no breeze blowing, all was quiet. His breathing resounded in his ears, together with the rustle of his bare feet on the damp grass growing in the middle of the path. He had walked in fog before, many times, but a preternatural trepidation had begun to envelop him now. Peering almost blindly into the grim murkiness, he started to realise that the trek to look for Mary Moore and the children might take a lot longer than he had anticipated if the weather was this bad! He stumbled onwards some more and began to consider turning back and trying again another day.

He was looking around him to see if he could establish some reference point on the road when suddenly his eyes were drawn to a number of ethereal shapes floating in the heavy mist before him. He stopped in his tracks, a sliver of dread shooting up his spine, a primal fear holding him fast, rooting him to the spot. What could they be? He was instantly transfixed by the vision of grey figures swaying delicately in the miasma, as if swimming underneath some grey and listless water. Too startled to cry out and too terrified to run, he dropped his sack and muttered a prayer of self-preservation. Were they the ghosts of James' family coming to him or perhaps the ghosts of James himself and some of the Wexford rebels? Emotions spilling over, he fell to his knees momentarily, supplicant to the visitation, but then rose and drew nearer, pulled closer by some inner force driving him to discover what he was witnessing.

The slightest of breezes rose up and the fog swirled around lazily in the flow and dispersed briefly. As it cleared he saw, with mounting horror, that the incorporeal spectres were in fact the bodies of three men swinging from a gallows at the side of the cross-roads! Ropes clung tightly around their necks and their heads hung grotesquely to one side with mouths open and tongues displayed hideously between their teeth. Rags of shirts barely hung on their shoulders, remnants of britches hardly clinging to emaciated waists. Bile rose in Laurence's throat at the gruesome sight. It struck him that they must be some of the rebels from the battle at Mountainstown, who had gotten lost or were too injured to continue and were captured and strung up as a warning to the populace. Their presence at the junction must have been a recent act by the authorities because they hadn't been there when he and his father passed through on their way to Smarmore several days ago.

He stood immobile, mesmerised by the ghoulish scene and blessed himself repeatedly, offering more quiet words of prayer for their souls. He didn't know how long he lingered beneath them, but he felt a strong urge to tarry a while longer, to act as their witness and honour them in their short tragic lives. His vigil before them soon turned to successive bouts of fury at their treatment and vengeance against the perpetrators. The various government actions he had encountered this past few weeks, culminating in the event before him, had resolved any final doubts he might have had, making him now sure about what he wanted to do, even if his own life would become forfeit from his subsequent actions.

Slowly the mist began to dissipate in the rising temperature of the morning. The road junction became visible and he could see how deliberate and prominent the gallows were positioned, as anyone travelling on the road couldn't help but notice the dead men. A house diagonally across the junction stood dark and empty. Had the inhabitants fled when they realised what was being erected in front of them? It would indeed be a macabre sight for them to witness every time they came out their door. Almost reluctantly he decided to move on, before others came and saw him standing beneath the bodies, wondering why he was braving the site, rather than scurrying away in trepidation. He gathered up his food sack and hurried on, trying to make up for lost time.

*

Even as the fog steadily evaporated, he remembered little of the rest of his journey in the morning brightness, his mind continued to be filled with images of the men on the gallows. Along with James and hundreds of others, he had been witness to Michael Boylan's public hanging at the Tholsel in Drogheda two months before and that too had been a difficult event to stomach. Yet there had been a measure of comfort in the crowd that surrounded them and he hadn't been able to get close to Boylan's gallows. The corpses hanging at the cross-roads had affected him rather more; their final humiliation on the gibbet searing him like a skinning knife.

Reaching Leabby Cross almost unknown to himself, he stood looking at the junction for a moment before realising he was now near White Mountain. The day had cleared up and huge tall clouds sailed slowly across the sky, heralding possible thunderstorms in the afternoon. Before he began his search, he sat by a mearing and consumed his cold potatoes and buttermilk, then emptied his bowels against the back of the ditch. His stomach no longer rumbling, he made his way down the White Mountain road, back again to the same place, where he and his father had been several days before.

He contemplated calling to John McQuillan's house again to see if he had heard any further news about the disappearance of Barney's family. All was quiet on the road to Smarmore. He noted again the patch of uneven ground at the side of the road where John Matthews had been temporarily buried and further on, Barney Moore's burnt out cabin. Arriving at McQuillan's neighbouring cabin, all was quiet, but on the other side of the road he saw John and a number of other men out in a crop field, their backs stooped as they made their way down the drills towards the road, throwing clay-covered potatoes into woven peillics. The gate lay further down the road but Laurence jumped across the ditch into the field and waited to see would John notice his presence. The other men were picking in a line abreast, all of them slowly working down the field towards where Laurence stood. John McQuillan happened to look up from his exertions and saw Laurence gesturing at him. Without signalling that he saw him, John looked around at the others but weeded on for a little longer, leaving Laurence to wait.

A few minutes later and becoming impatient, Laurence called out to him. 'John, 'tis Laurence Moore… here again! Can I talk to you? I'm just wondering if you've heard any more since I was here last?'

John McQuillan stood up, clutching a couple of praties in each hand. He threw them into the bag, grabbed his stick and walked slowly over to where Laurence stood. He looked back at the others in the field, one of whom was now standing upright, watching inquisitively. He eyed Laurence with his peculiar sideways look. Then he spoke, quite loudly, so the field-workers could hear him.

'What do you want, a mhic?' Laurence wondered at the loud voice and he so near him. McQuillan drew closer, whispering urgently.

'Make sure they can't hear you when you speak.' Laurence nodded, not quite understanding his meaning.

'You're a shocking man to be annoying the people round here,' he began, still whispering. 'And 'tis dangerous to be prowling along the lanes and roads. Be on your way now, lad.'

But Laurence stood his ground. McQuillan was being his irascible self and he figured if he stayed strong he might still get something out of him.

'John, I'm not leaving 'til I find them or someone tells me what happened to them. You and my uncle Barney were neighbours and friends. He would do the same thing for you.'

John wiped the sweaty strands of hair from his brow. He drew closer to Laurence's ear.

'Listen, 'tis not right that I be talking to you. The yeos are still about, riding their big horses through the fields and roads, searching and searching, still looking for...who, I don't know. Would I be right in saying that? And there is someone new in the field with us today. He says the Taaffes sent him up from their yard! But the divil only knows who sent him. The rest of us don't know him at all.'

Laurence grew cautious and decided to be non-committal. Something had happened that was worrying John since the last time they met.

'But you helped us before,' Laurence reasoned. 'All I am asking is if you've heard any more news?' McQuillan was sweating profusely, his lank hair plastered to his forehead, refusing to leave his face despite his best efforts at parting it. He repeatedly looked back at the other men working in the field. Laurence wondered should he just move on.

'Listen, a mhic,' John almost hissed, beating his stick rhythmically on the ground, 'I did what I could for ye when ye were here before. Maybe I did too much. Those yeos yesterday, they stopped at several cabins, even dug through the ruins of Barney's cottage. What are they looking for, I am asking? Your family seem to be drawing soldiers back to bother us agin and 'tis not what we want around these parts. We don't want trouble here.'

John was growing fidgety, even petulant. Laurence could see the man in the field, still standing, watching them intently. He was about to leave, feeling there was no more to be gained by questioning John. He didn't want to aggravate him more than was necessary but he was concerned to hear that the yeomanry units were continuing their searches. Did they think James was still alive? John directed him back to the road, encouraging him to be on his way, not wanting to be seen talking to this young stranger any longer than was necessary.

'You'll be on you travels now son. There's no work here for you.' He was talking loudly again, for the benefit of the field workers, but then added quietly. 'There is one thing you might want to hear. I only heard this hour from one of the men here, that a woman with children was spotted up near the fairy fort at the top of White Mountain. Lismore they call the fort. Beneath it you should be able to find Patsy Rogers' old cabin. It's supposed to be empty, so perhaps someone is staying in it. Go up there now and see who is there - and don't be annoying us down here.'

He gave him a grudging wink, then left Laurence on the road and returned to his potato drills. Laurence heard him in conversation with the others in the field, saying that he was only a young spailpín, on the look-out for work in the area. He was thankful that McQuillan, who was awkward and irritable, had been verbally shielding him from his fellow worker's curiosity. He began to walk back the way he had come, the road gradually rising before him. In detail, he considered the meeting he just had with John. He was a man whose demeanour had changed since their previous one. He was much more evasive now, afraid of something; something perhaps that was said to the yeos. Laurence knew he would need to be very careful now. Who could you trust anymore? Walking on, he computed the sun's position. It was afternoon and the big clouds he had seen earlier in the day were now quite close and looked dark and full of rain. He hurried on before the deluge hit him.

*

97

He made his way up the west side of the furze and fern covered hill that was White Mountain. Still warm, the dark thunderclouds drifted ever closer and occasional spits of rain landed on his face. He wasn't sure exactly where Patsy Rogers' cabin was, but there wouldn't be many up on the brow of the hill. But to be certain, he decided to go all the way to the top and look from the height in search of it. The small fields soon thinned out into commonage and higher up it became a coarse heather and furze-filled landscape which slowed his ascent somewhat. He tore his feet more than once on sharp stones and furze stems and spent some time on the ground massaging his soles and stemming blood with dock leaves.

The rain began in earnest as he reached the summit. And he quickly came upon what McQuillan had called Lismore. His first impression was of a kind of fairy fort - and he was wary of those stories and did not fancy being left alone close to where they might dwell! With a brisk wind bearing in the rain from the west, he struggled initially to climb up onto the circular rampart of the fort, which was partially covered by parapets of furze. Retreating back down to the ground, he walked round the large circular enclosure until he came to an entrance gap on the northern side. Warily, he sidled in and was confronted almost immediately by several sheep grazing inside. They fled from him immediately, away to the far side. The overgrown walls of the ancient fort afforded him some protection from the rain, now coming down in torrents. The sheep eyed him suspiciously but remained where they were and soon returned to their grazing, oblivious to him and the rain.

Evening drew in, the rain's intensity lessened out but still lingered and the western sky became luminescent with the setting sun reflecting off the cloud mass. Yet, even though he was in a relatively sheltered area, the cold and wet soon seeped through him. He curled up for as small as he could, with his arms around his raised knees, not really knowing what his next move was. Spending the evening in the fairy ring was beginning to intimidate him and, realising that it was now too late to return to Killary, he decided to leave and look for this cabin.

He eased off the ground and scaled the shallow earthen embankment to have a look around. The rain had stopped but the wind hadn't softened with the onset of evening and it continued to buffet him. Yet despite the chill he was overcome by the enormous vista before him. Whichever way he turned he could see away to and evening horizon. Multiple shades of green rolled down the hill and away towards the limits of his sight. James had told him of the magnificent hills around his home, but he had paid no heed to them, until now.

In a gap in the furze cover, where he was positioned at the highest point of the fort, he slowly swivelled around, catching the huge panorama of other domed hills, lower-lying farms, tracks and the vast late summer sky. He marvelled at the contrast of the claustrophobic fog he had encountered that morning and the vastness of the hilltop now, and all in the same day! Up here, he felt fleetingly like he was king of the world, ready to take on all-comers, yet ultimately, he still didn't know how he could find Mary Moore and this was the sole purpose of his journey, to try and locate her. She was down there somewhere; John McQuillan had more or less confirmed it. But where was she? Where?

So, before the dusk filtered out most of the light, Laurence made a final effort to look for a cabin in the slopes beneath, a cottage, a hut, in fact, any kind of habitation. John had mentioned Patsy Rogers' cabin below the fort, so he concentrated on anything that looked like a cabin on the west side, which would be directly up from the road. One or two mud-built structures were partially visible down the slope, one with a tree-lined field adjacent. On a whim he decided to check on that one and if not it, maybe the family inside could direct him to the Roger's abode.

Leaving the solitary confines of the fort, he made his way slowly down the hill, seeking out paths that would get him close to the cabin he had spotted. With the last vestiges of light receding in the west, dusk had descended on the land and he had to manoeuvre carefully through the undergrowth as he negotiated the rough sheep track he had found, leading down from the hill.

Darkness gradually enveloped him and only for the vision he

retained of the cabin's location, he would now be lost in the expansive slope of White Mountain. The sky grew clear and a gibbous moon had risen above the hill. Its light afforded him dim images of tracks, hedges and openings. And, before long, he had reached a gap, which led into a field surrounded by dark shadows of trees. It was the tree-lined field he had seen next to the cabin! No animals were in the enclosure and so he was undisturbed as he traversed it.

The vague oblong shape of a cabin grew in size as he crossed the rough pasture, sheltered in behind boughs and branches. He imagined a shadow, perhaps someone outside who was returning indoors, but with the little light and silhouettes of trees moving in the wind, he could just have been mistaken.

Forcing a brave face on his solitary mission, he crossed a low wall and came up to what was the front of the house. All around the perimeter was dark and not a flicker of rush-light flickered from within. He hesitated for a minute, uncertain whether to call out and make his presence known, or to approach the door and knock. Some of the trees bordering the field cast long rippling shadows onto the cabin, weak moonlight interwoven into the darkness.

His nerve-ends were tingling and that shiver went up his spine again, the same as at the crossroads that morning. If only he had a firelock or knife now, any weapon, he mused ruefully? Feeling defenceless, he rooted out a broken length of branch from nearby and let it rest firmly in his hand.

Reaching the door, he could have sworn he heard voices, like distant low whisperings coming from within the building. Perhaps it was Mary and the family after all! Could he really be that lucky?

His sense of fear receding somewhat, he banged lightly on the door with the stick. Here was no response. He paused briefly then he struck the door again. Again, only silence met him. He considered moving on down the hill, as this house seemed to be vacant, derelict even.

Then, with a suddenness that sent him jumping in fright, a grating noise came from within and the door was suddenly pulled inward, scraping loudly along the dirt floor. A dark shadow in the entrance moved across the space and the figure of a man swiftly emerged from the dark interior, aiming a pistol directly at Laurence's chest.

# Chapter Nine
## Arklow

The all-pervasive smell of the Arklow Fishery was close to overpowering James as he began to come to. Despite the rankness of the air, he gulped in as much as he could through the threads of the dusty sack, which was still over his head and pulled tightly around him. His legs were tied securely and he could only breathe with difficulty. He started shouting out. Immediately a muffled voice hissed into his ear.

'Whist outta that lad, there's none that can hear you. The bag's coming off now, but if you make a sound, back on it goes.'

He could feel the rope being released and the hood pulled off him. His jaw felt numb and ached when he opened it, but nevertheless he breathed in a proper lungful of air. He was in a small room with only a bench and a few stools. He was sitting uncomfortably on a three-legged stool. Warily, he eyed the two men standing before him.

'We hear you've been asking a lot of questions,' the taller man said, leaning in close to James. The other one, ragged in loose jacket and britches, stood back but added, 'Aye, you're looking for Mr Tyrell. Why is that now?'

Through a groggy and tired head, James was trying to assess just how much danger he was in. He had revealed little or no information to anyone in the town, yet these men were taking exception to his asking for Tyrell. Why? The two were looking at each other.

'We think you're some sort of informer or spy,' the shorter one said. 'And you know what happens to them? Captain Tyrell doesn't take kindly to those kind of people and nor do we!'

The shorter one drew out a gutting knife and looked at it menacingly. James realised he had to do something quickly. So he told them his story.

'Dominic O'Farrell, from this town, is up in the mountains fighting the redcoats. I was with him and Michael Dwyer and his men for a few weeks but I need to get home to the county of Louth now. Mr O'Farrell told me to get to Arklow and make contact with Andrew Tyrell; that he would take me up the coast and land me close home.'

He reached into his pocket and took out the small parcel of hooks that O'Farrell had given him. He held it out.

'Dominic said to give these fishing hooks to Mr Tyrell. That they would prove it was him and I was here in good faith.'

The taller of the two men grabbed the pouch then left the room, while the shorter man, wielding the knife, glared at James with suspicion. He was fearful of what would happen next. Then the second man also departed and James could hear him in the next room, making himself busy, before going quiet. Later, James stood up and tried to hop around to get some feeing in his legs but he soon fell over and it took all his effort to regain the chair. He lay his head on the table and fell asleep.

Dark had brightened into day and still in a fitful sleep he was roughly shaken awake when three men entered the room, the two that he already knew and another man. The fishhooks were thrown onto the bench by the newcomer.

'So these are supposed to satisfy me of who you are?' the newcomer said. James remained silent.

'I am Andrew Tyrell, the man you asked for. My men here say you told them that Dominic O'Farrell directed you here, and those are his hooks.' He looked at them again. 'I recognise them as the special hooks he made himself. But how do I know you didn't steal them from him or take them by some other means?'

James had no answer to that and shrugged silently. Tyrell began pacing the room, over and back, looking at James, then down at the floor, assessing his captive. He asked the other two to leave before deciding what to do with him. As soon as the door closed, he stood in front of him.

'My crewmen, Byrne and Kennedy, were a bit rough on you, I grant that. They assumed you might be an agent of the government people. This town is full of them since the battle in June.' It wasn't an apology from him, just an explanation. 'But now here I am and wondering why would you give me those hooks?'

James noted a subtle change in his tone. He sounded more amenable.

'I know they are O'Farrell's. Their shape is unmistakeable and they would be precious to him. So, if you didn't steal them, then he gave them to you for a very good reason. I will tell you about me and Dominic O'Farrell later. My gut is telling me to believe you lad, that you were with him in the hills and that he wanted me to help you. Otherwise, how would you know O'Farrell and Dwyer's names? But how can I get you up the coast? Going as far as Drogheda is seldom part of my voyage. My crew will be suspicious of where we're going. I don't know. 'Tis hardly worth the risk I would have to take. I think maybe 'tis best you be on your way.'

Tyrell was thinking that the lad was probably more trouble than he was worth and James was wondering how he would break the deadlock. How could he persuade him to make the journey north along the coast? Then an idea came to him. He fished in his pocket and drew out Sylvie Kavanagh's gold coin. He stretched out his hand. 'Maybe this will help you change your mind.'

James opened his palm and showed Tyrell the small gold piece he had been given. Tyrell's eyes widened.

'Where…did you…get this?' he gawped. He reached to take it from James, who immediately pulled away. But he had to trust his instincts now. He let it fall in Tyrell's palm. He looked at it with intense interest and even tested it's veracity on his teeth.

'The man who give it to me said, 'twas made of pure gold.'

Tyrell was soon satisfied with its authenticity. 'I know what gold is. I've seen some of it from the mountains.'

'It was given to me as a gift on my journey down from the mountains. 'Tis yours if you can get me up the coast.'

Tyrell eyed him quizzically. 'You're some lad for people giving you things. Do you sing songs for them? Do you play the fiddle or make up stories?' He regarded him with renewed interest.

'I could still have you dumped overboard. It would save me the bother.'

'You wouldn't do that, I know you wouldn't. I am but an honest lad, sir. I do not make up stories. I do my best. The redcoats killed my father and I must return to find my mother. That is all I ask of you; that you sail your boat and get me back up to the land beside the Boyne.'

*

The following morning, just after dawn, Andrew Tyrell woke James and arranged some cold porridge and a crust of bread for him. They then walked down to the harbour. James intuition had been right - and O'Farrell's too. Tyrell was a trustworthy man and he had made his mind up the previous evening to offer James a place on his boat.

The two stopped for a moment and Tyrell gazed at the sky, seeking out the horizon for signs of approaching weather. Tall dark clouds hovered out to sea, to the east, hardly moving, yet the breeze in his face told him they would be along this way - and soon. The tide was gradually filling the harbour where the boats were lying and the sun's early rays, escaping from the far-off low cloud, flitted among them. They were the first there, his crew of three would be along later, he told James. They walked towards where Tyrell's yawl was tied to its moorings.

'I havn't told the men yet why you are going to sail with us,' Tyrell advised. 'So, just point over to me if they say or ask you anything. You are to keep your mouth shut. Is that clear?' James nodded silently. He could sense the wary hesitancy in Tyrell's voice.

'Was Dominic O'Farrell your captain?' James asked, wondering how Dwyer's lieutenant in the mountains could be connected. Tyrell nodded.

'He helped keep my family alive, when we had nothing. He gave me work on his boat ahead of other men in the town.'

Reaching the boat he jumped up onto the edge of his boat, grabbing hold of the boat's gunwale for balance.

'Why did he end up in the mountains?' James continued and watched as Tyrell turned back to him, a scowl on his face. He was a man who wasn't used to questions.

'I owe him for helping *me*, not for telling what path in life he took.' James remained curious and Tyrell relented briefly.

'Look, he left his boat when the rebellion began around here in May. Some fishermen joined the fight, others didn't. But he took up arms and when the rebel army was beaten here in June, his yawl was impounded and a search was made for him, so he and a few of his crew took to the hills.'

James nodded, silent but satisfied. Tyrell climbed into the bowels of his craft, shouting back at James to wait while he carried out some running repairs to the wooden beams. James looked on with scant interest as Tyrell plied an area of timber in the stern with oakum, where water was leaking in. James looked around the small harbour. Boats were pulled up, their sails lying in the body of the craft. Others were without sails, lying sideways on raised sections of mud, seemingly under repair. A few fishermen had now come down to the shoreline to prepare their yawls for fishing. He looked on with interest at the waters of the tide rippling into the harbour, inching up along the rivers muddy sides, lapping at the bottoms of the moored fishing craft. He had never seen the sea before, he reckoned, just rivers and streams. Here, he saw the start of it, all mucky and smelly and wet.

Despite his days of walking, James wondered was he still doing the right thing. Dry land was preferable to the dangers of travelling by water, but recent battles and subsistence living on the hills were hollow in his memory now and all he wished for was to see and comfort his family. The quickest way home was on a boat and it certainly seemed to be his best option. But he was unsure how he would fare out in this new, unknown form of transport. But if it got him closer to home, well then he would take his chances out on the water.

\*

Several fishing boats left the harbour simultaneously; easing through the channel, their sails in bloom, catching the wind as they headed out on their seaward journey, well beyond the shelter of the coastline. Sails were trimmed and despite the wind and dark clouds coming from the south, a fair wind soon drove the small flotilla northwards, making a good speed up the coast.

James was wary of Tyrell's crewmen, two of whom were the men who had abducted him. Yet he was also mesmerised by the spectacle of riding the waves on the puny little wooden craft, with flimsy canvas sails to propel it along and was quietly impressed by the seamanship of its crew and the pace of its passage. However nature soon intervened and his stomach began to rebel at the unnatural movement it was experiencing. His head was soon positioned over the side, endeavouring to bring up whatever modicum of food that lay in his stomach. The three crewmen, Byrne, Kennedy and Doyle, sniggered at his visible discomfort. Tyrell smiled and pointed behind him to some seabirds following the craft. 'You are feeding the gulls their breakfast, lad. Soon, they will be waiting on you for their dinner.' James was too drained to respond to their laughter.

The six boats sailed on, the captains of each observing the waters, trying to determine from their experience where the shoals were located. Though the boats were separated by a distance and fishing independently, they signalled to each other with a shout, if fish were spotted or other signs that they should be aware of. Off Dublin Bay, they came close to an English frigate, sailing towards the harbour, her white ensign flapping in the wind. A few on board the vessel looked at the small fishing boats beneath them as if they were insects.

North of Dublin the captain of the yawl closest to Tyrell called out to him, gesticulating at the sky to their rear. Tyrell directed his gaze to the rear and noted the dark mass of thunderclouds building in the distance, with the southerlies drawing them progressively towards the craft. In turn he passed on the warning to the next captain ahead of him.

It was after noon and James watched as the weather slowly changed around them. The sky grew heavy and murky and the sea had developed a surge, which tossed the boat in a sickening fashion. His stomach still heaved uncontrollably with the yawl's rise and fall in the choppy water. Waves began to splash over its bow and its mainsail flapped violently as Andrew Tyrell and Ned Byrne wrestled it down the mast. Despite reducing the speed, Kennedy and Doyle struggled with the fishing net as they dragged it in from the water and across the stern. Tyrell groaned as it cascaded into the boat. He had thought their struggle with the net might have been the burden of fish in it, but, for the second time, the catch was abysmal, just a few herring and some mackerel jerking around in the netting at the bottom of the boat. Byrne ranted at the meagre contents.

'That's two casts today, and what have we got? What have we got? A single creel, half-full of sprats, hardly fit to feed any of us on the journey back.'

The others on board looked disconsolately at the results of their labours but said nothing. Tyrell grunted to Byrne to help him hoist the fore mast back up. James scanned the horizon to his left and could just make out the long thin shoreline under the low cloud. No physical features were discernible but Tyrell had deduced that they were sailing north of Dublin and that they would be coming up to his dropping off point at the Boyne sooner rather than later. Though Tyrell was courteous enough to him, even giving him a cut of bread, which didn't stay down too long, the three man crew were not so forthcoming. If their work drew them close to him he could hear their mutterings under their breaths, especially from the two who had incarcerated him. James would not be drawn and eased himself up towards the aft end where Tyrell was manipulating the sail ropes and tiller.

'Don't pass any remarks of the lads,' Tyrell said. 'They're only concern is catching herrings. They're crabby enough because we have netted so little.'

James smiled wanly, his stomach continuing to heave. He had noticed that the other boats were turning round and heading for the coast. At the front Ned Byrne was in a volatile mood, with much hands waving and pointing at James. It appeared Tyrell had still not them the purpose of the extra-long voyage beyond their normal fishing grounds. Byrne had also noted the deterioration in the weather and that the other fishing boats had decided to head for shelter and were now no longer visible. He voiced his concerns to Tyrell.

'The weather's worsening. Shouldn't we heave about and head towards shelter?' Tyrell was looking hard at the sky, unsure now whether to proceed ahead of the storm or pull the boat to port and look for refuge closer to land. Byrne sensed his dilemma.

'And while we're at it,' he complained, 'what about this lad here, with no sea legs? One day he's for stringing up, the next you have him on your boat.'

Tyrell eyed him coldly. He knew the others had come to rely on Byrne to act as their mouth-piece and Tyrell had had to put him his place now and then, since he joined his crew last year. But he was a good fisherman and had learned the ropes with little tuition. Tyrell usually tried to be even-handed with him. They had scrutinised James warily but had said nothing when he boarded the yawl that morning. However, Tyrell knew the question would be thrown at him at some stage. He sighed and, showing James how to keep the tiller arm steady, he edged closer to his crewmen. Amidst a gentler yawing of the vessel he ushered them nearer.

'Men, like you, I was once a young fisherman. I was indentured on Dominic O'Farrell's boat out of Arklow when I was fourteen. He was a hard but fair captain and he knew where the herring were. He could almost smell them beneath the boat. He learned me the best places to search, some unknown even to the other fishing boats. I was up as far as here with him a few times. He had a saying, "From Wicklow Head to Clogher Head, there is where we earn our bread." And if the wind and tide were favourable the boat would struggle with the weight of fish.'

His crew eyed him silently as he explained the reasoning for going this far. Did they believe him? He wasn't sure, but it would have to do. He continued. 'Young Moore here, he is a friend of the fisherman, Dominic O'Farrell, who I learned the trade with. He is up in the mountains now, but he wants me to help this gossoon out.'

'By giving him a place on this boat, like an apprentice?' argued Byrne stubbornly.

'No, by sailing him as far as the Boyne, where we will let him disembark. We are giving him a seat on the boat and that is all we are doing.'

'So, our nets are empty because we are to deliver this lad somewhere beyond our normal fishing grounds and not worry about the catch.' Byrne's voice rose above the wash of the sea and the rising wind. Tyrell, tired and hungry but content to carry out this favour to O'Farrell back in the mountains, was now tiring of Byrne's petulance. He looked at him impatiently.

'Ned, we will catch the fish, when we drop him off. We are nearly there.' But Byrne, stubborn-headed now with the lack of bounty and the extra sailing, would not back down. The other two sat silently. They had seen Byrne like this before. He was standing up, balancing himself on the swaying boards of the boat bottom, facing Tyrell.

'We've missed two days fishing,' he shouted at his captain. 'Two days of food and a price at the market, and you have us wasting our time on some... some favour!' He looked at James in a threatening manner. 'I should have gutted him when I had the chance.'

Despite Byrne's rising hostility, Tyrell was still casting his eyes on the deteriorating weather. He looked for the shoreline, which was barely visible in the near distance. He nodded at James to hold steady on the tiller again, showing him how to grip the front edge while resting his arm along its length. Then he stood up and leant forward into the wind to have a few final words with Ned Byrne, to try and calm him.

Overhead, the sky had filled and with a massive clap of thunder, the wind picked up malevolently and began to shear ferociously across the yawl. James grew alarmed and with presence of mind, located Sylvie's gold ring and placed it tightly on his little finger. By then, it was all he could do to hold the tiller arm firm, yet his eyes were locked on the two men, meeting in the middle of the boat, ready to challenge each other.

With little warning, sheets of rain descended and hit them squarely, in what quickly became a wind-blown deluge, blasting against the boat. Momentarily he raised his hands to his face to wipe his eyes from the buffeting wind and rain. The tiller, like a limb possessed, whipped from side to side, whacking against the stern. The yawl suddenly lurched to one side, throwing everyone on board into the sodden bilge. James was swamped in rain and torrents of water washing on board. He could see nothing in the sudden maelstrom. The boat swung erratically, lurching, heaving, like a living thing. Tyrell was shouting, as if from far away, screaming at his men to grab the tiller, to lower the fore mast. In the squall James could hardly see in front of him but he struggled up from the bottom boards and reached out for anything solid, anything that he could hold on to.

The boat lurched and a body washed by him, arms flailing, whoever it was, shouting hysterically. James was too shocked to reach out. Was it Tyrell? There was an ocean of seawater everywhere now. It was in his mouth, over his head, pulling him under. He felt the yawl was going down - and he with it. He shouted out for help and was pushed back down into the bottom of the boat. Through a break in the pounding waves he glimpsed Tyrell at the aft section, desperately trying to control the wild movements of the boat. There was no one else around. Had the others gone overboard? Tyrell was half out over the stern, trying to force the rudder back, despite no tiller arm; then reaching out for the boom to bring down the main sail. The boat was juddering and swaying, water sluicing in and out of it, almost full and then nearly emptied. It seemed to race away, surging forward erratically. Tyrell was shouting - maybe at him - for James could see no one else aboard. Panic set him on a frantic attempt to extricate himself from the sinking boat. But the rain and wind hurled itself upon them in all its fury, forcing him back into the bilge again. He coughed up more

111

swallowed water. Peripherally, he was staggered that this tumult had come upon them so quickly. Even Tyrell, who had been preparing to deal with Ned Byrne's obduracy, had failed to comprehend the impending danger of the tempest developing behind them.

Under the immense pressure of the heaving, broiling sea and the accompanying cyclonic wind, the yawl began to break up. James held onto whatever fabric of the boat he could grip on to. Timbers and crossbeams soon splintered and were torn apart, washing away in all directions. Both masts, the large foremast and smaller mizzen mast, snapped, toppled over and plunged into the sea. James became trapped under the wooden boom and folds of the aft-rig as it swept by him into the water. His last image was of the boom swinging towards him and knocking him down, before dragging him overboard and into the maelstrom.

# Chapter Ten

## Boyne Valley

The morning heat had quickly evaporated any lingering fog along the valley of the Boyne. The harvest was in full spate and with the mixture of rain and sun the cornfields were now burgeoning with their bountiful crop of barley and wheat and ready for reaping. But fields of grass would be cut first and lap-cocked, they too were top heavy with crop and men were plentiful in the meadows scything and tossing and finally stucking the ripened fodder.

Thomas Gettings' nose was filled with the smell of freshly cut grass, as he journeyed out of Slane along the Navan Road. Retracing his route from the previous week, he rode past the scene of the recent executions on Carrickdexter; the bodies still hanging, up on the hill; silent reminders of the consequences of rebelling against the authorities. Cognisant of his own part in executing the sentences, Thomas kept his eyes on the road, refusing to look at his grotesque handiwork from the week before.

And other uncomfortable considerations also occupied his mind. As well as attempting to interdict with the group of rebels sheltering in the trees opposite Bellevue House, he had also received, that very morning, a hand-delivered directive from Speaker Foster, about a further sweep of the river area. It would be conducted by amalgamated Slane, Kells and Collon yeomanry units as early as the following morn. This inevitably would mean that Rothwell would be involved and would be in his sights sooner than he would have hoped.

However his most immediate concern was to find these rebels in hiding on the banks of the Boyne. He hadn't figured out exactly how this was going to transpire but he would venture to the approximate position where he had heard them the previous night and hopefully establish some kind of contact. That was his basic plan, but he knew it was fraught with all kinds of dangers. Was he naïve enough to think they would even talk with him? Would they pose a danger to him on his approach or perhaps they might even flee at his arrival? Formulating a cogent strategy was proving eminently difficult and the more he thought of just riding up to them the more he realised they would be unlikely to accept his bona fides.

He stopped his horse in mid-stride on the road and dismounted, beginning to have second thoughts about his wild scheme. Leading his horse to the roadside to graze, he stood reflecting, knowing he had so much to lose over what he was considering. Yet his very life as a yeo officer had become offensive to him and his thinking this past few weeks had been leading up to just such a venture. It many ways it didn't come as a surprise to him, what he had proposed to undertake this morning: to try and talk to the other side, possibly reason with them that what they were doing was wrong. Yet he was prepared to listen to their story and if he could help them leave the area, he would endeavour to offer some assistance. No one knew of this project, not even Emma, the one person who he confided in most. She alone understood his struggle with this battle weariness he had. But she knew nothing of this endeavour and he shuddered inwardly. He briefly contemplated her anger but she didn't realise the depth of his despair. No one was to know what he envisaged, for if it failed, he didn't want either her or his father to have any inkling on what he was undertaking, for fear of possible retribution.

Reining in his horse, he remounted but continued to agonise over his next move. Perhaps he would return to Slane, cross the bridge and venture back to Bellevue and see if there had been any developments since the previous night. Maybe he could find the steward there and establish if he had noticed anything untoward recently. Settling on that, he swung his horse around and backtracked on his route, re-entering Slane village, turning right at its junction, then down the hill, across the bridge where he took the road to Navan, along the

114

southern stretch of the Boyne.

Still unsure of his motives, nevertheless he forced his horse onwards, concentrating on the rhythm of his mount beneath him. He took a short-cut through Fennor townland and was soon drawing near the entrance to Bellevue estate. He would say - if he was questioned by any sentries - that he had mislaid an item of clothing from the previous evening; that Emma had dropped it down by the river bank. That would draw him close to where he wanted to be. It was a ruse that he hoped would hold tight, for the time being anyway.

Turning into the avenue, some labourers were removing the lanterns that had illuminated the route for the previous evening's guests. Bidding them good-morning as he passed, he proceeded onwards casually, as if he had every right to be there, and eventually reached the house itself. There was no one around, save a couple of large dogs lying in the shade at the front door. He tethered the horse on a tree at the east side and decided to approach the steep path down to where the river lay. That end was shaded by a series of large ornamental bushes and trees and offered good cover as he walked on. Working his way down the stone steps he spied a steward on the lower lawn, who was busy cutting and trimming a series of low hedges. Without hesitating Thomas reached the bottom and walked over to introduce himself to the groundsman. To prevaricate at this stage would be his downfall. He must exude a calm exterior yet be brash enough to bluff his way to success.

'Hello! I am Lieutenant Gettings from Slane.'

An elderly man turned towards him and tipped his cap slowly in acknowledgement. The gardener had a loose-fitting shirt on, dampened with sweat over dark britches tied with cord. A round, haggard face scrutinised the visitor, yet the man also looked fit and sprightly despite his advancing years.

'How d'you do, sir. How might I help you?'

Thomas adopted a courteous style. 'Firstly, may I ask your name, sir?'

'Certainly lieutenant, 'tis Denis O'Rourke you're speaking to.

I'm one of the groundsmen here and also assistant steward.'

Thomas tried to read his face as he spoke, watching for any uncomfortable pauses or unusual gestures.

'Good man. The reason I'm here is, I'm on an errand following last night's soiree. As we took a walk around here, my fiancée happened to lose one of her gloves. Somewhere over by the river, she thinks. Do you mind if I go and search for it? I shouldn't be too long.'

Thomas noticed the gardener's smile wane ever so slightly. He was mumbling something to himself, before suggesting an alternative to Thomas's idea. He waved his hedge clippers back up to the house. 'If you wish to wait back up there, lieutenant, I will have a quick look and see if there is anything along the bank belonging to your lady. If I find the glove, I will bring it right up to you.'

Thomas, not wanting to be outmanoeuvred, dismissed his proposal outright. 'That won't be necessary, Mr O'Rourke. It is but a small silver-lined glove, easily overlooked. You can help me search for it if you like?'

Thomas made to step towards the path that led down to the river. O'Rourke panicked and tried to side-step him to block his way. Thomas saw a shard of fear flick across the man's face. What was wrong with him looking for a mis-placed glove? Getting's decided to increase the pressure on the unfortunate O'Rourke, to see would he give way.

'Look, Mr O'Rourke, you mustn't obstruct an officer like that. Do you want me to report you to Mr Barton?'

Thomas slipped to the side and headed down the path. Denis O'Rourke shuffled after him, calling for him to stop, to wait. Thomas pushed on, through a path in the trees until he heard the flow of water close by. The river bank was near and he hoped the groundsman would back off and let him carry out his secret search for any rebels nearby.

In front of him, he saw a small wooden boat pulled up onto the bank, its oars lying beside it. It was wet and had fronds on it and appeared to have been recently used. Thomas stood looking at the small craft, his curiosity piqued. From memory, the other side of the river was exactly where he had heard the men talking the night before. Now, looking at the wet ground underfoot, he discerned prints in the flattened grass. There had been a gathering here, a landing perhaps, from the other side? He turned to O'Rourke who was following close behind.

'What has been happening here, Denis? Would you care to enlighten me?'

O'Rourke stopped a short distance away. He looked fearfully at Thomas, his mouth opened but no words issuing; his mind trying to come up with a plausible story. Thomas helped him along by pointing at the boat.

'Should I deduce from this evidence that there was a recent transfer of men from one side of the river to the other?'

Denis O'Rourke stood stock still, his face blanching, eyes turning to the left and right to see was anyone else a witness to the accusation.

'As God is my judge, sir, you are holding the wrong opinion of me. I was only preparing the craft for a short trip on the river for Mr Barton and his lady. Sure it belongs to the house.'

Thomas eyed the spot, noticing the amount of traffic on the wet uncut grass adjacent to the river verge.

'There's more than one set of prints here,' he offered, 'that I can see anyway. Were you, per chance, the captain of this craft as you ferried someone across from the other side... a group of men, maybe?'

As he forced Denis into a disclosure, Thomas felt a pang of guilt for the groundsman, whose features had dropped with alarm. O'Rourke now saw his livelihood, and possibly his life, crumble away before him.

'See here, I do not propose to pursue this further,' Thomas said evenly, 'but, you must tell me about the men across the river. Are they rebels... croppies, who are they?'

O'Rourke blinked rapidly, his mouth open, words still not forming, shock at how his actions were so easily discovered. Thomas had been quick to determine that the O'Rourke was implicated with the hidden men and his discomfort before him seemed to prove it. Perhaps now was the opportunity to relay Thomas's own view of the situation. He drew near to the man who was visibly shaking before him and urged that he listen closely.

'Well, surprised as you might be, but if you've helped some of these men, well that pleases me. My duties as a lieutenant include defeating them in battle, hunting the remnants through the fields and ditches and executing as many as possible. It's a job I no longer feel suitable for and wish no more part of it.'

O'Rourke's eyes grew wider as he looked at Thomas, amazement on his face at the young lieutenant's utterances.

''Tis not right for you to say such things, sir.'

'Mr O'Rourke... I will call you Denis. I have taken you into my confidence about my intentions here today. I hope you will do the same with me. I want to meet some of these men; listen to their stories of why they fought in vain against the might of the government. If I can I will help them. I have done enough killing. Are they still around the place?'

Denis was speechless, consumed with self-preservation and unsure how to extricate himself from this conversation. Could he trust this young lieutenant, who was unbelievably speaking words of sedition and treason? But if he rejected his request to see these men on the run, what was to stop him reporting to his masters in the big house above?

O'Rourke reluctantly decided he had no alternative but to accede to the officer's request and, leaving the clippers on a bench, he nodded for Thomas to follow him. They proceeded beyond where the boat lay, into an area of thicket and undergrowth where the path along the river soon disappeared. Over to the left a series of willow and copper beech trees had been landscaped into the riverbank and he could hear the ripple of the river quite close to them. Thomas kept his eyes focussed on O'Rourke who was leading him into an inaccessible area of the riverside, covered in heavy thorn and deep thicket.

Ahead of him Denis suddenly stopped and turned to Thomas with his finger to his lips. Soft murmurs of men's voices came through the dense growth. O'Rourke drew close to Thomas' ear.

'These are some of the Wexfordmen that came across the river

118

by boat during the night,' he told him, watching his eyes intensely to see was there a sense of betrayal in them. But Thomas only felt a nervous excitement. This was the scenario he never dreamed he would encounter but had secretly hoped for this past few weeks; to meet with some of the rebel survivors, hear their views and hopefully, have some kind of meaningful discussion with them. Denis carefully pulled back a leafy branch for Thomas to glimpse them better. What he saw shocked him.

Half a dozen men lay sprawled on the ground, covered in rags, their emaciated limbs moving slowly and dark hollowed eyes telling only of flight and hunger and death. Two or three whispered quietly in a subdued fashion, the others lay on the ground, too weak and exhausted to contribute meaningfully. Thomas watched them for a moment before turning away, troubled and disheartened at their condition. What had he expected, a Sunday school discussion with bright-eyed pupils listening intently to his evocation of redemption? O'Rourke whispered beside him.

'As you can see, lieutenant, these are hungry, defeated men. They are in no state to enter into talks with anyone. With the help of God, I will lead them out of this estate tonight and show them the way south; point them to the town of Dunshaughlin and pray God they keep heading that way. There is little more that I can do for them. It is indeed God's will that they have any chance of returning to their native county. There are a few more on the other side of the river, who will be brought across tonight and they will too be sent through the woods. They have been hunted for a fortnight now. Some are eating the heads of nearly ripe corn, they are that hungry. And they stuff their pockets full of barley seed for the journey. All I can give them is some of my food from the lodge. I even saved for them, scraps of food for the dogs from above at the house.'

Thomas nodded silently at Denis' exposition, in awe of this ordinary simple groundsman and what he was doing for these young renegades from far away. Denis nodded towards where they lay.

'Do you still think it wise to speak with them? I fear you may

119

not get much of a reception.'

He was unsure now, doubtful as to what he could actually do or say to them. They looked as if they were beyond help. Would they even understand his strange accent and educated ways? Mistrust and suspicion would lead to a one way conversation. They would be apathetic towards him at best. He turned to Denis.

'Have you been able to talk to them, find out their motives, why they are so far away from home?'

'Look sir, they hardly know who they are or where they are. They have walked and rode all the way from Wicklow. That, I do know. And before that, they fought battles in Wexford. Many of them were massacred in a bog near Nobber and those that escaped have been lying, cowering in ditches or being caught and strung up at the nearest crossroads. Discussing their views on the whys and wherefores of joining the rebellion is the last thing they want to do. There is only one thing on their mind now and that is get back home, if at all possible.'

Thomas backed away from the hidden den where the men lay, gesturing for Denis to do the same. They walked away slowly, cautiously, his mind draining of effort. He was devoid of an initiative now. What had he really intended to do with them, carry them all to Wexford on his horse? With hindsight, it had been a ludicrous idea to come here. They spoke quietly as they repaired to the path.

'Denis, it is an admirable thing that you do for these unfortunate men, really admirable. You are giving them genuine assistance and I cannot fault you in that, together with putting your own life at risk too. And I realise now that my talking to them won't solve their problem, so all I can do is tell you now that the authorities mean to sweep each side of the river early tomorrow morning for any survivors. I received word about the operation earlier today. If there are more men to be brought over, you must to it tonight and have them all away from the river before morning or they will be surely captured. Do you understand what I say?'

Denis O'Rourke nodded sombrely, his mind in turmoil over Thomas' presence and the urgency of the work he was carrying out. As they approached the spot where the rowing boat lay, he turned to Thomas.

'Lieutenant, I am trusting you not to breathe a word about this work here. Already I am feeling the breath of young Mr Barton on my back, as he has begun keeping an eye on me over the last few days. I fear he may have noticed my unusually busy presence down here whilst I rowed the river over and back with some scraps for the men.'

Thomas grew nervous at this news. If discovered, Gustavus Barton would have no hesitation in seizing everyone connected with this conspiracy being carried out, literally under his nose. There would be little mercy for those in hiding or indeed for poor Denis.

They passed by the grove of trees and the boat and made for the steps up to the house. Thomas felt he needed to be away from this place, away from the intrigue of those lost souls lying in the trees, awaiting their escape. He knew in his heart that they were now beyond anything he could offer and whatever could be done was being undertaken by Denis O'Rourke. They reached the tall bushes, just in front of garden steps. Denis looked around then turned to Thomas.

'Can I trust you with what you have witnessed, lieutenant?'

Thomas nodded that he could. 'I will not say a word of these things, Denis. But you must be very careful. You simply must. There are many out there who will demonise you, if you are caught. And shortly after that they will hang you from the nearest tree!'

Denis nodded wisely. As he did he looked up at the house above and saw a familiar face gazing out of one of the windows. He turned back to Thomas.

'Lieutenant, not to worry you unduly and please don't turn around, but we are being observed from the house. It looks like young Gustavus is taking a keen eye on us.'

Thomas did not respond, other than to say, 'Undoubtedly our simple parley looks innocent enough. I will talk to him when I go above. But Denis, don't forget to move the men on before the round-up tomorrow. It is your only chance to save them.'

The two men briefly shook hands, then parted; Denis back to

his garden duties, Thomas taking the steps up to where his horse was awaiting.

*

Above them, in the big house, the contemplative eyes of Gustavus Barton peered through the dining-room window, puzzled and intrigued by the sight of the two men talking earnestly in the lower garden, both of them glancing around as if part of some mutual conspiracy. One was O'Rourke, the old steward, who he had been observing recently, his movements not in keeping with his daily ritual of tending to the outside work.

And the other person with him, in ordinary clothes, younger and taller, who might he be? From this distance he was dammed if it didn't resemble his fellow Slane officer, Lieutenant Gettings! In fact, it was him, and out of his uniform too!

Barton brooded long and hard after the two men parted company beneath him, a mixture of bemusement and irritation floating through him. Who, he wondered, would be interested in this odd encounter? Maybe he should have a quiet word with Baron Conyngham, or perhaps Edward Rothwell? Gustavus pursed his lips, intrigued at this supposed secret liaison he had just discovered. He would have words with Denis O'Rourke later but first he wanted to hear what his fellow lieutenant had to say.

Just as he had climbed the steps and fetched his horse from under the trees, Thomas heard the crunch of feet on the gravelly stones covering the front esplanade. Turning round he saw Gustavus Barton approach. Caught off-guard, he squared himself towards Barton and quickly decided to brazen out this meeting and not let panic set in. In all facets of their working relationship, Gustavus and he were of identical rank so Thomas was reluctant to allow Barton browbeat him.

'Ah, Lieutenant Gettings, I see you're using the tradesman's entrance to meet with some of my staff.'

Thomas stood his ground as Barton drew closer.

122

'Yes, lieutenant, a nuisance more than anything, I must say. My fiancée, Emma, you may have met her last evening; she mislaid a glove at the soiree, somewhere on the lower lawn. I've come to locate it and return it to her, nothing more.'

Thomas used a reserved tone, which was imitated by Barton. 'And did you find what you were looking for?' he enquired.

'No, unfortunately not, and she will be disappointed at its disappearance. However your steward has advised he will keep a weather eye out for it. But now, I must be on my way to prepare for our operation along the Boyne on the morrow.'

'Oh, yes,' said Barton, 'likewise, likewise. Pray God, we shall have another successful sweep of the area and weed out what remains of these agitators in our midst. What say you, Gettings?'

Thomas looked at him coldly, knowing he was trying to draw him out. With a nod brief of closure, he mounted his horse, briefly tipped his hat towards Barton and made for the avenue. Barton watched him depart, a trail of dust rising in his wake, his suspicions still not assuaged.

Gettings had indeed been acting strange of late. His reticence on the hunt for rebels; at the hangings the previous week; his peculiar questions and answers at the meeting at Foster in Collon and likewise in company at Bellevue last night; all added up to an impression of an officer who was straying into dangerously disloyal territory.

Gustavus understood his own limitations on understanding a man's mind-set. Essentially, Gettings had done nothing wrong and his story of a lost glove could well be true, but he wasn't one to deliberate too long on issues of loyalty. To him, it was a simple matter of expediency. You were either loyal to the Crown or you were an enemy of the Crown. There could be no middle ground.

His deliberations on Gettings led him to think that a few people in his immediate officer group would be more than interested in his observations of the Welshman and there might even be some who would be willing to take appropriate action, accordingly and decisively.

# Chapter Eleven

## White Mountain

The gun held by the mysterious occupant was pointing menacingly in Laurence's direction. Whoever it was confronting him was also possessed of a raspy nervous voice - and he had a local accent as well!

'Who are you? What do you want?' the gunman threatened. 'I *will* shoot you.'

Laurence heard the click as the hammer of the weapon was pulled back. 'Stop! Stop!' he pleaded, dropping his stick and raising his hands. 'Don't fire, please! I'm Laurence Moore, Barney Moore's nephew, from down the hill. Please stop!'

The pistol was still aimed at him and Laurence stood stock still, his hands in the air, unwilling to move, for fear of the stranger deciding to shoot. His eyes closed involuntarily, certain he was nearing death, but a brief glimpse, seconds later, showed rush-light coming for the house and a silhouette before it, someone moving towards the door. A woman's voice shrilled from within.

'Dan, for the love of God, put the gun down, please! 'Tis Barney's nephew... Laurence Moore. I know his voice. 'Tis him, I'm sure of it.'

Laurence saw the shadow of a small woman come round beside the man and faced the door, holding a small child swaddled at her side.

'Come in, Laurence, come in.'

He recognised his aunt, Mary Moore, who they had been looking for this past week! He couldn't believe his luck! The gunman stepped away from the door, allowing Laurence entry into the gloomy interior. With what little light there was, the shape of a shadowy, low-ceilinged kitchen, slowly emerged from the darkness. Save for a couple of broken stools at the fireplace, it was empty of furniture. Along the back wall some of the thatch from the roof had fallen through, leaving the space above open to the elements. A breeze, coming down from the hill, blew through it and the light flickered, threatening to extinguish at any moment. Apart from the stranger and his aunt, he could just make out some small shapes huddled in a corner, covered by a selection of rags. Sounds of shivering and stifled coughing came from there and the covering rippled as those beneath moved around. Were some of the children underneath, his young cousins? Laurence stood staring at the scene, speechless.

'Aunt Mary,' he said at last. 'We've been looking for you all week, father and me.' Beginning to cry, she clutched his hands, wanting to be certain he was real, that someone from the family had found her at last. She wiped her eyes with the palms of her hands, pushing away strands of grey hair hanging loosely down her face.

'I came looking for you,' Laurence said, 'for you and the children. A neighbour showed me where Uncle Barney is buried.'

Mary nodded, a small groan of comfort coming from deep within her.

''Tis well I know it, Laurence,' she said tearfully. 'This man here, Dan Kelly, he kindly removed Barney's poor broken body from the roadside and took it to Smarmore graveyard and gave him a burial that he wouldn't have got anyway. The neighbours were afraid to go near him and we had no priest either.' She shook her head, disconsolate, morose.

Laurence could just detect the man hovering in the dim shadows, quiet now, unmoving. His name - the name his aunt had called him - was recognisable, from somewhere. He wracked his brain. Then a coughing fit began from a dark recess. One of the children was sick, struggling for breath. Mary stood, wringing her hands, before disappearing into the corner to tend to her child. She returned a moment later when it had settled and Laurence dropped down before the candle and squatted there, beside her, already feeling the chill and damp of the hillside cabin.

'They all have the croup,' she explained sadly, 'those that are left.'

'How many?' Laurence asked, concerned.

'One died, the day after Barney; Christopher, the baby. Patrick left us on the second night. When I woke he was gone, gone away. I havn't seen him since. I just have three here now.' With tears falling, she had recalled the names matter-of-factly, as if reciting a litany. Laurence looked around at the cold dark interior.

'Is this Patsy Rogers' cabin?' he asked. 'I was told to look for his cabin. Is he here too?'

Mary nodded at the question. 'He's gone since last winter,' she told him, 'gone to his sister and no one has taken it yet.'

Laurence could barely see her face above the quivering flame. The catching up stopped and the room was quiet, save the rasping wheeze of one of the children. Laurence suddenly wondered was the man Dan Kelly in the cabin, the one who reported Michael Boylan. But before he could ask, Mary spoke up, wiping her eyes, continuing her tale.

'We hid in the clump of furze beyond our cabin for two days and nights after Barney was killed. We only had what we wore and it was wet. It rained a lot. The furze bushes wouldn't keep you dry. That's when baby Christopher died, on the first night. He didn't wake up the next morning. I couldn't wake him.' Again she spoke in a monotone, beyond emotion, barely choking back a sob.

'On the second night, at dusk, I went to our cabin, what was left of it, to bury the child beside where he was born and that's when I saw Dan lifting Barney's body from the front of the house. He told me he was a friend of John Mathews and he was going to bury both bodies up in the old graveyard.'

The thin voice of Dan Kelly escaped from the shadows, adding to the story. 'I found John Mathew's horse and cart abandoned, out in a field below Leabby Cross and used it to bring the bodies for burial. I dug the graves meself.'

126

As Dan spoke, it occurred to Laurence where he had heard the name. He turned and asked was he the same Dan Kelly that had sent Michael Boylan to the gallows in Drogheda. The man in the corner remained silent. James had told Laurence the story of Dan Kelly's treachery against the United Irishmen of Louth. The figure in the shadows drew closer towards the only source of light in the room.

'Indeed, I am that man,' he replied quietly, his outline shimmering on the near wall.

'So why are you still around?' Laurence said. 'I thought you had been run out of the place after Boylan's funeral.'

Kelly drew closer still, as if to draw some warmth and comfort from the meagre light.

'I went away after that,' he said. 'I told John Mathews I was sorry for what I did. But the committee should not have delayed our march to Tara; they should not have done it. The men were more than willing to go to fight. We had been preparing for months. It was a stupid mistake not to go. In a way, 'twas the top United men who betrayed us because the ordinary men were willing but the committee shied away.'

But Laurence was not prepared to let him away with his excuses. 'Yes, but you still went to the authorities with your information. That is the work of a traitor.'

Dan Kelly began to massage the pistol in his hand, pointing the muzzle towards the ground. Laurence flinched at the motion. Dan lifted the gun, looked at it minutely, then got up off his haunches and walked to the door. He stood there for a moment before disappearing into the darkness. Mary turned towards Laurence and harangued him.

'You shouldn't say those things to him. He guided us up here last week, to safety. He took some food to us every day and he buried Barney's remains. Whatever wrong he did, is he not now trying to make up for it?'

Laurence didn't care. Much of the chaos they were engulfed in, all of it pointed back to the break-down of the United Irish strategy at the end of May and then the likes of Kelly running to the authorities exacerbating the situation. Next to him, his aunt broke his thoughts as she flinched at the sound of her offspring's laboured breathing.

'The children are sick, Laurence,' she wailed into her hands. 'They're all coughing and full of the fever. Owen has barely spoken this past few days and the younger ones, Ann and Bryan, are breathing very poorly. Don't make things any worse with Dan, please. Pray that God and his Mother look down on all of us now.'

He put his arm around her shoulder, offering slight comfort, before rising and going over to the corner where the three young ones were cuddled together. He could hardly make them out in the faint trickle of light, just the tops of their heads as they curled up against the wall. But even through the chill he could feel the heat of fever on them and heard the congestion in their lungs. There was nothing their mother could do to help, there was nothing he or Dan could do, nothing. Tenderly patting their heads he lingered with them but felt he had to leave the room to get some fresh air, some solitude.

Outside, a weak moon flitted through sparse clouds and above, the dark heavens were awash with myriad constellations of stars. He gazed at the sight in awe, at how miniscule and insignificant he felt under God's great ceiling. And yet, he pondered bitterly, if He could make such a grand design, could He not spare a brief moment to aid some of his poor people here on earth? Laurence moved further away from the cabin and had just enough light to see Dan Kelly beyond the walls, feeding his horse.

'John Mathews' horse?'

Kelly nodded at the question, not looking up, still feeling resentful. Laurence looked around. There were several trees close by and more over towards the nearest field. He saw the outline of hedges along the path down the hill. It was secluded, even sheltered. Surely, no one would find them up here.

'And his cart?' Laurence queried.

'I left it at the graveyard. What use have I for it now, or the horse for that matter? I prefer to walk anyway.'

The two stood in the dark, saying nothing, Laurence listening to the silence of the dark hillside.

'I have no life now. I'm a dead man.' Dan Kelly's voice came from close by, a quiet, resigned quality to it. Laurence turned towards his dark shadow.

'Whose fault is that?' Laurence retorted. 'There's a woman in there who has no life either and 'tis not her fault.'

'I helped save her life.'

''Tis no life she has now.'

'I did my best for her. Before that, I did wrong, I know I did wrong. But I did it for the right reasons. I told you, our leaders were no good. It is they that ruined the rebellion. If we had the French and their guns and cannon we could have taken Dublin. The men were ready to fight. They were.'

Laurence was becoming inured to Dan's trait of agitating. It meant nothing now. 'If the French wanted to help a rising of the people here,' he said, 'they would have arrived before now.'

'Maybe they're on the way,' said Dan. 'They've been organising for months to sail to here. Surely they can't have reneged on us.'

Laurence let him be. He had heard this talk of the French before. But behind all the conflict with the United Irishmen, hadn't he, after all, helped James' family? Mary and the children would have died had Dan not intervened. He could hear her inside the cabin trying to console the distressed children. It seemed to be a lost cause, Laurence thought grimly, a lost cause. He turned to the shadow.

'I saw three men hanging from a gibbet at crossroads this morning, just this side of Lobinstown. Out of the fog they appeared to me. 'Twas a hellish sight and is some vision for the people to see as they go about their business there.' In the darkness Dan nodded. 'They think by doing that, it will cow us,' he replied. 'But they don't know us. The more of us they kill, the more memories those that remain will store for the next time. Mark my words, Laurence Moore, there will be a day... and it might be soon enough... when their shameful treatment of us will come back to haunt them. One day we will have proper leaders and we won't be so easily defeated.'

*

The next morning, the two men buried Mary's child, Ann, behind the cabin. Laurence and Dan had slept at the door throughout the night and had heard the child's intermittent death throes and they knew by the disconsolate look on Mary's face the next morning that her daughter had succumbed to the sickness. It was a small pit they dug at one corner, beyond the gable-end. Dan had found a large stick to break the earth while Laurence scraped away a depth of soil with a sharp, flat stone. Mary removed her shawl and wrapped her daughter's small body in it, before placing her down in the earth. A palpable sense of loss and anger swept over Laurence as they covered her small body with soil. Soon, feelings of vengeance spilled through him, like molten iron yet to be hammered.

They left Mary grieving by the grave and Dan told Laurence that he would have to leave soon.

'I'm away to Navan on the horse,' he said. 'There are some people there that I stay in touch with and I will sell her at the market. I've done all I can here for your aunt. At least she has family with her, now that you're here. But I will be back at some stage. Keep your head low Laurence and save your energy. You might be needing it sooner than you think.'

'Where do you get the food for them,' Laurence asked, knowing he had no means to pay for sustenance.

'Wherever I can lad. I might take some tubers from the ground. I might steal some leftover gruel thrown out for the pigs. Taaffes' castle, beside where I buried Barney, there might be something to take from there. Be careful though lad, for there are still many yeos about the place and people willing to betray you.'

Laurence watched him turn away, hearing the irony of his words; Kelly being the one who had given up Michael Boylan to the authorities.

130

Dan had a few quiet words with Mary, then throwing his bag onto the cart he grabbed the reins and quickly urged the horse towards the blackthorn-edged path, which led to the road below. Laurence watched him depart, grateful for Dan's help but anxious now for the future of Mary and the remaining children. He had no idea how he could save them, all he could do was forage for some food and maybe stay for a while to help. She was comforting her two remaining children, Owen and Bryan, inside, when he told her that he would go and look for food for them. She barely heard him.

The days fused together as he continued to prolong their lives. Mary had told him of a source of water that crossed the hill path and with a leather peillic that Dan had left behind, he transported enough water back to the cabin to help sustain them. The old man, whose house they were in, had abandoned a tinker's can out the back and, noticing little wrong with it, they used it as a drinking utensil. And in the mornings, Laurence would head off early, down the rutted thorn-lined track, its branches arcing across the top as if he were in a shaded tunnel.

Out onto the Smarmore road, he would alight, reluctant for anyone to know he was around, not even John McQuillan, who he felt might have offered him some help. He took new potatoes from their drills; a few here, a few there, resting the foliage against their neighbours so that they would not be missed. He even ventured as far as Taaffe's castle at Smarmore, skirting the outer trees and surreptitiously drawing close to the outhouses. On one of his forays there, he found an old coat in a loft and later, a small knife and a near fresh loaf of bread in a pantry, and secreted both away in the darkness. When he returned that evening he placed the coat across Mary and the sleeping children and the next morning, with the boys still weak and coughing, everyone chewed through the chunks of bread and pieces of raw potato he had cut for them.

The next evening, he took a bundle of kindling and twigs into the room and, with a shard of quartz he had discovered on the track, eventually managed to strike a spark with the knife and ignited a small flame. He had built the fire under the hole in the roof, allowing most of

131

the smoke to escape through it. The two boys lay nestled under the frieze coat, while his aunt drew near the fire and placed some bits of a broken stool on it. She crouched close to the flames, drawing a degree of comfort from it. Laurence noted a trace of contentment from her, the first time he had seen the furrows of pain absent from her brow.

''Tis fair and good the way you mind us, Laurence. Your Uncle Barney would be proud of you.' She tried to stifle a tear. 'My poor, poor Barney. I still cannot believe he has been taken from me. May the Lord have mercy on him.'

''Tis little enough I'm doing, aunt. And I'm glad I can help.'

'But what would we do without you?' she repeated.

'Your James would have done the same for my family,' he said. 'Sure, didn't he save my life? These are terrible days for us, Aunt Mary. We are at the mercy of the redcoats and because Barney and James and me were involved in the rebellion, they seek us all oover now. Our house was burnt, as was yours. My mother was engulfed in the flames. Now we are destitute, exiles from our homes. We'll be walking the roads like the tinkers, soon enough.'

Mary took to keening softly to herself, rocking over and back before the crackling embers, trying to block out the misery and death around her. Beyond any discussion of their current state, she had only two children left from the seven she possessed, a few short weeks ago. And those left were her life - what was left of it. Laurence fixed his eyes on the flames, sympathetic to her cries. Later, she ceased and all was quiet, even the children.

'We cannot stay here much longer,' she confirmed, 'no matter how sick the boys are.'

'And where will ye go?' he answered quickly. 'At least you're safe here.'

'I have a sister in Hurlestone,' she posited. 'Catherine and her husband might take us in there. I think they might take us in.'

Her voice faded. Laurence wasn't sure whether she was thinking clearly; the sickness and death around her were driving her demented, he reckoned.

'I will stay here for as long as it takes,' he said, offering her a morsel of comfort. 'Maybe the boys will get better and we can make our move then.'

She sighed and nodded, then rose and went to the corner where her sons were sleeping fitfully.

Laurence was conflicted; a mixture of loyalty to Mary, a thirst for fighting back against the injustice around him and a longing to have his life back, the way it was before he and James had become inextricably dragged into this relentless fight for survival.

# Chapter Twelve

## Termonfeckin

Like a flush of ice-cold water, consciousness washed over James' body and spurred him into frantic action as he coughed up a quart of saltwater. His mouth opened involuntarily in the swirling wash of the inrushing storm-tide but there was no air to breathe. Gulping in more saltwater, he struggled against a thick fabric wrapped round him, clinging tightly to his upper body, pulling him down, drowning him. He vomited the contents out his nose and mouth into the water then struggled upwards, searching frantically for air. With waves continually pounding above him and the wet canvas from one of the sails wrapped around him, he was being continually dragged under. Yet, inexplicably, the piece of sail also gave him enough buoyancy to push for the surface.

Then, almost unconscious, his head breached the surging waves and his outstretched legs touched solid ground beneath, the stone-filled sea floor. And gradually there was more of it to gain purchase on and he gulped and gasped his way to a kneeling position on cold gravelly shingle. Standing and falling over again, the stormy waves continued to wash over him. He made a final valiant effort to extricate himself from a section of sail and slimy lengths of seaweed which were stuck to him. And he did stand up, his feet sinking into the rolling slippery silt, gaining purchase in the sand. He forced himself forward and the waves grew less fierce and his hands and feet burrowed into the wet sand and then he was away from it, away from the all-consuming water.

Finally, tossing away the last remnant of canvas, he staggered towards the safety of nearby sandy hillocks, rising like a bulwark at the high point of the beach. Rain continued to lash the seashore but the storm was passing over, away to the north and the wind had slackened noticeably. He shook his head and wiped his eyes and, with the last of his energy, made for a grassy mound in the near distance. His feet sunk into the soft sand as he gained some height through a path in the dunes. There was shelter here, not from the relentless rain, but at least from the wind and the waves. Exhausted beyond recall, he slumped down in the nearest available clump of dune grass and passed out, curled up in a ball, oblivious to all around him.

At several stages he woke to a kind of lucidity but couldn't determine for how long he was unconscious between the blackouts. Light filled the sky above the tussocks of long grass around and above his head. He could barely move his limbs, his breathing was laboured and it was all he could do to remain still and slowly regain his senses. His mind drifted and cleared, then his eyes closed again and darkness resumed. Later, he awoke, opening his eyelids painfully, grains of sand lodged under his lashes. He was lying on his side, dune grass pressed into his face. His mind was clearer and he eased his face away for more space. His neck felt stiff, but and when he moved to sit he could only do so gingerly before causing pain. Instinctively, he felt for the gold ring on his finger. It was still there and returned it to his pocket. After rubbing the grit from his eyes with his thumbs, he slowly looked around. The sky was bright. It looked like morning, early, the sun shallow in the sky and lay across the sand-dunes, rising from the sea. Lying on his elbow, not knowing whether to sleep or get sick, his head spun, not helped by the low-level flight of a number of swallows, swooping through the dunes, deftly avoiding him, their small beaks open to catch any air-borne insects in their path. Feebly he marvelled at their dexterity.

His eyes focussed on the strand, the scene of his recent brush with death. They lingered on the rise and fall of the sand, the ebbing water trapped between the gentle undulations, as seagulls circled and landed in search of sustenance. Off to his left, he made out a bulbous green headland pushing out into the water, while, on his right, the beach he had struggled from, swept away off into the distance. A little later he spied movement between the dunes. People!

As if appearing from nowhere, a number of them came into view off to the right, close to an outrushing flow of water, a small river, running into the tide. There were three of them; women, girls, he couldn't quite make out. Sitting up to see better, he watched as they began to comb the beach with wooden forks, gathering sea wrack tossed up by the storm. Bringing it up beyond the high water mark they laid it out in strands to dry in the morning sun. He watched them at their work for a long time; all morning they were there, it seemed to him. The group seemed to be a woman and two younger girls, all three in dark dresses with their heads covered in black shawls.

The one toiling nearest him drew his attention. As she carried out her tasks, she hummed a soft refrain, over and over, the same melodic notes. And sometimes she would rise from her work and stretch her arms above her, loosening her limbs from the tedious nature of her chores. At one stage, she took her shawl off to adjust it and he could see her shoulder-length hair of black curls, and her young pale face enhanced by the faintest rose-blush of cheeks and dark humorous eyes. She indulged in fixing the length of her shawl, humming away all the while, smiling secretly to herself, oblivious to his attentive gaze.

As if the day had stopped, he watched her and grew entranced by her labours and temporarily forgot his hunger, his bruises and the continuing trauma of his near drowning. But his predicament soon returned like a bully, harassing him into submission, compelling him back onto his back, where he quickly closed his eyes closed again.

He woke later, the sun somewhere behind the dunes now, low in the evening sky. A nearby sound had stirred him, a refrain, floating towards him in the air, ethereal, familiar. He had heard it before, recently. It was the girl's song! Had she returned to work on the sea-wrack? He sat up - too quickly - emitting a painful groan, but much too loud in his ears. Suddenly concerned at revealing his hiding place, he lay low again. But the girl's interest had been aroused.

'Who's there?' she called out, like a challenge. He could hear her moving closer.

James lay flat in the sand, his nose to the ground, blowing

grains away with his exhalations. He didn't want to be found, not in this condition.

'Hello! Is there anyone there?' Bravely she stepped up through the dunes. 'I heard you, whoever you are. Why are you hiding?'

There was little fear in her voice, more so curiosity. She was close now, her feet getting ever nearer to where he lay. Rather than fall over him, he knelt up, reticent and distrustful. She squealed at his sudden appearance, her hand rising to her mouth.

'Shh! Don't be alarmed,' he said. 'I'll do you no harm.'

She stood still, wary, gauging his presence, looking back to see how close her colleagues were. He presumed she would run away and he stretched out his hand towards her, to placate her. She placed her hands on her hips, as if somehow cross with his antics. 'What are you doing lying in the sand?'

He made to get up. 'We could be here all night if I were to tell you my story.'

'Well I havn't all night to listen,' she admonished him. 'I must gather the kelp into a basket and be at Rath before dark.'

He stood up unsteadily, his feet sinking into the sand and began to topple towards her, just regaining his balance before knocking both of them over.

'I'm sorry… I'm not meself,' he said, shaking himself down. 'I near drowned yesterday… or perhaps it was the day before and I'm not the better of it yet? A fishing boat went down in the storm. I was on it and just made it ashore before I died. I fear for the lives of the others aboard.'

The girl was listening to him but was already turning to make her way back down to the beach, where a basket lay beside the lines of seaweed. James followed her, his uncertain steps like an infant.

'Where *I* work,' she said, 'they were talking about the storm and the wreck. Some bodies were washed ashore, up there, close to the Boyne River.' She blessed herself self-consciously.

'May God rest them,' James intoned. 'They were good men to let me on their boat, for I was trying to get back to Ardee, to my family there.' Then he asked, 'What is your name?'

She was busy positioning the basket close to the seaweed. She looked up at him, her dark eyes piercing him.

'Well, I am Mollie... Mollie Devin, and you are far from Ardee here, wherever that is,' she said, but suddenly paused.

'I believe I might have heard of the place though.' She reached for a clump of seaweed. 'We are near the village of Terfeckin. That's what we call it but usually the people in the big house call it Termonfeckin. This is the strand belonging to it. Drogheda is the big town not far from here. But I mustn't be talking to you now, for I have work to be doing here. The others are already gone back with their loads.'

Noting that they were now by themselves on the beach, he watched her, fascinated, as she began piling the dried kelp into the wicker basket. The seashore breeze toyed with her hair as she circled the seaweed around and around in coils inside the creel. Terfeckin, near Drogheda, he mused. So, not a great distance from his destination after all. He was cheered at the news, while simultaneously marvelling at Mollie's speed and deftness as she toiled before him. She was certainly no novice at this beachcombing work. Occasionally she would glance over at him, deliberating on him. Was she wondering what to do with him, James thought gloomily? Was he a liability? She would surely leave him here to fend for himself.

Finally, she tested the weight of the full basket and looking up at the darkening sky, attempted to place it on her back.

'Wait, Mollie, I can help you with that.'

'And, if you weren't here, who would help me?'

Despite his weakness, he lifted one side and she smiled at him in thanks. Her features suddenly lifted his heart. She had a tantalising smile. It was warm, homely, inviting; a pleasantry he had not laid his own eyes on before. Reaching for the side of the container, he beamed back at her. It was the first time *he* had felt like smiling in weeks. Holding each side of the basket, he followed her away from the strand and they proceeded up a narrow track through a track between low hedgerows. She told him that the workmen on the estate spread the wrack on the land as fertiliser; that it was for helping the crops grow better. She looked back at him.

'You never told me your name. Have you a name at all?' she chuckled mildly, teasing his bashfulness.

'Of course I have.' He was indignant, knowing she was playing with him. 'I'm James Moore from White Mountain, a good morning's walk from Ardee.'

'And what were you doing on a boat this far from your home?'

'As I was telling you, 'tis a long story.'

But, he tried to relate some of it to her anyway, and it took him the length of the lane to tell her even that much. Mollie, acknowledging his injuries, allowed him to draw breath and speak. Occasionally, she turned her eyes to watch him converse, a mixture of curiosity and intrigue in her, as if he were some exotic animal recently let loose. They let the sea-wrack down and rested for a minute. James could see a farmhouse at a distance up ahead.

'So you have escaped from the soldiers many times,' she summed up his tale for him, 'and here I am now, harbouring you from your enemies. What's to become of me if *I'm* caught?'

There was that mischievous twinkle in her eye again, as she goaded him gently. He offered her another of his sheepish grins and began to understand, that despite the perils of his journey that had taken him close to death, there was the occasional encounter, such as Sylvie Kavanagh, Andrew Tyrell and now Mollie Devin, which confirmed that many he met were still possessed of decency.

\*

Mollie hid him in one of the outhouses at the back of Rath House, where she worked. It was nearly pitch-dark inside the shed, as she guided him over to the ladder that led up to the loft.

'When I'm working here,' she whispered in his ear, 'I sleep in a basement close to the kitchen, at the back of the house. So, in the

139

morning I will try and bring you some food. Do not stir till you see me.'

She gave his arm a gentle squeeze, but before he could respond, she disappeared into the night. He looked around for somewhere to sleep and, deciding on a corner in the loft, settled himself as best he could. Despite the trauma of the last few days, sleep didn't come easily and he found himself preoccupied with the nocturnal sounds around him. There was the scuttle of some small creatures in the corner of his hiding-place; mice or larger vermin, he couldn't tell. A horse whinnied close by and the rattle of carriage wheels crunched on gravel.

But his mind's eye returned to Mollie and how generous she had been to him, a complete stranger, lying rough in the dunes. He had not been one to give the eye to any of the young girls about the neighbourhood of Smarmore. He knew he was shy when it came to talking to them and anyway, his father wouldn't hear tell of it. There was work to be done and then more of it after that! Yet Mollie was different than the few he had known before. And, incredibly, he had seemed not to displease her somehow, for she had gone out of her way to lead him from the shore and provide him with shelter, and hopefully something to eat in the morning. Despite the pangs of hunger in his belly and the after effects of the near drowning, he finally settled and drifted into a deep sleep with a small speck of hope to rest on.

She woke him early the next morning, calling out his name, quietly but insistently, from the shed door. He rose and climbed down the ladder. She was even prettier now, in the morning light and his rejuvenated eyes lingered on her rose petal cheeks and gentle brown eyes for longer than they should.

'Don't be giving me your glances, James Moore. Have you not seen a girl before?'

None so pretty as you though, he mused silently.

'Surely James, 'tis your stomach that needs attention this minute? Am I right?' From beneath a cloth, she removed a small bowl of buttermilk and a big crust of oaten bread and offered them to him. Greedily, he reached for the food.

'I saved these for you, but you must eat up quickly for this

140

place will soon be busy with workmen. We need to get you away from here.' Through his munching and slurping, he thanked her and asked how she was going to accomplish that. She flared at him, her eyes fierce.

'So now it's up to me to save you, is it? Maybe I should just send you on your way and be done with you.'

Finishing his food, he apologised and told her he appreciated all she had done so far; that it was too much to ask.

'Well, maybe it is,' she agreed. 'But I am obliged to go home, to my family in Bellcotton, not far from this place. I am not wanted here for the next week or so. Anyway, mother is unwell and my brother cannot tend to her. Perhaps I can bring you with me. You can stay in our shed while you are with us. We can carry a parcel of kindling, or something as we leave. It will make us look busy about the place and not be noticed too much.'

Abruptly she went away but returned soon enough with someone's tattered jacket and a hat for him to wear. Peering out to make sure no one was watching, she took him round the back of the shed where bundles of tied kindling lay.

'Here, put some of these across your back. I will carry the smaller ones.'

Keeping his head low, the two of them walked down the avenue and turned left onto the road towards the village. James was relieved that their movements had drawn no suspicious response; everyone was too busy in the yard or out saving the harvest. This part of the county seemed to be quiet and peaceful and they continued their trek towards Mollie's house unmolested.

They walked into the small village of Terfeckin, as she called it. Passing a row of cabins on the right, one of them a blacksmiths, James noted the tall spire of a church off to his left. But Mollie had him turn to face west and down a narrow track with the bundle of sticks still balanced on his shoulder.

''Tis nor far from here,' she said cheerily, 'just up towards the end of the track here.'

'You mentioned your mother only,' James noted from under the parcel of sticks. 'Is your father…still with you?'

'No, he's not…around, anymore. He went off a few weeks ago. He said he was going to meet some men outside… Ardee.'

She turned to him, her eyes bright with recognition. 'Now *that's* where I heard the name of the place you come from. I remember father mention it to mother the day he left. "He was going to Ardee," he said, for a few days.' Her voice caught briefly, a little melancholic sob in it. 'And he hasn't darkened our door since.'

She went quiet for a bit, unnaturally so to him. For such a spirited young woman he hadn't seen her subdued like this in the short time he knew her. James hadn't mentioned his own father's demise in his tale to her and he didn't think it would help by revealing it now. He stayed behind her, saying nothing, but carefully contemplating her words. Had her father gone to Ardee to join up with the United Irishmen on their failed march to Tara? *His* father had said that there were men at Blakestown that night from all corners of the middle and southern part of Louth. It seemed more than likely that Mollie's father had been there too.

*

James had spent a week at Bellcotton with Mollie, before the compulsion to move on became irresistible. At first he was overwhelmed by the place she lived in, barely existed in. The months since her father's disappearance had seen the cabin and yard fall into disrepair and neglect. As Mollie had noted, her mother was unwell and sat by the cold fireplace throughout the day. Even when James was introduced to her, she hardly raised her vacant eyes to look at him. Mollie told him she had been like that ever since their father had left. Some days she would not rise from her straw bed on the floor. Their cabin was only a little less dilapidated than the burnt-out shell that was his at Smarmore. It turned out that Mollie had a younger *and* older brother. She revealed that the older one, Patrick, was in the militia in

Drogheda and the younger John tended to the tasks as best he could.

'Does your brother, Patrick, not help you or your mother?' James was inclined to ask one day, when he was helping outside.

'Don't talk to me about Patrick,' she answered stonily. Her mood darkened with the mention of his name. 'He thinks he is someone, now that he has a fancy red uniform to wear. Whatever King's shilling he earns doesn't come back here to this house. My few pennies from working in Rath are all that we have.'

He could see how much she cared for her mother and younger brother. She was up first thing in the morning, stoking the small fire into life and preparing some stirabout for them, always humming her favourite little tune. And just enough was made to bring some to James, residing in the outside shed. And after a day and a night of rest, he rolled his sleeves up and helped her catch up on the chores that her father would have been doing.

James first job was to clear up the unsightly dunghill outside the door with John. Using a fork, they threw the dirt nearest the door over the other side and tidied round it. Next, they found a little lime in the shed and James mixed it up and whitewashed the whole cabin, giving it a bright clean exterior. Mollie weeded out the few drills of potatoes and cabbage to the rear of the house. They even borrowed a scythe from a neighbour and James spent an exhausting day in the field cutting the heavy unmown grass. Their whitehead cow eyed him suspiciously as he mowed towards her. Mollie was helping him build small lap-cocks one day, when he noticed a tall uniformed man, on a large slate-grey horse, riding up the lane, passing the cabin and on towards a large farmhouse beyond.

'That's the Major,' she advised. 'Major Phillips. He owns all the land around here, including father's field.' James, keeping his head down, spied him surreptitiously through his forkful of hay, noting his rigid face and long sideburns. He averted his eyes, not trusting anyone in uniform these days.

Despite his increasing fondness for Mollie, come the end of the week, the tension to be on his way back to White Mountain to locate his family, had gradually increased in him. On one of the balmy evenings, after another busy day weeding, cutting and cleaning, they took a break to sit in the small field next to her cabin, with a cock of hay at his back and she by his side. There was much outdoor work to be done during his days there and at times he barely saw Mollie, with her responsibilities indoors due to her mother's debilitation. Yet he had secretly grown to admire her dark-haired looks, together with her strength of character in doing the right thing for her family.

Sitting in the warm evening glow, the air alive with insects and cawing birds preparing to roost, he felt it was important now to reveal some of his thoughts to her. She was chatting away contentedly next to him, telling him some tittle-tattle about their neighbour, the Major, and his ardent pursuit of one of the Brabazon women who visited the big house at Rath, despite him being married with children! Mollie was fully engaged in the tale, telling him of the Major's English wife in the house just up the track, when James dared to reach for her hand and grasp it in his. Her flow of words ceased suddenly and she looked at him openly, her brown eyes like dark pools he could willingly leap into.

'James, what are you doing?' she asked him, surprised, but didn't withdraw her hand. Instead her grasp matched his and she leaned a little closer towards him.

'Mollie, I am so thankful for all you have done for me this last week. When I was lying in the sand down at the beach, my life was ebbing away. I knew not where I was bound for... maybe for eternity, it seemed. And then you came along and put yourself in danger by saving me and giving me food and shelter. I have been very lucky to meet you. I have.'

Her hand clutched his tightly. 'You looked like a lost soul on the dunes, James. Your hair, your clothes, you looked like a ghost. I wanted to help you. I couldn't leave you there, hungry and close to death.'

'I told you some of my story, Mollie, but not about my father, Barney. Let me tell you about him. He was involved in that United Irish rally in Ardee, and me and my cousin became caught up in it too. And for that, the redcoats killed my father, burnt our house and scattered the rest of the family.' She turned to him, suddenly shocked at his words.

'I didn't know, James. You should have told me.'

'You had your own worries, Mollie. But, you see now, I must return to my home look for them, to see are they still there, still alive.'

'I know, James. I know and I *am* understanding of your plight. We are very grateful for the work you have helped us with about the place, and though mother is struggling with her nerves, I know she is thankful for your help too. It was great that we had a man to help us.'

Silently she steeled herself at the suggestion of him going away. Yet she must accept it. It was his will that he go, though secretly she would have had liked for him to stay longer, to see more of him. And there, sitting against the hay, as if it were the most natural thing in the world, she put her arms around him and hugged him tightly. He swallowed hard with emotion and held her, well aware of her generosity and patience for him.

Their embrace lasted longer than he had expected. His eyes were closed and he could smell her hair, feel the touch of her hands on his arms. Eventually, they parted but a sliver of inspiration suddenly raced across his mind. He reached into his pocket and withdrew Sylvie's small gold ring.

'Mollie, I would like you to have this ring to remember me by. When I was in Wicklow, an old man gave it to me as a gift for helping him. I would like you to have it now for helping *me*. Please take it. Say you will.'

Before she could answer, he held her hand and tried to place the band on her finger.

'James, what is this. I cannot accept this from you. In truth I cannot.'

'But why not Mollie? I want you to have it. You deserve it, more than anything else.'

She stood up and he followed suit. She examined the ring in the evening light, the last rays of sun trailing down through the hayfield and illuminating the lustre of the tiny band. But she handed it back to him.

'James, you must be off about your business now. You have important things to attend to, none more so than finding the whereabouts of your family. You said so yourself. And after you find who you're looking for and if it suits you, why don't you return here and then you can give me the ring properly. Would you do that for me? 'Tis for the best.'

Realising just how wise she was, far beyond her youthful years, he knew she was right. He knew that, in the long run, what she said was the correct thing to do.

'With my last breath, Mollie, I will try and do that,' he said and, on an impulse, like a fledgling taking its first hesitant flight, he drew her close to embrace her properly. And, just as quickly, she turned her face towards him, raised her mouth and kissed him gently on the lips. The surprise and longing in both their eyes, when they parted, was a fleeting, magical thing for him. But those few seconds of her touch and warm embrace was a moment James would remember and cherish in his heart.

# Early Autumn 1798

*But, hark! A voice like thunder spake*
*The West's awake! The West's awake!*
'The West's Awake.' Thomas Davis (1814-1845)

# Chapter Thirteen
## Kells

*"27th August 1798.*

*For the attention of: Thomas Gettings,*
*Lieutenant, Slane Yeomanry Unit*

*Sir,*

     *Following recent discussions between Speaker John Foster Esq.*
*of Collon and Capt. Rothwell of the Kells Corps, pertaining to the*
*threat emanating from the recent French landing, your temporary*
*transfer has been agreed upon to Kells Yeomanry District, and you are*
*hereby required to report to Capt Edward Rothwell's unit in that town,*
*with effect from 1st Sept 1798.*

    *Your obedient servant,*
    *Henry, Earl Conyngham,*
    *Slane"*

Emma tore her gaze from the letter and gazed at Thomas, her eyes welling up after reading its contents…and their cruel implication on their relationship. She forced herself to read the missive again, making sure there was no misconception of its message. Yet, there it was, the Baron's unmistakeable seal of approval embossed on the paper. She continued to stare at it, long after construing its contents. Thomas sat beside her on the embankment overlooking the Boyne. She reached for his hand, squeezing it tightly.

'Rothwell's machinations are all over this instruction,' he fumed, taking the note from her. He crunched the paper in his fist before forcing it into his pocket.

'Despite this French threat in the west, Rothwell is insisting I go under his command, no doubt to scrutinise my military weakness. The Baron's argument will be that he has two lieutenants at Slane, Gustavus and myself. So, seconding me to Rothwell's yeo unit to bolster his force should not weaken the existing force at Slane.'

Thomas brooded unhappily as his emotions twisted and turned at this latest turn of events. Having received the letter two days previously, the consequences of his move to Kells were beginning to weigh heavily on him. Emma was lost in her own deliberations too. Though cognisant of Thomas' misgivings about his imminent transfer, her feelings were more personal, such as when would she see him if he was based so far away? And what if this French army in the west were to advance as far as Dublin, would Thomas and his comrades become embroiled in the conflict?

Thomas had taken part in a series of follow up cavalry sweeps along the Boyne valley in the previous weeks, led by Rothwell and Foster, both of them equally zealous in their push to cleanse the area of any remaining insurgents. Thomas was conscious, in the first of the raids, of those men whom Denis O'Rourke was hiding at Bellevue. But despite the intensity of the search along the banks and to Thomas' great but concealed relief, none were captured or spotted. It would appear Denis had gotten them away following the warning.

And now this blow! He had assumed the security situation had been stabilised and that the district was returning to normality; he had even considered relinquishing his lieutenant's position and returning to civilian life, but the pursuit of that was now seemed like a pipe dream.

Emma had risen from her grassy perch and began to pace up and down the shallow embankment that was part of the Boyne's earthen seawall. She gazed across the filling river, seeing the white-washed cabins of Mornington on the other side. Their wedding plans, little discussed since the rebellion began in May, would be further suspended now with Thomas' imminent transfer. She turned to him.

'What about us, Thomas? What of the preparations we talked

about? This war is dividing us yet again.'

When he stood up, she reached out for his hand and held it tightly, an idea crossing her mind. 'I wonder Thomas, can you refuse this request?'

He said nothing, shaking his head slowly. They walked away from Queensborough and west along the riverside road leading towards Drogheda. On his last day of leave before reporting to Kells, Thomas had arranged to meet Emma for lunch at her parent's house. The letter's contents had been burning a hole in his pocket as Emma's father entertained them in his usual style at the dining table. His stories normally concerned his work as a customs officer on the river and the characters he met when boarding and occasionally seizing non-excised goods from ships approaching the port of Drogheda. Thomas smiled abstractedly at his anecdotes, having heard most of them before. He acted the good escort to their daughter throughout, but as they left the house that afternoon for a stroll along the estuary, he couldn't hold his tidings back any longer.

'Thomas, you must resist this move,' Emma was insisting. 'If your principles are telling you to avoid further senseless loss of lives, where will that leave you in front of a French army?'

He stopped in his tracks and turned to her.

'They will call me a coward if I resign now, before these battles, which must surely come, against the French. I have no option, Emma, but to accede to this order, much and all as I would to decline the request. Peace would have meant leaving the Slane yeos as an officer who had served in time of war. But with the French now on Irish shores, I must continue as part of my troop.'

As he spoke the words aloud, he knew for certain he had no means of escape; that this new invasion in the west had put paid to that.

Later that evening, after advising her parents of this latest mission, he offered his goodbyes to Emma beneath a setting sun.

'We've talked about this before, this reluctance I have for killing. Yet I am trapped in this quandary, Emma, of at once, detesting violence against my fellow man, yet as an officer I must carry out my duties. I am not a coward and nor do I fear adversity. So I fear I must report to Kells on the day after tomorrow. I have no other alternative.'

Emma drew him close. She knew his hard words were a shield for him, a buffer to sustain him in the days ahead.

'Thomas! Thomas!' There were soft tears in her eyes. He ran his hands through her hair, brushing it over her ears, whispering words of endearment.

'Thomas, you must do what your heart is telling you. I cannot force you otherwise. But I am sad, so sad, at your leaving for faraway places, and I fear I will cry tonight after you go; knowing I will not see you until God knows when. Perhaps it will be a very long time. Say you will write as often as you can. Your words will help sustain me during your absence.' He nodded forlornly.

They walked back to her house along the riverbank, watching the rising tide sweep up river towards Drogheda. They said little, both knowing the inevitable conclusion to this last day together. Before he mounted his horse, he reached for her in one last embrace.

'My dearest Emma, you will be in my heart, always. And when I return we will surely be wed as soon as is possible, I promise you this.'

Reluctantly, she bid him Godspeed and with that he was away towards Drogheda, leaving her at the gate, her hand raised, already stifling the tears she knew were close.

*

Just after dawn on Saturday, the first day of September, Thomas left his home above the Boyne in Slane and, under a heavy sullen sky, rode the country roads to Kells, arriving, in heavy rain, over an hour later. He entered the quiet town, enquired as to the direction of the barracks and rode towards it, emotions swelling in his heart, boundless misgivings in his head. He knew that this request from Rothwell, and he was sure other officers were called as well, was a bid to test his resolve. The Kells captain, on the pretext of preparing for battle against the

French, was going to examine the mettle of his lieutenants, and in particular, Thomas.

Someone must have had a word with Rothwell recently, he presumed, someone who might have had suspicions of Thomas' lack of enthusiasm in his duty of mopping up the remnants of the rebels about the Slane district. And as Thomas rode in through the gates of the barracks and tied his horse up, he tried to figure out who would have done such a thing. He had toyed with various notions on his journey over, but discarding his wet cape and seeking out Rothwell's rooms, he put it in abeyance for the present.

He found Lieutenant Francis Manning from Collon already waiting outside Rothwell's door. Manning stood up to greet him. Thomas acknowledged him warily, knowing him peripherally from operations over the last few months and noting well his distrustful eyes and attentive ears. He had been told that Manning was one of the few junior officers who had the ear of Rothwell. Thomas wondered who, of any of the officer corps in the area, was trustworthy any more. They sat down on two stools opposite each other, a heavy silence ensuing. Manning broke the uneasy impasse.

'So, you also have been seconded to the Kells Corps.'

Thomas nodded faintly, as Manning added, 'It must be quite serious, this French assault, for the captain to be augmenting his forces here, so far form the danger area.'

Manning, seemingly aware of developments, elaborated further. 'I overheard Speaker Foster only yesterday in Collon. It appears that the French have landed in the county of Mayo, with the intention of setting up a provisional government there, amassing as many rebel followers as they can and perhaps advancing as far as Dublin. However, I presume Rothwell will be able to tell us more.'

As he finished speaking, several groups of uniformed men had entered the hall, all of them dripping wet from the weather. They began to congregate around the periphery. They were mainly officers but some attached militiamen took a cursory glance inside before being told to remain outside and await orders. Cursory discussion soon established that most of them were from the outlying areas, all of them being summoned to Kells by request from Rothwell.

Thomas rose and strolled over to the window and looked out onto a saturated courtyard, milling with militia and many tethered horses, all caught out in the downpour. There was certainly a build-up of forces now for the coming confrontation. The government must indeed be fearful of this French advance from the west.

The musings of the assembled men came to a sudden halt when a door opened, with Lieutenant Ogle appearing to summon them in. Thomas and Manning were the last to enter Rothwell's office. It was almost a bare room save for a desk and chair and a Union flag upright in a corner behind him. Thomas sidled up against the back wall where he could just see Rothwell's face through the men standing in front of him. He was comfortable where he stood, in his anonymity, not wanting to be visible to the Captain, when the speech was being delivered to them. Eventually, Edward Rothwell stood up, his tall frame allowing his eyes to view most of the dozen men in the small room.

'Fellow officers, some of you will be aware of why we are gathered here this morning. But for any of you still unsure, let me read out a short statement issued in the last few days by Lord Cornwallis to all field officers in the counties of north Leinster. Lifting a note from his table and placing glasses on his nose, he read aloud:

*"To all Yeomanry officers…*

*Please be aware of the immediate threat emanating from the county of Mayo, where a French expeditionary force, under one General Humbert, is seeking to extend its ambitions further east and, from recent intelligence garnered, purports to march on Leinster and perhaps Dublin. My own army and that of General Lake are endeavouring to prevent their progress, but all yeomanry units and their militia cohorts are now requested to prepare for the defence of their counties and to make haste, if required, to the aid of our gallant armies fighting the enemy in the field. May God be with us at this critical juncture and reward us in our quest…"*

Rothwell laid Cornwallis' note on the table and gazed steadily at the silent men before him.

'With this order in mind, Baron Conyngham of Meath, together with Speaker Foster of Collon, has directed many of the captains within these counties to amalgamate into a combined counter-insurgency cavalry and militia force. This new group will then hasten to the counties of Westmeath without undue delay and seek to bolster the local garrison, together with a yeomanry group heading there from Cavan. From his missive, it would appear that the bulk of the regular forces are chasing the French party. So, it is up to our units to try and hinder or stop them in their tracks as they advance towards us.'

He paused to allow the information to sink in. Quiet murmurings buzzed around the room. Thomas, at the back, learned from Rothwell's words that they were now being placed on a war footing - just when everyone assumed that the trouble had been quelled! At the front, Rothwell was speaking again.

'… essential that we make haste for Mullingar, at first light. We will spend today mustering our men in this town, before advancing westwards. Every officer here must ensure they are acquainted with which yeomanry groups they gave been assigned to and are prepared and ready to move out at dawn. Have you any questions?'

Thomas wondered who he would be placed under but was not prepared to ask. He assumed Rothwell would advise them in due course. Rothwell terminated the meeting by directing them to wait outside in the courtyard where they would be allocated their units. Thomas and Manning were the first out, grabbing their capes in the hall and exiting into the damp, rain-filled morning, with the other officers close behind. Dozens of disgruntled militiamen stood in ragged rows, rain flowing down their hats, onto their faces, down the backs of their necks. The groundswell of grumbling subsided from them as the officers appeared outside.

Behind Gettings and Manning, Rothwell and Lieutenant Ogle appeared, with Ogle beginning to arrange men and officers into separate cavalry groups. Rothwell's eyes, however, were scanning the crowd and Thomas saw him home in on him, his hand raised, beckoning.

157

Momentarily he froze at the prospect of facing Rothwell in this crowded yard. Beside him, Manning also became aware of Rothwell's gaze and nudged Thomas.

'He wants us over to him,' Thomas murmured.

'Both of us?'

Thomas nodded. 'Come on, we don't want to keep him waiting.'

Rothwell stood at the door expectantly, as Gettings and Manning approached. Without a word he guided them out of the rain and back into his quarters. Placing himself behind his desk the captain ordered the two lieutenants to stand to attention before him.

'Now then, gentlemen,' he began, 'though we are mustering men to confront this French presence coming from the west, I have a special mission for you, Gettings. And I am also seconding Lieutenant Manning to assist you with this mission.'

Thomas remained still but his mind began to race, immediately growing suspicious of Rothwell's intentions. The captain continued.

'Gettings, I will be assigning you a small force of cavalry yeomen and this unit will begin a search for these young Moore ruffians who appear to be still at large.' He then turned to Manning.

'You, lieutenant, brought forward intelligence a few weeks ago of these Moores continued existence around the Smarmore area, south of Ardee, in the county of Louth. That is so?'

Manning nodded at Rothwell's information, having mentioned it at the meeting in Speaker Foster's house some weeks ago.

'It is imperative that you find them,' Rothwell pointed at Thomas, 'and when you have that completed, you will dispatch them forthwith. And as soon as you have achieved that, both of you, with your men, will reconvene with us at Mullingar, to where our units will depart for, this very morning. Do you understand?'

Both lieutenants advised they did. Thomas remained motionless, Manning likewise, waiting to be dismissed.

'Lieutenant Manning, you are excused for the present. I will speak to you later. Also…Lieutenant Ogle will advise you of the men being seconded to this new unit.'

Manning briefly looked at Thomas, before turning round and leaving the room. Rothwell eased himself into his chair and moved some paper around, leaving Thomas standing, waiting in suspense, curious of what Rothwell was about to say.

Rothwell left him standing. He seemed to be thinking, formulating some words to say. The captain finally stopped what he was doing and stared at Thomas over his glasses, with a look approaching disdain.

'At ease, Gettings. You look nervous, even anxious. Why would that be now?' Thomas engaged in the briefest of glances with him.

'I'm fine, sir. Just waiting for your orders, sir.'

'Are you indeed, lieutenant? Well, that is good.' He paused, still toying with his subordinate, a slight tic flickering in his eye.

'There is much to find distasteful with your military acumen, Gettings. You were given important responsibilities in hunting down and eliminating all subversive activity in your area…'

'Which I carried out to the best of my abilities, sir,' Thomas interjected.

Rothwell looked at him coldly then stood up behind the desk, rising up to his full height, Thomas following him with his eyes.

'Do…not…interrupt me, when I speak,' Rothwell exploded, his eyelid flickering spasmodically. 'I did not request you to remain in this room and be subjected to excuses from you.'

His tall frame lent forward, only the table width keeping them apart. Unnerved by Rothwell's tone, Thomas refused to allow himself be intimidated and returned his gaze steadily. Rothwell mocked him further.

'Certain people have recently talked to me, expressing some concern over a certain… reluctance you might have to engage in the purge of the enemy remnants. In fact it's not that long ago that you were throwing your menial officer rank in my face at Speaker Foster's house.'

Thomas blanched quietly at the dressing down.

'You are aware that once you have become established as a yeomanry officer under his Majesty's oath, that you are sworn to uphold the laws of this Kingdom and defend the rights of its citizens. That includes your full commitment to eradicate any attempt at rebellion or even unlawful congress. Do you understand what that means, Mr Gettings? You, with your nominal Welsh accent; what does your father say of your obfuscation, seeing as the Welsh have been our allies for centuries, hmm? Yet you seem to think you can bring your own morals into dealing with the enemy? You are no soldier Gettings, you are not what is needed now in these days of turmoil.' He paused, still locking eyes with Thomas, staring him down.

'May I be allowed to speak, sir?' But Rothwell carried on, enjoying his tirade.

'For one who showed such finesse in swordsmanship when under my tutelage, your inability to use that weapon on occasions of necessity, leaves me wondering, just what your motives are? It would appear, from this intelligence given to me that you, Mr Gettings, may well be in league with these very same subversives? How close to the truth would that be, I wonder?'

'That is completely untrue, sir.' Thomas said, eyeing a spot on the wall behind Rothwell, above the flag.

'I do not want to hear you speak Gettings, because I will not believe what you utter. As I said, I have heard enough from others to suggest you are a charlatan and not the calibre of man we require. There are many men out there you would be more suitable to don your uniform and fight for his king.'

Thomas knew he had become a lost cause before this man, who now seemed to be drawing him into some kind of snare, some entrapment, which would allow Rothwell wield a form of undue pressure on him. But nonetheless, he felt he must defend himself and protect his family name and reputation.

'I am no traitor, captain,' he said, with no little defiance. 'I have never sullied my reputation or denied by uniform. I have always performed my duties to the best of my ability.'

He stopped there, not willing to divulge in any way his aversion to the slaughter of these poor, uneducated, foolish rebels. Rothwell gestured toward him.

'You Gettings are an imported Welshman, an exile almost. My lineage is from Lincolnshire, also making me an exile of sorts. Yet we are here in this dreary isle to secure England's frontier. We both are officers in local militias. This uniform is not worn only for display. It empowers us to defend the realm against all its enemies, both near and far. And I cannot condone any form of leniency for rebels who have sought the help of our enemies. I even hear there is talk of amnesties and remissions of sentences, from Cornwallis and others. But I tell you now, it will not happen on my watch, or in my area. Every last one of these - I refuse to call them men - these traitors; I shall have them hunted down... and that includes those Moore villains who murdered my men outside Collon.'

He paused in his rant and backed away from the table, turning to the Union flag hanging in the corner. Lifting a section of the cloth he felt the fabric with his fingers. A patriotic gesture, no doubt, Thomas judged, trying to discomfort and embarrass him. Rothwell let the flag drop and turned to face Thomas again. His voice softened perceptibly, his eyes in motion, his mind formulating some conniving scheme.

'Unless,' he began, devising as he spoke, '... unless there is still some morsel of pride in the man before me, who hides in that uniform and the fidelity it represents. If you can prove to me that you are capable of dealing decisively with these Moore miscreants, I will desist in my campaign against your history of lack-lustre performances. That is why I have set this task for you and Lieutenant Manning. Seek these Moore wretches out and dispatch them without mercy and you will regain some of my confidence. Do you think you are up for it, Gettings? Do you?'

Thomas stood motionless, focussing again on the flag behind the desk, on the red and blue stripes curled around the pole. It was obvious he now had little choice in the matter. No matter how

161

vehemently he protested his loyalty, Rothwell was not prepared to accept his bona fides unless he could somehow prove himself. Along with Manning, he would have to accept this mission of Rothwell's and hope that it would be singularly lacking in conflict. It would also keep them away from any confrontation with this French army for the present. He rose from his brief reverie.

'I will carry out your orders to the letter, sir.'

Rothwell scrutinised him evenly, before sitting down on his chair.

'I am glad to hear that, Gettings . Perhaps we will make an officer out of you yet. Please instruct Manning to report back to me as you leave. I have some further instructions for him.'

Thomas saluted and turned on his heels. He left the room swiftly, quietly seething at Rothwell's treatment of him, yet equally relieved that his survival remained in his own hands - for the moment!

Thomas found Manning waiting just beyond Rothwell's door. Telling him he wanted him in, Thomas departed for some much needed fresh air, even if it was raining outside.

Manning closed the door behind him and stood before Rothwell.

'Yes, sir? You requested to see me, sir?'

'Yes, lieutenant. I believe I might need you to carry out some extra...duties...on your assignment with Gettings. Let me elaborate further.'

# Chapter Fourteen
## White Mountain

Laurence had just pulled the rabbit from the home-made noose and had been expertly twisting its neck when, from his peripheral vision, he spotted a distant, yet familiar outline, walking in the fields between the hills of Dunmore and White Mountain. Tucking the limp body into his britches, he stood up and looked long and hard at the person with the familiar easy gait, making his way slowly through the valley. He scratched his head, undecided about the apparent apparition walking towards him. How could this be? He had assumed he was dead; he hadn't even considered an alternative to that fate. He stood very still, shaking his head in wonder before rushing forward to reunite with his cousin.

He had spent the previous days caring for his aunt and young nephews, Owen and Bryan. Yet every time he approached the house on the side of the hill, he wondered would he find the cabin a morgue, their bodies curled in a corner, cold and lifeless. His inner demons were telling him that he should be away from here, off making plans, joining others in the fight for freedom, wherever that might now be taking place. Yet in the mornings, when he awoke, cold and stiff, he could hear Mary shuffling in the shadows, checking her sons and that would spur him on to go out and seek provisions for them. The boys were no better or no worse than before; remaining huddled under the old sack, an occasional cough or cry coming from one or the other.

He had talked to Mary at the door that morning. Dark rings surrounded her eyes and her face was gaunt, her cheekbones protruding from her pale skin. Her hands were like bony claws.

'I have some traps set for to catch rabbits and I will bring some water back with me in the peillic.'

She nodded slowly, hardly looking at him, her eyes downcast. He hadn't heard her speak in days, only soft sounds in the night as she pacified her sick children. Hope was fading in her, he could sense it. She was only staying alive because her boys were still alive, giving her some kind of faint hope. Dejected, he left the cabin and headed down the path towards the road, his usual route every day. There were still some pickings to be had in the fields and sheds along the road to Ballapuste.

*

In the valley, James Moore was walking westwards through a field of cut grass, turning his head to the left and right, familiarising himself with places he had previously known but had not been in recently. Looking up at White Mountain to his right, he recalled herding Taaffe's sheep up on it, not so many weeks before. Yet it seemed like a lifetime ago now.

The previous day, James had departed from the shed at Mollie's house as dawn began, before anyone was up… and also to save himself further embarrassment! He had wakened a couple of times in the darkness, and felt himself blushing at his behaviour the previous evening. Mollie must think him a right fool for revealing his emotions so candidly to her. She had much responsibility about the house, caring for her mother, her younger brother, the upkeep of the cabin and the crops in the field. In reality, she would have little energy for him, so he had done what he could to help her in the week he was there and now it was the right thing to do and move on, back to Smarmore and find out what had happened to his family. He was long overdue there. His only regret was that he may never see her again and that pained him greatly.

He kept the rising sun behind him as he headed west, plucking handfuls of ripened blackberries from the bramble bushes on his way through fields and lanes, always careful of who he might meet, especially those who were travelling on the same road as him. He took some chances too, by asking people on the road where he was and how he might get to where he was going. Walking along, keeping the sun on his left shoulder, he was told place-names he had not heard before, such as Sandpit and Galroostown and Ballymakenny and further west to Monasterboice and beyond there again to a more familiar place, the village of Collon.

When he was told he was near that village, he knew the name well, for just above it on Mount Oriel, hadn't he and Laurence helped save John Mathews from the clutches of the redcoats, on the day of Michael Boylan's hanging, back in June? How could he forget that day?

He walked past the bleach-green on his left and behind the cabins of Drogheda Street, he stopped to take some water from a wooden horse-trough, keeping his head low, trying to appear inconspicuous in the afternoon commerce of the village. Reaching the cross-roads he stopped and caught sight of a cortege of cavalry approaching from the south, moving slowly up the hill, towards the centre of the village. He stood under the shadows of a thatched cabin, watching as they passed through the junction, the riotous clattering of hooves and wheels forcing nearby villagers off the street. Some ended up close to James, muttering under their breaths about Speaker Foster and his daily coming and goings.

Slowing down, the column began to wheel into a substantial corner house, across from where James rested. All traffic at the junction had stopped temporarily as the three carriages and their attendant cavalry squadron wheeled through the archway of Foster's yard to the rear. It was then James noticed the officer on the large grey mare, his stern features familiar from some recent crossing of paths! Where *had* he seen him? And then he remembered. At Bellcotton, up the path from Mollie's cabin! That's where! What did she call him? The Major, Major Phillips! And now, all around him were yeos and militia, standing guard, on horseback, shouting orders, securing the area. James felt intimidated, afraid; he was too close to them, too close to danger. If anyone spotted him or called out he would surely be in trouble.

As soon as the street was clear, he crossed quickly over to the old church and graveyard and proceeded on the road west towards

165

Leabby Cross, where he would be close to White Mountain and home. Then, hopefully, he would begin to look for his mother and family again. He didn't invoke God much, he didn't know many prayers at all, unlike his mother, but now he called on anyone of a saintly nature to help him find them; Mary his mother, Ann his little sister and younger brothers, Owen, Bryan, Patrick and baby Christopher. He dearly hoped he could find them.

*

They sat behind the hawthorn bushes, speaking in muted but exited tones; laughing at the good fortune of their reunion, hushed as each of them told their stories since they had parted six weeks before.

Laurence told James of first seeing him in the valley, where he initially held his ground, staying behind some bushes, establishing that James was not being coerced towards him. But no one else seemed to around. Laurence was in a field of potatoes, pilfering some for Mary, when he saw James approach through a cornfield, with a large blackthorn in his hand, oblivious to being watched. But Laurence knew beyond doubt that it was his cousin! Incredibly, he had somehow survived after the battle at Mountainstown and he had come home again. It was then he stood out in the open and began waving excitedly at the figure drawing near.

'I thought you were dead,' Laurence said. 'You rode away with Whelan and the horsemen. I could hardly speak with my injury, but you got me home James. You got me home.'

'But what are you doing here, Laurence? Why are you not in Killary?'

For a second Laurence baulked at the question and its implications. He hadn't told James yet of his family's whereabouts. He deliberated briefly and looked at James squarely.

'I came looking for your family, a few weeks ago. I found them in Patsy Roger's cottage, up behind us on the side of White Mountain. They were being cared for by a man called Dan Kelly. I've being minding them since.'

James stood up, shock, amazement, delight, all etched on his features. 'I must see them, now. Why didn't you tell me sooner?' he turned for the hill, Laurence following him.

'Wait James, wait for me. There is something I must tell you.' He caught up with and drew alongside him. James pushed on, using the blackthorn for extra leverage through the field, intent on getting to the cabin as soon as possible.

'James, your mother, James, she's not well. The children...'

James didn't want to hear any more. He began to run, through the lower fields, then through a gap in the hedge and up onto the track that led to Rogers' cabin, Laurence continuing to chase after him. James' mind was a blank; he didn't want to think of what awaited him, but his cousin's words were insistent, echoing around in his head, "she's not well... she's not well."

Arriving at the old cabin, where they had kept the yeos' horses in the adjacent field, James flung himself through the half-hung cabin door. Calling out, he searched left and right in the shadows and saw the shape in the corner, sprawled, half hidden. He knelt down beside them, reaching out.

'Mother, 'tis James. I'm back. I'm here with you now.'

A head appeared and then a hand, a diminutive hand. It was his mother but now only a spectre of the woman he once knew. She looked vacantly at the dark shadow of her son above her. She gripped his hand, weakly.

'James?' she whispered, a frail croak of a word.

'Mother! Mother! It *is* me. Where are the others, mother, the children?' She responded with quiet sobs.

'They've all gone to their father, son. All gone away now.' She tried to choke back the words.

'But father is ...,' James couldn't finished the sentence. For a second he felt his father was alive, that *he* had the children. But no, that was not possible. He had seen him die, at the cabin. She squeezed his hand again, with what little strength she had left.

'We'll go back to the cabin,' he promised, not wanting her to confirm his worst fears. 'We'll build it again, make it fine. We will.'

She reached up and touched his face, her eyes wet. 'They're all dead, son. I've lost Barney and all the children. You're the only one left. You'll look after me. Tell me you will.'

Holding her hand, he turned his face away, saying nothing, trying to hold back the tears. Laurence loitered in the doorway, a dark shadow in the evening light. Fearing the worst, James drew back the cloth his mother was under and saw two small bodies curled up beside her, motionless. He reached down and touched them. They were stiff... and nearly cold. He could take no more and rose and went to the door, past Laurence.

'I told you. I told you, James. Me and Dan buried little Ann a few days ago. Patrick went missing after the fire at the cabin.'

James turned to him. 'And that's Owen and Bryan over there with mother,' he added, without emotion. 'I left the Wicklow mountains to come back home. I near drowned on a boat that brought me back to Louth. And I've walked for days and there's only one left... my mother!'

'I did my best for them, James. Me and Dan, we did our best for them. But they were not well; all the children were sick. Your mother is sick.' He looked across White Mountain, at the darkening fields.

'I did my best.'

*

Following the burial of Owen and Byran, James and Laurence tended to Mary for the next two days until she too, inevitably gave up her will to live. James held her emaciated body after her demise, gently rocking her, whispering soothing words that might have meant something to her. Later, as they prepared her for burial he hardly spoke a word. Even when they stood over her crude grave behind the cabin, where they laid her to rest with her three children, he couldn't bring himself to speak out. Laurence muttered some of the Lord's Prayer as they patted down the last of the soil on the grave. James remained silent, numb, paralysed with the thought that he was the only one of Barney's family left. He had wanted nothing more than to come home after all the fighting and killing; to find what was left of his family, to help rebuild the cabin, tend to the field of vegetables, to be the man of the house for his mother. Was he not finished with hatred and revenge?

That evening, Laurence had skinned and cut up the rabbit and, with a few potatoes, laid out a nourishing meal for them. James picked through his, hardly recognising its smell and taste. Laurence decided to let him be and left his cousin to mourn while he stepped outside into the evening air, the sky already filling with stars. Both their families were now decimated by the actions of the two sons. Laurence had already made his mind up to seek contact with Dan Kelly and prepare for any action he could take against the enemy. By his long absence, his father must have thought him dead by now, yet he only truly felt sorry for his sister Kate.

James rose before Laurence the next morning. Cold and tired, he stepped out of the cabin and went round the back to the grave, where he knelt on the cold ground. Laurence found him there later and cajoled him up on his feet.

'James, 'tis a hard thing to have to say but they're gone and only God in heaven can take care of them now. We must be about the business of the living.'

'And what kind of business is that?' James asked, running his hands through his lengthening hair, distracted. Laurence perked up. His cousin had found his tongue at last!

'Well, I'll not be one for sitting around fretting over what has happened to us. Our families have been taken from us, yes, but I'm off to find Dan Kelly and see if he has heard of any developments. We just cannot sit here and bemoan out fate. I'd rather lie down and die than to do that.'

'Then be on your way, cousin, for I've had my fill and more of all this.' He tried to think clearly, though his mind was still dysfunctional, still traumatised.

'Maybe I'll call to Killary,' James added, 'to see your father and Kate. Their all the family I have left now. What will I tell them, if I see them? That you're off to fight again?'

Laurence didn't hear the sarcasm in his cousin's voice, because in the distance, half way up the hill, he observed the outline of Dan Kelly making his way up the track.

'Declare to God, but look who's coming towards us.'

James followed Laurence's pointed finger. He was in no mood to listen to more tales of bravery and fighting and supposed victories of the United Irishmen? James made to leave, but Laurence grasped his shoulder.

'Just wait James and see what he has to say. Say you will.'

'I don't care what he has to say,' James said, yet he held his ground all the same.

Dan Kelly soon emerged from the undergrowth of the hill path and approached them, his face aglow and sharp with anticipation.

'God bless all...,' Dan had started his greeting and then saw James. He looked at Laurence. 'Who is this young lad?'

'Cousin James... James Moore... from down the road there. You were looking after his mother and the children here.'

Dan nodded at James. 'And how are they?' he enquired, looking around for activity.

'Dead,' James answered him. 'They're all dead.'

Dan was motionless, save for his mouth, which had dropped open. Laurence nodded silently in confirmation. Dan took off his cap and held it, lowering his head.

'Well, I'm indeed sorry to hear that... James. I really am. I'm at a loss for words now, and me carrying such good news too.'

He looked at the two cousins. 'I did all I could for them, I did,' he explained. 'I took them out of the furze behind Barney's house after he was killed and brought them up here to safety. And I had Barney and John Mathews remains buried in the old graveyard behind Taaffes. Whatever scraps of food I could find, I took them to Mary. She was a grand woman, indeed she was.'

He lowered his eyes. Laurence ushered him in to the cabin,

170

saying that there were a few crusts of bread left. James reluctantly followed them in, sullen and downcast. Dan threw his small bag to one side and they sat down, cross-legged on the earth floor. Laurence was anxious for Dan to reveal his tidings.

'Tell us this good news that you've heard.'

'Well, our dreams are almost fulfilled, our prayers have been answered,' Dan began with a flourish. ''Tis just short of a miracle, but word has spread that a French army has finally landed over in the west. Thousands of French with their horses and guns have come to help us. The English generals sent to oppose them are running around, floundering, with these Frenchmen giving them the merry dance.'

Dan was almost spitting out the words, his eyes wide and emotive. Laurence grew excited. This was intelligence he had been waiting for, something substantial that he could equate to, to drive him on.

'What is it they have done Dan? Have they defeated the English armies?'

'Well, they say, that a great battle took place in Mayo, in a town called Castlebar, where the French army and Irish rebels routed a large garrison under General Lake, sent them running out of the town.'

Laurence let out a whoop of joy. Even James' indifferent ears pricked up at this news. He interrupted Dan.

'John Mathews told us, when he was staying in our cabin, that a French army was on its way to Ireland. So, it has indeed come to pass.' He rose off the earthen ground.

'Yet, is it not too late now? Me and Laurence saw what the redcoats did to the Wexford army, the ones we were with for those few days. They were only a shadow of their former strength, defeated men, they were, but the redcoats chased them to the end. So who is left now to join the French? Will they be able to defeat the English armies on their own?'

But Laurence was excitable now and his blood was up. Now was the time for him to grasp this opportunity to do something.

'Cousin, they were men at the end of their tether,' he said.

'There were only a few left who offered up a defence; Timothy Whelan for one. But now we have a new hope. Surely men in the midlands will take up this gamble. We must travel and join them. Look around you, you have nothing here now. This is the past. Our future lies in the west.'

Dan too had stood up, leaving Laurence to gather up the few crusts left on the floor. Kelly was in his natural element now; discussing the future, planning ahead, his mind scheming out strategies for them.

'We will go to meet them, Laurence,' he advised. 'Me... and you and james here, and whoever else we can bring along. We will head west to meet them. The people will rise up when they hear of this. I am certain of it.'

James shook his head, unwilling to compromise.

''Tis too late now! It is Laurence. Can't you see that? 'Tis a great pity they weren't here months ago. The people will be afraid to rise up again. They wouldn't rise when we rode through Meath with the Wexfordmen, why would they do so now?'

Dan grew agitated. 'We could spend all day, all week, talking about this,' he said, 'but we are only delaying matters by being here. I came back to tell you the news, Laurence, not to stay and talk about it until we're blue in the face. Now, both of you know what this is about. You fought with the Wexfordmen. You saw men die. You saw how they hunted them down. The United men will rise in the midland counties if the French make for Dublin; places like Westmeath and Longford will rebel to help the French, and I am going to be there when it happens. I know Laurence here will come with me. James, be it on your own head if you wish to stay. We will not try to encourage you. After all you have seen, you must know your own mind by now.'

Kelly gathered his bag and made for the doorway. Laurence called after him.

'Dan, will you give me a minute to talk to James?'

Dan raised his hand and grunted wordlessly. He went to the beginning of the path and loitered there impatiently. The cousins faced each other in the cold, empty cabin; its walls and roof hardly fit to last through another winter. James looked around it; at the hole in the roof where the weather came in; at the other corner, where his mother and children had lain in their last days. This place would forever be associated with the loss, the total loss of his family. He turned silently to James, letting him have his say.

'Come with us,' Laurence urged him. 'We have something to fight for now.' James shook his head stubbornly.

'I will go down to our cabin and try to repair it, put a roof on it. Father would have wanted that.'

'James, you are wrong! That won't happen. The landlord will take it, knowing your father is gone, and repair it, then put some other poor tenant family into it. It will not be yours anymore.'

'I will not fight again, Laurence. I came home to get away from it. I have seen and done too much this summer.'

Laurence drew close, reached out to him.

'I am your family now and we must stick together. Father is lamenting his loss and can do no more, but I am going to make sure I give everything to this coming fight. I will never bend the knee to people who killed my family... and neither should you.'

James shrugged helplessly, but Laurence continued, relentless in his argument.

'We had no one to help us before, now we have an army marching our way. It is too late for me to change course. My future lies in this journey west to join with the French.'

Without waiting for a response, he turned and left the cabin, leaving James looking at his departing silhouette through the door. Squeezing his eyes shut and clenching his fists in frustration, James felt a searing fissure in his head, separating the overwhelming dilemma of whether to return to a semblance of his old life or follow his cousin into the unknown - again!

By remaining here he would lose Laurence again, having only just reunited with him. But by continuing their journey together, through thick and thin, he would be in the thick of action; something he had vowed to turn away from. And no doubt, in the near future, they would be fighting for their lives and perhaps bravely facing their last moments together. Standing at the door of the cabin, where most of his family had recently perished, he quickly realised he had little choice after all.

# Chapter Fifteen

## Lobinstown

Riding at the front of the column, Thomas Gettings was sweating profusely in the heat of the morning sun. From beneath his helmet, drops of perspiration seeped through his curls, down his forehead and into his eyes. It was uncomfortably hot for early September and Thomas dabbed his brow with a kerchief and loosened his tight collar, despite the action being against uniform regulations. But in this blazingly warm morning, as they patrolled in the hills around Collon and Smarmore, who was going to report on him?

Lieutenant Manning was riding behind him, checking on their cavalry detail. One of the yeos appeared to have a lame horse and they had to stop every so often to allow the rider check the source of its discomfort. Thomas wiped his face again and reached for the water canister to alleviate his thirst. Manning brought his horse close to him. He too was wiping his brow.

'We shall never make progress with this carry on,' he reported bitterly.

'This is only our first morning of the search, lieutenant,' Thomas advised calmly. 'Bring Corporal Brennan forward. He is from the Killary area over at Lobinstown. Isn't he a neighbour one of these Moore lads we are seeking?'

Manning gestured for Bryan Brennan to come before them. Thomas had removed his Tarleton helmet and was wiping his eyes again when Brennan approached.

'Is it your horse Brennan, with the limp?' he asked.

'No sir. 'Tis Corporal Allen's, sir. He is adjusting the shoe now, as we talk.'

Thomas drew his horse closer to him.

'Corporal Brennan, tell me more of what you know about these Moore lads, who Captain Rothwell is so keen to be rid of.'

'Well, I know one of them quite well; Laurence Moore, from Killary, who lived not far from my home. We captured... and dealt with... another neighbour of ours, Pat Sheils, who confirmed, under interrogation, that both Laurence and his cousin, James Moore, had murdered two of Lieutenant Rothwell's yeos outside Collon... in fact, on this very road that we are on now. They were spotted again in the rebel group who we fought at Mountainstown and we have been looking for them ever since. However, despite our best efforts, they have managed to elude us so far.'

'Indeed,' Thomas mused. 'Indeed. So, where could they be hiding? Would they have left the area, altogether?'

Brennan shrugged his shoulders, apparently bereft of ideas. Manning put forward a suggestion.

'Perhaps we should stop and interrogate some of the tenants around here. They may have seen them about the place.'

Thomas was agreeable to this and Brennan proceeded to steer the column of half a dozen yeos across the hill road through Belpatrick and on towards Smarmore.

After writing a brief letter to Emma and having it dispatched, Thomas had left Kells the previous morning with Manning and Brennan accompanying him. It occurred to him that Rothwell might have deliberately sent them along to watch him and report back any misdemeanours he might commit in their presence! They had stayed overnight at Slane, where the rest of the special unit assembled for the task of rooting out these young nemeses of Rothwell's.

As they set out from Slane early the next morning, Thomas remained dubious regarding the outcome of the task they had been set. Again he mulled over the recent meeting with Rothwell and the orders he had given to return to Louth rather than advance westwards to meet the French invasion, it all smacked of placing Thomas away from the action, with Rothwell's willing subordinates close at hand to monitor his behaviour. He was particularly wary of Francis Manning, who had

176

had several brief discussions with Brennan already, as they rode through Collon and up into the hills to the west of the village. He had even considered the fanciful possibility that Rothwell had engaged Manning to dispose of him, if the opportunity should arise! Though he laughed to himself at the absurdity of this, he felt it in his water that Rothwell was up to something and that he would need to be careful, very careful!

Lieutenant Manning took the lead as the troop descended to White Mountain cross and swung right onto the road leading to Ballapuste. The troop of half a dozen yeomen trotted along the dusty, stony track, with a few travellers on the road scurrying towards shelter as they drew close. Further along, Manning's raised his arm and the unit drew up close to the remains of a burnt-out cabin on the left-hand side. Manning turned to face them.

'That, gentlemen, from what I've been told, is all that is left of one of the Moores' home.'

From their vantage point on their horses, the patrol saw some men further up the path. Pointing to them, Manning suggested they interrogate them about any recent sightings. They galloped up to the field, where the men were going to work, Manning shouted for them to stop.

'I say, you men there! Stop what you are doing. We want to ask you some questions.'

Four labourers, all sweating in torn britches and jackets, turned around to face their inquisitors.

'Have any of you men seen one or two young lads from the area on this road in recent days? Moore would be their surname.'

Thomas watched as they eyed each other fearfully, reluctant to engage in any kind of conversation. Manning cajoled them.

'Come now, what about it? Have you no tongues in your heads?' Three men shook their heads vehemently; the other taller one remained still. Thomas decided to intervene and gestured for one of the men to come forward.

'What is your name?' he asked.

177

'McQuillan sir, John McQuillan I am. I was a neighbour of a Moore, back up the road, but he was killed a few weeks back and I seen nothing since, sir, nothing!'

Thomas queried the other labourers, who all answered in the same vein, except the tall one. Thomas became aware of a certain air of detachment from him and wondered had Manning noticed it too. It seemed he had! With a swift motion of his hand Manning waved three of them away and ordered the tall one to remain. The others skulked away to the field, afraid to turn back to see what was to become of their colleague. Manning dismounted and ordered him near.

'You're the quiet one, aren't you? You had little to say among your friends there. Have you much to say to us now, I wonder?'

The gangly labourer was perspiring under the sun and looking around uneasily until he satisfied himself that he would not be overheard.

'Lieutenant,' he began earnestly, 'truth be told but I am from Foster's estate at Collon. Speaker Foster wanted someone around here as his eyes and ears. But these men you spoke to don't know that. They think I'm from Taaffes, down the road here.'

Thomas senses were alerted. An informer! One of many that Foster was known to employ in the area. He pulled his horse close to Manning and the informant.

'We don't want your name sir, but only some intelligence you can relay to us, then,' Thomas asked, curious as to this new lead. 'Well, I am only here a few weeks and havn't had the chance to report back to Speaker Foster yet, but I can tell you that a young lad did call here over a week ago. He had a long chat with the man you talked to, John McQuillan, but I couldn't hear it. McQuillan said he was only looking for work. But he's a crafty one too, McQuillan and sharper than he looks.'

Bryan Brennan had steered his horse close to the conversation. 'What did the lad look like?' he asked.

The informer scratched his head. 'Well, I stayed in the field, when McQuillan went to him, so I only saw him from a distance. He was young, thin, had fair hair, freckly face. If he stood in front of us now, would I know him? That I don't know, sir.'

Manning looked at Brennan. 'Does that sound like the Laurence Moore that you know?'

Brennan removed his hat and wiped sweat from his brow.

'Yes, I suppose that is a fair resemblance of him. But the question is, why was he here in Smarmore and not at his home in Killary? Who was he looking for? It is said that all of Barney Moore's family died in the cabin fire, except James. So, was he here looking for James? It seems likely.'

The informer raised his hand to be heard.

'I would like to add something else, something I've only just remembered. Earlier this morning, we were just beginning to work in the far field, over there, just beneath the slope of White Mountain, when I saw some people walking down the hill path from a cabin up on the slope. See that long length of hedging, that's the path there. It seemed to be a few men, maybe three of them, but nothing more suspicious than that, except that when I asked later, John McQuillan grew uneasy and told me that the cabin on the hill was empty, that the tenant Patsy Rogers had gone away long ago!'

The two lieutenants listened intently.

'That is very interesting,' Manning said. 'We shall follow it up. Thank you for your help.'

He let the man return to his work and turned to Thomas and Corporal Brennan.

'Well gentlemen, it's not much of a lead, but we should investigate it all the same.'

They followed the informer's directions to the path and beyond to the cabin on the hillside. After an uncomfortable ride up the track, with the low overhanging blackthorns clutching at their epaulettes and caps, the troop finally reached the small yard and dilapidated mud cabin. Livestock grazed contentedly in surrounding fields, cattle in the near ones, sheep further up the hill. Dismounting, they looked around, leaving Corporal Allen to make further running repairs to his horse's shoe. There was little about the place to suggest habitation.

One of the men found a small steam and led the horses there to drink, leaving the others to reconnoitre the site. Thomas removed his hat and stepped inside the dwelling, initially thankful for the coolness of the interior. He quickly noted its dilapidated condition, with just a few broken stools strewn about. One of the dark corners contained some rags, all strewn about. The smell of smoke assaulted his nose; something had been lit lately…and there was something else in the air, the fetid odour of… excrement! Somebody had definitely been here recently. He retreated quickly out the door, taking in some much-needed fresh air. Brennan came from round the corner and signalled for Thomas to follow him. They rounded the gable-end and Brennan went to edge of the small yard.

'Look sir, a burial.' He pointed to a large clay mound. 'Someone's been interred here, and recently too.'

Thomas, reluctant to form any immediate opinion, squatted down and felt the fresh loose earth.

'It could be the farmer from here… anybody,' he offered, non-committedly. Brennan called Manning over, also showing him the grave. He too knelt down and sampled the newly-dug clay.

'Somebody was obviously buried here. Maybe they were killed here. We do not know. But could this be something to do with the men who Foster's informant saw, coming down the hill?'

He stood up and looked around. Thomas replicated his movements, proffering an anxious demeanour. The two lieutenants considered their next move.

'Let us follow the men that left this place this morning,' Manning ordered. 'See what they're up to.'

Thomas nodded, acceding promptly to Manning's plan. He did not want to demur on the task, yet neither did he want to flaunt a false sense of conceit in Manning's face. Inwardly he remained steadfast to his own resolve. He would not be cowed by Rothwell or indeed Manning's directives.

'I agree,' he said, 'but where would they be heading? They

could be travelling in any direction.'

'We mustn't delay then,' Manning said. 'We will stop everyone we meet on the road. Someone is bound to have seen them.'

Soon, all six were remounting and, with Thomas leading the way, they descended the hill and commenced the chase in earnest.

*

Just below Leabby Cross, they happened upon an elderly woman, shuffling along the road, her back bent from carrying a bag of corn. Fearful of trouble visiting her, she grudgingly told them of three men who she had encountered a short time previously, heading towards Lobinstown. Even better news was that, on further probing, she revealed that one of them was probably Barney Moore's son.

Riding away with the information, Manning whooped in triumph with Brennan also shouting exultantly. Thomas kept his face bright and eager, knowing he was under some kind of observation, his reactions being diligently monitored.

'They're on the road and walking only,' Manning rejoiced. 'By God's grace we shall overtake them yet. Come on, gentlemen, to the gallop.'

The horsemen increased their pace, heading west, the sun lowering gradually into their faces. The horses hooves kicked up copious amounts of dust on the dry path and, glancing behind him, Thomas could hardly see those in his tracks. As they passed the entrance to Heronstown House, Manning, just ahead of Thomas, shouted an order to stop. Thomas pulled up beside him.

'What is it? Have you seen them?'

Manning gesticulated with his arm over to the left. 'Look over there, across the fields, those men running, do you see them?'

Thomas was shielding his eyes from the sun, but just caught sight of three figures hurriedly making their way through a recently cut cornfield. One had stopped and turned back, spotting the yeos on horseback. He seemed to signal to the other two and they made off for some outbuildings in the distance. Manning was furiously gathering the men together.

'It's them, men! Follow me and don't let up until we have them. And no clemency is to be shown. They are to be cut down without mercy. Those are Captain Rothwell's express orders. Does everyone understand that?' As he said it, he looked tellingly at Thomas.

With that he encouraged his mount through a gap in the fields, with Brennan hot on his tail. Thomas cajoled his mare through the gap and picked up the gallop behind Manning; hoping desperately that this would be over quickly, for it seemed certain now, once spotted, these men would stand little chance against an attack by armed cavalry.

In the distance, maybe two fields away, the men had begun a frantic sprint through the corn stubble, towards the nearby buildings. As they entered the second field, Thomas could see them climb through a hedge and into a yard with sheds surrounding a courtyard. Brennan drew alongside Thomas, his sabre unsheathed, pointing it out before him.

'They've gone into Parsonstown. They are entering the yard and stables of Parsonstown House,' Brennan roared at him. 'We must get to them quickly to stop them from hiding.'

Thomas chased after Manning, who was jumping a shallow ditch, the last before the yard, looming in the near distance. But the men had entered the yard with the six yeos galloping through the open double gates seconds later. A couple of stable-boys, who were leading horses from a shed, looked on in disbelief and stood stock-still with their horses as the yeomen dismounted before them. Thomas ordered the yeos to gather round, while Manning barked urgently at the stable-hands.

'Have you seen three men running through the yard just now?' They both said no, shaking their heads rapidly, afraid to move. Manning grew anxious.

'We must *not* lose them now and we so close to them. They are around here somewhere. Lieutenant Gettings, you take Corporal Allen and go through the stables on your right, checking each one. I will take the left side with Corporal Dolan. And you Brennan, you and Teelan go round the back in case they try and escape that way. Tread carefully for they may be armed. Go!'

Everyone scattered to their positions and Thomas nodded for Allen to join him. They ran to the first stable on the right. It was empty, just stalls for two horses with a little hay in the corner. But there was a narrow passage at the back that led to the next stall, meaning there were front *and* rear entrances to the stalls. Thomas called Allen to him.

'You watch the front door of each stable and, after I check through it, I will call for you to move to the next. That way, we have both front and back covered.'

Corporal Allen, drawing his pistol, nodded silently and they proceeded on to the second stall. Thomas also had his pistol out and held it close to his body. A nervous energy ran through him as he inched through the initial rear corridor. As the stables were not all the same length, he encountered blind corners as he moved in to the next section, so he treaded quietly and carefully on the dusty dry floor, aware that one of these fugitives could be waiting with a pistol aimed at him.

Despite the danger, he considered this demonstration of loyalty, which might indeed be enough for Manning to report back to Rothwell; a report suggesting that he, Thomas Gettings, was an officer to be trusted and had carried out his orders to the letter. He just required this errand to have an orderly ending and he could be back with Emma, making his plans for their future together. If this was over soon, and he prayed silently that it would now end quickly and mercifully for these men on the run, he would force himself to do what he had to do; report to Rothwell at Mullingar and hope the French would be beaten or have surrendered by then. If only that scenario would come to pass!

He dragged himself back to the present and entered the second horse stable, where he heard a scurrying noise close by, from the next stall perhaps. It sounded like a soft rustling, nothing more than a series of light movements. It would seem someone was hiding in there!

He looked across to the front of the shed but couldn't see any movement from Corporal Allen. Perhaps he was in the courtyard, moving between the two doors. Thomas eased the hammer back, held his pistol up and took a furtive look round the dividing wall into the next stall.

# Chapter Sixteen
## Killary

In the stable, James Moore's heart was thumping so loudly that he felt it would be heard out in the courtyard. The redcoats, searching through the stables, were close now, very close. He could hear one of them cock the hammer of a flintlock, preparing it for firing. The sound of his heart filled his ears. Would it be the last thing he would hear, for surely the yeo couldn't help but locate him in this, his final hiding place? He cowered under the straw and waited for the end.

Earlier that morning he had followed Laurence and Dan, his mind quickly made up following his cousin's parting words. With his mind set, he ran to the grave of his mother and family, patted the cold earth with a grim finality then hurried after them as they headed down the hill. Little was said on the road to Lobinstown, except Dan Kelly advising that they would keep walking towards the setting sun and reach the town of Kells and then further west to Granard, where he had heard the United Irishmen were rising to meet and join with the French army.

James secretly admired Dan's single-mindedness. It seemed nothing was going to stop *him* from his objectives, whereas for James, he just wanted to go home. It was a phrase that had become familiar in his vocabulary in the last few weeks. But in reality, he had no home now, nowhere to call home anymore. They walked quickly and purposefully away from where he was from and for a few brief moments, his mood lightened, thinking of the happiness he had found with Mollie, over at the village of Terfeckin. She had made him feel important and wanted in his time with her and he nourished these thoughts for a time, enjoying the small comfort they gave him, until suddenly Laurence, who was behind him, hissed urgent words of warning. 'Christ, there's a redcoat patrol behind us. Redcoats, lads! My God, they've found us!'

Immediately they took off at pace, running blindly for all they were worth. Luckily, near them were the outside sheds of a big house and reaching open gates, they ran through with no one around. Dan Kelly and Laurence rushed towards doors on the left, while James, hearing the thump of horses' hooves not far behind, fled into an open stable door on the right, fear flooding through him. Already he could hear redcoats dismounting in the yard, so he ran into a back section of another stable and beyond into a third. There, a heap of straw lay in a corner, piled up as bedding for the horses. He threw himself and his stick under a rail for tying animals and quickly covered himself with the bedding, lying as still as possible; his heartbeat monstrous in his ears.

One of the yeos was close and he could hear his firearm being made ready. Shifting slightly, he pushed deeper into the straw. Should he have kept running? He was trapped now. He closed his eyes, waiting for the end, for he would surely be found. Under his cover, he could make out muffled shouts and men running, but much nearer, one of the yeos was entered the stable, his muted steps halting a short distance away. Then a voice spoke, quietly, almost soothingly.

'Give yourself up and I won't harm you. I know you're under the straw. I can see your stick poking through.'

James trembled at the words and clutched at the stick defensively. He had been discovered already, hardly having time to conceal himself. Unable to move, frozen with fear, he waited for the yeo to fire.

A shot rang out. James jerked in anticipation, tensed for pain, for the final blackness. But, incredibly, it wasn't directed at him; it was outside, away from the stable. Then a shout came from someone, almost a scream. He stood up, disorientated, the straw falling off him. A pistol was pointing at him, hardly an arms-length away with a tall yeo standing behind it, nervous, sweating in his redcoat and helmet.

'Don't move, don't run,' Thomas Gettings ordered.

'Don't shoot me,' James replied, unsure what to do with his

hands.

'I won't. Just stay quiet ,' Thomas said. He was uncertain now of how he would deal with this supposed capture of one of the rebels. Despite his loathing of the unpleasant business of eradicating them, it would be justifiable to just dispatch the boy and, ungodly as the act would be, at least he could say he had proven his effectiveness in Rothwell's mission. But in his heart, he knew he wouldn't carry out that deed.

'What's your name?' Thomas asked quietly, casting an eye around to see where Allen was.

Hesitating, James told him. Thomas regarded him silently.

'So, you're one of the infamous Moore cousins?' he said, almost disappointed at the ragged, emaciated appearance of the enemy. 'You're but a slip of a lad.'

James raised his head, puffing out his chest, facing the officer and his gun bravely in what, he presumed, were his final seconds.

'Did you have to kill Captain Rothwell's men?' Thomas asked him, matter-of-factly. James considered his reply, beyond fear now.

'They were going to hang a friend, a friend of the family, John Mathews. We were trying to save his life. You would have done the same for a friend of yours.'

Thomas was surprised at the lad's forthright response; this wretched young lad, in tattered shirt and britches, barefoot, seemingly unafraid of his fate. Another disturbance came from outside, somewhere in the courtyard… shouting, followed by gunfire and somebody's long drawn-out groan. A second later, Corporal Allen shouted out from the front of the stables, enquiring as to Gettings whereabouts. Thomas stiffened for a moment then raised a finger to his lips, signalling for James to remain still.

'Yes, corporal,' he called out, 'I'm just re-checking the stalls in here, looking for the others. I'll be out shortly.'

Thomas lowered his pistol and drew close to a nervous James.

'James Moore, you are the first rebel I have said words to, during this uprising. I wanted to talk to more of your kind, to find out the reasons for your rebellion. Maybe, for me it was a stupid idea, but unfortunately I have no time to discuss it with you now, why you do what you do.'

'Everyone fights for different reasons, sir,' James tried to explain his motives. 'We just wanted to be left in peace, but the government won't let us be. My whole family were killed because of it. We die when we do your bidding and we also die when we rise against it. What choice have we got?'

Thomas nodded, a kind of understanding coming to him.

'There are tyrants in all walks of life, young man, believe me, I know. But recently I took an oath that I would not kill another one of you. There has been enough killing. But for this stand, I now must deal with tyranny in my own life.' Thomas reflected on both their words then came back to the present.

'Do you see that window behind you? Make your escape through there now and keep running. Try and go back home and rebuild your life. I am willing to allow you to do that.'

James stood dumbfounded at this apparent escape from certain death. Thomas nodded briefly in affirmation then urged him to flee out the aperture in the wall as quickly as possible, just as footsteps drew near. Before James forced his way through the opening, he looked back briefly at Thomas, a look that acknowledged what he had just been given. Then he leapt out and scrambled away into a grove of trees. At that moment Corporal Allen ran into the stables, winded, with gun drawn, looking for Thomas.

'Has anything happened to you, sir? Are you alright?'

'Yes, I'm fine, Allen,' he said, dusting himself down. I was searching through this straw, thinking I had heard something. What has happened outside? I heard shots.'

'Corporal Teelan has been shot. We chased after his assailant and managed to return fire. It was an older man we shot, not one of the Moores. The man's last act was to push one of them out of harm's way before he stood and faced us.'

Thomas nodded grimly at the news and, as they returned to the courtyard, the realisation hit him that his action in allowing the young Moore lad to escape, had pushed him over the parapet of loyalty to the Crown and towards the realm of collusion and aiding the enemy.

*

James ran around a large holly bush and plunged straight into a bed of nettles. He crawled out, whacking away the stinging plants ineffectively with his stick. All but oblivious to the increasing pain from the numerous stings, his only feelings were that he had been allowed escape with his life. The redcoat officer, with the strange accent, had, unbelievably, released him from certain death in the stables behind. How had that happened? Was the redcoat secretly a United Irishman or why had he offered such leniency to him? Whatever the reason, he whispered a silent prayer of thanks and pushed on through the undergrowth, the irritating nettle-stings on his arms giving him something else to think about, yet flight still his overriding ambition.

He could hear the commotion of the yeos, continuing their search for him back at the yard, thinking that he was still in the vicinity. If only the officer who saved his life kept his silence, which would give him a chance to make good his escape. He had broken through the tree cover and come to the bank of a small river. Deciding to follow it, as it seemed to be leading him west, he was now out in the open, the only cover around being the hedge which ran along the stream. Crouching behind it, he ran close to the perimeter as fast as he could; stopping only once to cup his hands and drink from the water. But he forced himself on, trying to put as much distance from him and his adversaries as possible.

With his limbs aching, he left the riverbank, crossed over some fields and spotting a hedge, with a road beyond, he crossed the mearing, hardly believing his fortune in not being spotted. Standing close to the hedge, he held his hips, gulped in a lungful of air and tried to steady himself. Gradually gaining some of his composure he looked around and studied the area he was in, and he slowly realised that he was close to Killary, where Laurence came from. And off to his left, in the next field, he could just make out the ruins of the old castle that Pat Sheils had hid in. It was also where he and Laurence had set off on their quest to find the Wexford army several weeks ago. The irony of the situation was not lost on him!

He sidled down the roadway, thankful that no one was on it. Deciding that his best option was to make for the castle and then focus on what to do next, he struggled through a gap into the field and rushed for the castle walls. His emotions were in turmoil. It would seem from the gunshots in the yard that both Laurence and Dan had been injured or even killed. If that were the case then he knew that he was now on his own and he would have to decide what he was going to do. He was trapped too, trapped in that he had nowhere to turn, no option to return home, for he had no home. Should he push on and make his way west to join up with the United Irishmen and the French? But he was only one person. What good would he be to them? No horse, no weapons, no incentive to fight for the cause. At the heel of the hunt all he wanted was to return to his former life - but that was now beyond him!

Entering the castle, he drew some breath and sought out a place to rest. He sat on a dry grassy patch among the collapsed stonework, trying to come to terms with the bleak future he faced. Would he walk up the lane to Geraghty's and tell his Uncle Henry that every one of his family were now dead, that he was the only one left? Perhaps it was the only thing left for him now.

Above the broken parapets of the castle, the afternoon had grown overcast with dark autumnal clouds building from the west. He rested for a little longer on the ground, closing his eyes, unwilling to formulate a plan, not knowing what his next step would be. And there he stayed the night.

*

He was cold and agitated when he woke the following morning. The residual burning of the stings in his arms was still there, but the rumbling in his stomach soon outweighed his other discomforts. So deciding he had no other viable option, he left the rock-strewn confines of the castle and made his way across the road and up the lane, past the ruins of his uncle's cabin. Geraghty's house was a little further along, where Laurence had told him his Uncle Henry would be staying. Knowing the danger of the redcoats' relentless search, he decided he would not linger there too long. And not for the first time this summer, it was his cousin Kate who recognised him as he drew close.

'James Moore, well I declare,' she said as she sighted him. 'And we had given up hope... that you were...!'

She stopped herself but, like the other times when he returned to the fold, she exclaimed her delight in seeing him again.

'You're like the lost sheep who keeps returning. I am almost used to saying hello and goodbye to you when you come back. But come in, do come in.'

He stood out on the track, embarrassed and reluctant to advance but she ushered him to the yard and preceded him into the cabin, where Mrs Geraghty was stoking the fire. Soon, his Uncle Henry and George Geraghty appeared and a quiet commotion ensued on his unexpected return.

Henry clapped him on the shoulders. 'And there was us thinking you were another casualty of these troubles ... along with poor Laurence.'

The mood deflated somewhat as they reflected on the recent deaths. Over some buttermilk and newly-baked oaten bread, James recounted his adventures in Wicklow and how he had managed to return to Smarmore. He told of his meeting with his mother and being there with her in her last days.

'Then, Dan Kelly came and told us of the landing of a French army over in the west somewhere and how they were advancing towards us, trying to make for Dublin.'

Henry shrunk on the stool and put his head in his hands at this news. Surely to God, there was not more tumult coming their way, surely not?

'So, we left Smarmore and were walking towards Lobinstown and then onwards to Kells when we were overtaken by some redcoat cavalry. I hid in a shed and was... I was blessed to escape. But there was shooting all around and I fear both Laurence and Dan were...' he hesitated at the import of his words, '...might have been killed.'

Henry, who hadn't seen his son in a fortnight, grew ever more dejected at James' words.

'Why did ye do it lad,' he asked quietly. 'What hope did ye think ye had of beating against the might of the government?'

James was too downcast and weary to consider answering. It was all in the past now anyway. They had done what they had done and nothing could change that. He lapsed into silence.

Henry and George exchanged heartfelt commiserations on their respective family tragedies; the deaths of loved ones, destruction of their dwellings. 'These young hotheads,' George was saying, 'did they not realise the effect their actions would have on the rest of us?'

Henry turned to James. 'You need to consider your actions, nephew, both you and my poor son Laurence. Do you not see what has happened because of what ye did in Collon? Taking the lives of those yeos has brought the wrath of the authorities on us and ruined all our lives. And then you called here for him and brought him away on that foolish journey to meet the Wexford rebels. Do you see that, boy? Do you?'

James flushed briefly with anger. 'Laurence had a mind of his own, uncle.'

There was silence in the room after that. James left the cottage to seek refuge in his own thoughts. Kate ran after him and stopped him.

'James, don't be angry at father. He has lost so much. Do you not understand that?'

'I'm not angry, Kate. Really, I'm not. I'm just sad at all that has happened.'

'Father hasn't been the same since they raided the house,' she said sadly. 'He goes back to the yard, feeds the cow, takes a few potatoes from the drills, but he has no heed in it anymore. His life is gone. We are away to live with John, his cousin, in a day or so.'

James was afraid to catch her eye, knowing now what they felt about him. He looked away from the cabin, towards the quiet lane, the fields across the way, thinking deeply, mulling over what had happened, what was to happen.

'They are evil men who come to kill families; taking revenge on innocent men, women and children, for the honourable actions taken in the heat of war. Me and Laurence slew two yeos because they were going to kill John Mathews, yet they kill tenfold in taking their revenge.'

'Violence begets violence James,' Kate countered. 'All it brings is more death.' James nodded gently in agreement with her.

''Tis such a tragedy indeed, he said. 'All the poor people dead and ne'er a priest to bury any of them. We had to do the burying ourselves. What is to become of us at all?'

She shrugged helplessly, although sympathetic with his sentiments.

'Truth be told,' he continued, 'I wanted to go home and start my life again, but when I met up with Laurence, he was full of fury and was all for the settling of scores. It was he and Dan who were heading west to meet the French when we were attacked. Maybe, all I have left now is to fulfil their wishes, for there is not naught left for me here.'

'James, come back to the house, please,' she implored.

'Not right now Kate. I left my good walking stick at the ruin. I must go and fetch it. And, I feel the need to clear my head too. You go back in. I'll be along later.'

Reluctantly she returned to the cabin, leaving him to mull over his future. He drifted down the lane to the road, crossed over and made for the castle ruin to retrieve his stick. He found it where he had left it, lying against a crudely-cut arch stone. Sitting down, he considered, yet again, his next move. He knew he was no longer wanted around here. He was an outcast now, from his home and family, neither of which existed anymore.

He fretted quietly amongst the stones and broken walls of the

193

old ruin, tapping his stick on a flagstone stone at his feet. The scorching hot day had turned cloudy and a breeze had picked up. Dark clouds gathering above portended a wet evening. As he searched for potential shelter for the night, a sound came from behind a wall. He turned sharply, his hackles rising, to see who had made it. The familiar voice said,

'So, cousin James, we meet up in the same place again!'

# Chapter Seventeen
## Delvin

Edward Rothwell reined in his black stallion and checked behind to see that his column of yeomanry was keeping pace. Stretched out for some distance and partially hidden by a bend in the road, were several dozen cavalry interspersed with over a hundred militia infantrymen. The extended line of redcoats, on the road west from Kells to Oldcastle, both on horseback and on foot, caught the eye above the unyielding drab greenery of the countryside they were marching through.

He tried to restrain a certain thrill that was rising in him, one of imminent engagement, of confrontation and battle. This is what being a soldier was about: fighting and beating a proper military opponent. Chasing glorified brigands carrying pikes and green flags around the fields of Meath and Louth was all well and good; catching them and seeing them swinging from gallows for their wrongdoing was even better, but the thoughts of opposing a real army, a French army, coming to do battle in England's back yard, made the hairs stand on the back of his neck with anticipation. It was what he was born for.

Soldiery had been in his blood from an early age. His father had been in the Irish Volunteers in Dublin twenty years ago, when he was a youth and had encouraged in him an interest in uniforms and weapons at an early age. Now, it was his vocation, his life. Women and relationships had never seemed to interest him, only the camaraderie and regimen of fellow soldiers, weapons and battle.

He couldn't abide peace-loving intentions, like those which Lieutenant Gettings seemed to be so fond of. It rankled like buttermilk in his aggressive, militaristic mind. A few conscientious mavericks, like Gettings, weakened the resolve of others around him during critical affairs, such as they were in now. Behaviour like the Welshman's was anathema to all he stood for. So this affair with the Moore lads, who had killed his yeos outside Collon, would hopefully resolve two problems at once; as soon as the special group found and disposed of them, then Gettings would be taken care of afterwards. He would have carried out his duties in chasing them down and then paid the penalty for showing unwarranted softness in his recent duties. Rothwell rarely smiled but now he raised a chuckled at the ingenuity of his scheme.

Satisfied that his column were in order, he was about to lead off again when he noticed a horseman gallop towards him from the rear. It was Corporal Brennan, who pulled up close to him, saluting smartly.

'Yes Corporal Brennan, I see that you have made it back from your mission at Smarmore. Tell me, how well did it go?'

Bryan Brennan could not look at him squarely in the eye, for the news he brought wasn't what Rothwell would want to hear.

'After making our enquiries in the Smamore area,' Brennan began guardedly, 'we managed to chase three insurgents down to the outhouses at Parsonstown Demesne, just outside Lobinstown. Unfortunately, one of them had a pistol and fired on us, forcing us to take cover and allowing the others to flee. Corporal Teelan was mortally wounded in the engagement but we managed to shoot and killed the perpetrator. However, sir, it gave the two Moores a chance to make their escape. We spent the rest of the day in pursuit but ceased our operation as night fell.'

Rothwell glowered at Brennan. This was not the news he sought, not at all!

'I send some of my valuable men away to carry out a simple instruction and now I find they are not up to the task.'

'Yes, sir,' Brennan agreed weakly.

'Well, where are the others, then?' Rothwell asked, deflated now, the nervous tic appearing again, affecting his eye.

'Well sir, Corporals Allen and Dolan have taken Corporal Teelan's body to the infirmary and Lieutenants Manning and Gettings are making their way here to join us, as I speak.'

Rothwell considered Brennan's summation.

'Yes, well tell both of them to report to me when they get here; that if they have the alacrity to catch up with us.' He shrugged out of his irritable disposition; it made him sound petty. He stared at Brennan.

'However, we have little time to ponder on this now. We are to make for Mullingar in the county Westmeath at the greatest speed, for the latest intelligence suggests the rebels are massing there a rather substantial amount of men and arms.'

Brennan saluted and veered away, thankful that the dressing-down had been less caustic than he anticipated. It was apparent that the captain's views were on more urgent matters.

Coming to the outskirts of Delvin, Rothwell received a messenger riding back from Mullingar, advising that they proceed to the north of the town, where a large force of rebels was gathering. He ordered his cavalry unit to proceed quickly through the main street of Delvin, leaving the infantry to march in behind them. A few inhabitants acknowledged the column's progress by giving them only a cursory glance. On the outskirts of the town they were to convene with a yeomanry group from the area and then proceed west towards Mullingar. Rothwell drove his cavalry group on inexorably, leaving his infantry further and further behind, yet knowing that for them to falter now would lessen the chances of a confrontation with the enemy up ahead.

At the junction called Turin Crossroads the Kells unit took the road to the right and proceeded forcefully towards the village of Crookedwood, where they then had to wait, impatiently, for the arrival of another force of yeomanry from Castlepollard, recently assembled by Thomas Pakenham of Tullynally Estate. The orders for this joint force were that they would then advance, at great speed, to the contested area north of Mullingar.

*

Thomas was growing uneasy at Manning's odd behaviour. Not

197

knowing him all that well he became wary of any ulterior motives he might have been assigned to do harm to him. Manning's recent demeanour seemed as if he was being forced to confront a difficult internal decision. Thomas sense of self-preservation had heightened dramatically when he realised that his life may now be in imminent danger from his fellow lieutenant.

Their departure from Kells had been delayed when Thomas insisted that they inform Corporal Teelan's wife of his demise in the line of duty. They left her modest town cottage later with her bereft cries still ringing in their ears. Thomas shared brief sympathies with her, but he was aghast at Manning's unsympathetic behaviour towards her and his insistence on being on the road as soon as possible.

They proceeded west at a moderate gallop with Manning's big horse thundering down the road, leaving Thomas endeavouring to keep pace. But his mind was also racing with many unanswered questions. Their mission to eliminate the Moore cousins for Rothwell's had proved to be unsuccessful. Both of them were still at large with Thomas been instrumental in one of their escapes. His action had gone unnoticed by the rest of the group, yet the overall failure of the mission would prove to be a detrimental sticking point with Captain Rothwell. How Rothwell would resolve the issue of the failed mission was now moot. He had more or less insinuated that Thomas' future in the yeos was predicated on a successful outcome in the hunt for the rebel cousins. It would seem that a fraught exchange with the captain was now a certainty.

Up ahead Manning continued to force the pace and Thomas, assuming now, that Rothwell wanted him dealt with one way or another, was going to have to be circumspect as the journey proceeded. Also the fact that Brennan had rode on ahead earlier, to break the news to Rothwell, further reduced his chance of a benign outcome to proceedings.

Despite the pace, he held the reins briefly in one hand to check again that his pistol was primed and his sabre was close at hand in its scabbard. He thought bitterly that you could never feel safe enough when your life was in jeopardy from the intrigues of others.

It was late afternoon and after an hour of hard riding the pair rode into the town of Delvin. Manning pulled his horse up close to a wooden water trough.

'We'll get some water for the horses here.'

He busied himself with his thirsty mount, refusing to make eye contact with Thomas. Thomas led his own horse to the trough and the two men stood adjacent watching the two horses drinking thirstily. Manning turned to Thomas.

'Perhaps we should find a hostelry on this street and seek some food before we attend to catching the main column. What say you?'

'Yes, I agree,' said Thomas. 'You appear somewhat irritable this day, Lieutenant Manning. Perhaps some food and a little respite may suit us both.'

Manning, his eyes glancing at Thomas suspiciously, shook his head.

'You are wrong Gettings. My humour is fine. I'm just anxious we return to the developing fray as soon as possible.'

They walked towards a nearby inn on the main street. Thomas was unsure whether cavalry officers would be welcome here, but Manning pushed on as if he knew of the place and had frequented it before. Thomas decided to query him further.

'And how will you explain our lack of success to Captain Rothwell.'

'As accurately as possible, I hope. He will be disappointed, I have no doubt, but perhaps the imminent engagement with the enemy will have him preoccupied instead.'

Reaching the door, the two entered a low-ceilinged tavern with a few men sitting across some wooden benches, drinking quietly. Silence ensued when the locals saw the red uniforms, but the owner scurried towards them offering immediate hospitality and soon they had arranged fodder for their horses and were sitting down to two platters of stew and a jug of ale each. Few words were exchanged between them, both men hungry and thirsty from the journey. As the food and drink were near finished Manning ordered two more beers for them. Thomas, enjoying the food, nonetheless grew suspicious.

'I thought we were in a hurry, lieutenant? You seem to be settling in for a long sojourn here.'

'It has been a tedious few days on horseback, Gettings, don't you think; scouring the countryside for rebels, exhausting both men and horses? Rothwell's main column will already have reached their destination and mind, we are still a full day behind them. Perhaps if there is a room here, we should stay overnight and proceed at full tilt after them first thing in the morning.'

Thomas nodded indifferently, yet had just noticed that Manning's first jug of beer was still near full, while his was almost empty! Was he trying to get him drunk and if so, for what nefarious reason? The second round of beer was brought to the table.

'Come on Gettings, drink up. Quench your thirst man. Enjoy this opportunity to imbibe a little, let your weariness dissolve, for tomorrow we travel west, meet up with our unit and try and stymie the French advance.'

'Yet I am sure Captain Rothwell will have something to say about our mission's lack of success,' Thomas observed.

'You worry too much about what our captain thinks. We can deal with it when we get there.' He raised a jug in salute.

'As you wish, Manning, but I will let you do the explaining when we arrive.'

'Oh, I will explain alright. I have no doubt he will want to hear from me.'

Thomas' instincts twitched in alarm, for he was near certain now that Manning was up to something; trying to create an opportunity to dispose of him somehow. Despite the comforting haze of the alcohol, he tried to keep his senses vigilant. His pistol and sword were by his side and he resolved to play along with the lieutenant until a chance presented itself where he could break away from whatever trap was being laid for him.

Glancing around Thomas noticed that the bar-room they were in was now deserted, the only occupants being the landlord and the two officers. Manning raised his jug of beer, insisting that Thomas do the same, a smile snaking across his face, good-humoured but somehow forced.

'Drink up, I say, Gettings.' He waved his hand to the counter. 'Landlord, if you please, two more beers over here and thank you kindly. Stay put Gettings, for I must relieve the pressure on my valves!' He chuckled brightly as he left.

Thomas waved him away with a forced belch and a swing of his jug, but as soon as he was out of sight, he spilled the second jug of beer onto the clay floor beneath the table, some of the liquid splashing onto his boots. He was dammed if he was going to allow Manning to have him succumb to intoxication and then probably have him deal a deadly blow in a nearby ditch. He must keep his wits about him.

Darkness had fallen and both men continued the subterfuge of increased inebriation. Manning used the pretext of periodically checking on the horses on the street; bringing his jar with him, to empty it outside, while Thomas also drained more beer in a large spittoon in the window. Manning sat down beside him after another jaunt outside.

'Come Thomas, 'tis about time to find a stable for the horses. The innkeeper tells me he has a shed for them at the side of the establishment. Let us unsaddle them and bring our valuables inside.'

He affected a slurred speech pattern and Thomas responded in a similar vein. 'After you, Francis. Sure it's late for the horses as well as ourselves!'

Only for the developing situation being so serious, Thomas felt like bursting out with laughter at the pair of them trying to dupe each other. However, as they bade goodnight to the innkeeper and exited into the cool of the night, their respective masks of levity soon fell away when they witnessed an unruly throng of men brandishing pikes and torches coming menacingly up the street towards them.

'What is this?' Manning cried out in alarm. Thomas looked at them in alarm.

'It's a band of United Irishmen,' he said, seeing the pikes raised in the air. 'And they've spotted us and our horses. Quickly, we must get back into the inn!'

They turned towards the door, just as it slammed before them and a crossbeam clamped shut behind it. The crowd drew inexorably closer, their torches held high, throwing dancing shadows in the night; the sound growing noisy and ominous. Someone let out a shout. 'Redcoats ahead.'

Their military apparel was made ready and they began to raise their weapons in preparation for an attack. Another roared. 'No redcoats will get in our way tonight boys. Take them!'

'The horses,' Manning shrieked, ''tis our only chance.'

The mob, brave in numbers and with bloodlust awakened, were rushing toward them, gathering momentum, their pikes lowered in attack. The two yeos made a desperate dash for their horses, both of whom were prancing wildly and trying to break free from their reins, as they were tied up in the space between the lieutenants and the attacking crowd. Nervous energy pumped through Thomas, who reached his horse just ahead of Manning. He jumped onto the saddle, the crowd continuing to bear down on them.

Manning was in a fever of fright and as he grabbed his horse's reins, he also attempted to withdraw his pistol, in a vain effort to get the charging men to stand their ground. But in doing so he lost crucial seconds in mounting his horse and making his escape. Shouts came from the pack.

'There'll be a few less of ye to meet the French and more of us.' A cheer went up.

The nearest pikeman drew near him, like a fearsome apparition, the torchlight throwing ghastly shapes around him. Manning, losing control of his horse, raised his pistol and fired at him. His attacker tumbled forward in a death throe, his impetus hurling him and his pike to the ground, just before Manning's feet. He turned to the already retreating Thomas, his eyes wild with fear and fury.

'Damn and blast you Gettings, and all belonging to you. You are the death of me now.'

As he endeavoured to draw his sword, a pike was thrust towards him and lanced his side. He crumpled, letting the reins go. His horse skittered away. More rebels closed in for the kill.

'Help me, Gettings,' he gurgled, blood spilling from his mouth. 'Tis all Rothwell's fault, I swear. Help me.'

By now Manning had rolled onto the ground, his legs kicking spasmodically. Thomas steered his horse to and fro in a fruitless attempt at intervening, but it was obvious Manning was beyond saving. Kicking his spurs into the mare's flanks, she kicked her hind legs and drove forward, away from the murderous scene. Thomas' last, lingering sight of Manning was of his body engulfed in flames as several torches were thrown onto him, setting his hair and jacket on fire.

Thomas, shaken at the sight, sped away, shouts and insults from the gang tossed ineffectually after him. He galloped west, into the night, not knowing if he was on the right road but just glad to be alive. Yet, with Manning's final words ringing in his ears, he was now certain that Rothwell had instructed him to have Thomas killed and therefore no longer a burden or threat. It was a terrifying development.

# Chapter Eighteen
## Cloone

James had been astounded by the unexpected appearance of Laurence in the castle ruin at Killary. After their initial exuberance of seeing each other alive, they both calmed down sufficiently to allow Laurence relate his experience at Parsonstown. After Dan Kelly had sacrificed himself to allow his escape, he had hidden in the stable's rafters, lying on old canvas rolls that had been stored there. During the night, when all was quiet, he slipped away quietly and made for Killary, where he had rested up in the castle.

They discussed at length their next moves, knowing that they had stood in the very same spot less than two months previously, deciding on a very similar path.

'But what has changed cousin?' James asked sadly. 'Those weeks have brought us nothing but misery and death. And yet here we are again. We seemed to have learned nothing at all.'

'Well, we have learned that the enemy will not rest until they have us at the end of a rope or in a shallow grave. I know we are repeating the same words, but I for one will not rest until I join this French army somehow. It is our one chance of victory. If we don't take it, we will regret it forever. I know I will.'

James grew exasperated. 'But we are doing the same thing all over again, following the same path. The last time we travelled to meet the Wexford army at the Boyne. Look where that led us? And now we go in search of this French army. For all we know Dan Kelly could have been told a ball of lies about them. Maybe he made the story up himself. How do we know?'

Laurence looked him straight in the eye. 'I think Dan has finally atoned for going to the authorities about Michael Boylan. By forfeiting his life, he has given us a chance to live, to fight. The one thing he would have wanted to see was the French army helping to free Ireland from English oppression.'

James was full of cynicism. 'Aye, I hear Dan Kelly's words. He did wrong and he knew it and now he's gone because of his actions.' Then something the yeo had said to him in the stables seemed to make sense. 'Perhaps lifting one tyranny might leave us open to the tyranny of another.'

Laurence studied him earnestly. 'Those are big words cousin, coming from one so lowly in life, as indeed I am. You have been mixing with the wrong people lately. But let me ask you one thing, seeing as you are so full of doubt. Why did you leave White Mountain and follow us over here then?'

James didn't reply. He couldn't either, for he hardly knew the reasons himself. Having no alternative to their present circumstance was a weak excuse for following his cousin. But Laurence let him be.

'How are we going to travel west then?' James asked eventually. 'We can hardly walk all the way, can we?' Both considered that problem and could think of no simple answer.

In the end, they decided to take George Geraghty's black and white cob, Ginny! She recognised Laurence from the journey he and his father had made to Smarmore. Laurence was full of remorse when they stole her away from her tether; telling himself resolutely that she would be returned as soon as he was able to. It was a hard thing to do, to steal such a valuable possession as a horse on a man who had been so kind to their family. They took a little food too, just enough for a couple of days and crept off into the early September evening. They mounted the horse further down the road and made off to the west.

Laurence knew the path to Castletown and, reaching there, they took the road to Moynalty after that, not pushing the cob too hard. With the two of them on her, he kept her at a gentle trot. They slept outside Mullagh on the first night and the next morning they were guided onto the road for Virginia. The villages they passed were quiet, with a few going about their daily chores. However a woman outside Virginia told them that a lot the young men had been making their way west in the last day or two. When pushed she talked of them 'going to meet the French.' This knowledge drove them on with even greater enthusiasm.

Leaving Mountnugent on the second morning of their journey, they saw military activity in the near distance, crossing over a junction they were approaching. Stopping temporarily to allow the column to clear the junction they travelled on, cautiously and slowly, too slowly Laurence felt.

Further west, they noticed an appreciable increase in men going in the same direction as them. Passing one, his head down with a large cap covering most of his face and hardly looking at them as they passed by, Laurence drew up the cob and they both jumped off. While he went to relieve himself in the ditch, James asked the man directions for Granard.

'And why would I tell a stranger like you that?' he answered sullenly, not looking up.

''Tis a simple question I ask. We are going there to... to meet some people. We want to know the road, that's all.'

James saw his face. He was young, red-jawed, his cheeks pockmarked. He wore a dirty jacket and torn britches, but his eyes showed a latent strength in them. James decided to test him.

'Are you going to meet the French, to join the United Irishmen with the advancing French?'

The stranger looked at him, stupefied at this young lad with the strange accent, who seemed to be foretelling his plans. James tried to placate him but he grew restless. James remained calm and persevered with him.

'We too are going west to meet up with this new force, to help them beat the redcoat army. Can we travel with you? I'm James, James Moore.' He pointed to the ditch. 'And that is my cousin Laurence.'

Before the traveller had time to say anything, James dug out a piece of crust for him.

When Laurence reappeared, he found the two hunched on the roadside, chewing through the remains of the bread. On the onward journey he stayed with them, telling them he was Patrick McGovern, a Cavan man. Only twenty, his older brother had gone to Granard, to the United men rising there, in preparation for the arrival of the French. Despite his father's wishes, he too had fled their homestead that morning to join him. James nodded, understanding. They too had done the same thing.

'There must be dozens flocking to the cause,' Laurence said, pointing ahead, observing the road with many others now on it, all heading in a westerly direction. The three stayed together but there was little talk between them. Ginny had grown tired with the constant travelling and the two-man load she was forced to carry. They decided to leave only one on her while the other two walked alongside. Throughout the afternoon, the skies clouded over with angry grey clouds massing, brimming with rain. As they walked, Patrick revealed the names of some of the places they passed through, including a large lake to their left, Lough Sheelin, its surface rippling dully under the grey sky.

Up ahead, a large group of men were gathered on the road, some of them talking excitedly, others shouting, arms gesticulating. The three men drew close alongside numerous stragglers from Granard who were arriving from the other direction.

'I tell you, the United men in Granard have been beat,' one declared loudly, a broken pike shaft under his arm. 'We ran up against the garrison twice, as hard as we could, but they had many weapons and no end of powder for their guns. We were a sorry sight by the time we broke.'

'So, where are the United men now?' another asked.

'They've spirited away, those that were left, after the redcoats charged at us with their bayonets and horses. We were scattered to the winds, half of us were killed or maimed.' The man knelt on the ground exhausted.

'And the French... what of the French?' Patrick McGovern asked. 'Are they near?'

A few turned to look at the three men and their tired cob.

Another man, small framed, in a tattered coat, his face smarting from a blow of an instrument took over.

'Lads, if ye mind my words, I'm telling ye now, be off home with ye, as fast as ye can. I've heard it said only this very day, from a Leitrim man I met, that, around the same time as the Granard yeos chased us from the town, the French army was in Leitrim and heading south towards Longford.' He clutched at his injured jaw but continued to speak to those listening, some agog with his words.

'Hear me now...but so are two armies of the English, chasing them all the way, with General Lake and General Cornwallis at their head.'

A few men, who had been talking, quietened, listening to him; he knowing more than the rest there.

'There are still United men holding fast outside Mullingar, I heard, at some hospital. But what hope have they either? Yeos from Cootehill and Mullingar are bearing down on them and they have little or no weapons.'

Men nodded and muttered knowingly under their breaths.

'Why do you say that?' Laurence piped up, challenging his view. 'The French will come and retake the countryside for us. They will be a match for the English, won't they?'

Silence swept through the men on the road. The man who had outlined the current situation stood up painfully, his cheek swelling further as he shook his head.

'You might say that son, you might say that. There are hundreds of men lying dead around the streets of Granard, who believed that. Some that got away, some of you standing round me, might think that the French will save us. Away ye go then and raise yer pikes with them, but my home is down this road and I'm lucky I'm so close. I'm going there now, and I'm going to hide away in a corner until it gets quiet. That's what I'm going to do.'

With an awkward shuffle he stepped through the ring of men and headed east, down the road James, Laurence and Patrick had just come. The two dozen men on the road stood looking after him, lost in their own contemplations; some having serious doubts, others willing to continue their trek. The Moore cousins and Patrick looked wistfully into the distance.

*

The journey the men made over the next day turned into a never-ending challenge of circling drumlins, avoiding bogs, crossing streams and water-logged tracks and even making moderate progress on the occasional passable roadway. Following a brief talk in the rain, a dozen or so, who had stood heeding the survivor from Granard, vowed to carry on with their journey. The French were only a day away it was assumed and it was too late to do anything else. Wasn't that why they had come this far anyway?

Fortuitously, a few of those accompanying them knew the approximate route north into Leitrim and, together with dribs and drabs of men joining them, some with ponies, and mostly those who escaped with their lives from Granard, this motley band made their way to the north of the county of Longford. In a field of rushes outside Aughnacliffe, they lay overnight, tired and hungry, with a few stunted hawthorns above them, giving the barest of cover.

The next morning, after several hours walk, the man leading them slipped away without anyone noticing. Those close to the front looked up from their feet, only to realise that he was no longer leading. They stopped to take stock of their situation. McGovern dismounted from Ginny and led her to grass. James and Laurence sat on a low stone wall, tired and demoralised.

'How far have we to go?' James said, leaning forward to rub grit and muck from his bare soles.

'I don't know, but we've been on the road near three days. If I wasn't convinced with what Dan Kelly said and those men we met back there, I would think this is some kind of nightmare.'

'Should we turn back then?'

Laurence looked at him. 'Turn back to where? We don't know

209

where we are. Only that one or two of these men have an idea of the roads, we might as well lie down and die.'

A few spoke up. A man, who had joined them that morning, said he was from up the road at Legga and knew the paths. He had heard some fortuitous news the previous day; that the French were approaching Keshcarrigan and were proceeding southwards.

'Aye, that's the good news, but they have the redcoats trailing them all the way. The man who told me had fled from the Irishmen attached to the French army. He was afraid for his life, but said the French turn on the enemy every so often and drive them off. But they need as many men to help them as they can. I say we should keep going. We will be in Leitrim shortly. Are ye with me?'

A weary murmur of assent was voiced by the men and they picked themselves up, mounted the few horses they had and followed the man along the track.

The next village on the road north was Cloone, the man at the front told them. Darkness had drawn down quickly over the countryside and from a distance before them came the dissonance of peoples voices; many people it would seem, talking and shouting, echoing across the hills and down towards the small rebel group. The sound shook them for they knew not whether it was friend or foe! They had rounded a small lake, Keeldra Lough they heard it called, its water still like darkened glass, and were now heading north on the Drumlish to Ballinamore Road. Neither James nor Laurence had been on Ginny for most of the evening. McGovern had dismounted and given her back to them as she was visibly struggling. Her head hung heavily and they had to cajole her to keep moving. Busy motivating the cob, James had not heard the noise. The men in front of them had begun to look at each other, fear in their eyes, wondering could it be the English coming their way.

The leader, who was walking them through another junction, stopped in his tracks, listened and looked around for any sign of an ambush. James now heard the muffled cacophony too; a lot of people in the distance, milling around, horses neighing, cattle lowing, the clang of iron and … drums!

''Tis the sound of an army,' he said aloud.

'But whose?' Laurence replied beside him.

'It can't be the English,' the man up front said. 'They wouldn't be that boisterous, surely.'

But he waved them on anyway, fear of going back overriding that of moving forward. Up the long straight incline they trudged, trying to judge each footstep and gap between each other. James' feet were painful with blisters and beside him Laurence hobbled along with the cob. Ahead of them the sky became illuminated with the glow of newly lit fires and the sounds grew stronger. To James, it sounded like a boisterous night after a cemetery patrun. If it was the French, they certainly weren't trying to hide themselves from a pursuing enemy. Cloone stood on top of a hill and was a single-street hamlet with a small collection of cabins either side. As they cautiously drew near, a field on the right looked to be the epicentre of the commotion. It was filled with groups of men, talking loudly in an unknown language and beating drums around where the fires were lit. Laurence was just ahead of James looking on in awe. He turned back to him, his eyes dancing.

''Tis the French, James! It has to be. Look at them. Look at all the blue uniforms and their strange words. And not a redcoat in sight either.'

James voice was lost at the sight before him. Many locals were out of their cabins providing food to the hungry men. Many horses were tied in a row along the field wall and the field itself, sloping down to a stream, was gradually filling up with these foreigners. Further up the street, many more were emerging from the darkness, mainly Irish rebel volunteers marching with the French force. They were exhausted and hungry, and some were injured and being assisted by comrades. The flood of men entering the village continued. Most were on foot, a mixture of French and Irish, some arriving on horseback, a few pulling small artillery pieces and ammunition wagons, all filing into the already crowded village.

Camp fires had been lit in the field and James saw a young

bullock being manhandled by villagers. It was grounded and swiftly slaughtered then butchered with the help of two moustachioed grenadiers, who shouted, 'Merci, merci, mes amis' to the providers.

On his left James saw more animals being brought forward for killing and consumption by the hungry soldiers, while on his right, two large iron gates, which someone said belonged to the Protestant churchyard, had been taken off their hinges and manhandled onto wooden blocks on the street. And again, villagers came to their aid here, with bundles of kindling and timber provided for lighting fires under the gates, which acted as huge griddles for roasting the freshly cut beef. Buckets of water were brought up from the stream to quench the soldiers' thirst and from somewhere beer and small bottles of whiskey were produced. It seemed as if the whole village and surrounding townlands came to offer what they could to the visitors. It was a bedlam of activity with all the mood of a festive occasion.

The group James and Laurence had walked into Cloone with, dispersed rapidly; it was every man for himself now, as they sought out a morsel to eat and something to slake their thirst. Laurence led Ginny to searching for some water and fodder. James walked slowly through the crowded street, bemused and nearly overcome with emotion at the extraordinary scene.

For the past three days, he had been trekking west, through stream and bog, constantly hungry, ready to return to his native county at every turn, his mind empty and unable to fathom what his intentions were. Even the image of Mollie had eroded to a distant memory in him. So now, in this unknown part of the midlands, he was suddenly immersed in the weary but good-natured spirit, which this exotic army from a foreign land had brought to the area, even if only for this one evening.

More French soldiers were arriving from around the curve of the street, led by a few officers on horseback. A mixture of young recruits and old veterans, they quickly disassembled and sought out comrades already settling for the night. The older grenadiers, fatigued after a day of marching and rear-guard fighting, lit up their pipes and stood in quiet contemplation with others of their vintage. The younger ones were louder, eagerly grasping the brief respite from battle and launching into song with their peers around the fire, grasping at hot pieces of meat being distributed and slaking their thirst with local beer and even the evil-tasting poitín.

The cannon and ammunition train had been wheeled into a defensive circle in the middle of the village and soldiers who were fed, took turns to stand guard over the precious weapons, for it was these that had kept the enemy at bay for the past three days as they marched east. Towards the end of the cabins the forge was opened and put to use, making running repairs to horseshoes and other equipment. James even spied pike-heads being manufactured by one of the smiths.

And yet, it appeared that not all of the column had arrived. Perhaps what James saw was just the vanguard or the main body of men. Grabbing a piece of bread and meat, he looked on as a cavalryman, his uniform a mixture of green and brown, rode down the street and drew up close to where James was standing. A half-dozen mounted men followed close behind.

'Make way,' the horseman shouted, dismounting from his horse. 'Make way for General Humbert. Has anyone a drink for the general? He thirsts so!'

James was astonished to hear an Irish accent emanate from his mouth; an Irishman in French uniform! Yet more horsemen cantered in, a combination of French and Irish. James stood back captivated, as they congregated in the centre of the village.

Someone in uniform shouted out, 'Captain Teeling, here is some drink for the general,

'Thank you. He arrives shortly.'

And from the darkness another large squadron of cavalry entered, led by a man in a long dark coat with a cravat covering his neck; his eyes quickly taking in the spectacle of his army encamping for the night. He dismounted, drank from the jug put in his hand and spoke to Captain Teeling briefly, in French. Teeling mounted his horse and called loudly for some silence.

'Quiet please. Quiet, I say. General Humbert wishes to speak a few words to both his soldiers and to the local people gathered here this evening.'

A large space was cleared for the two men and the general began to speak eloquently in French. Many of his soldiers drew close, listening to his words, while some remained at the fires, having heard his heroic speeches more than once before! When he finished he spoke quietly with Captain Teeling, who advised aloud that he would translate the general's words into English.

'This is a fine place that we rest in tonight,' Teeling related Humbert's words. 'I see the people have been generous to our men and to our Irish allies. We come in the name of the Virgin Mary and the Directory of France to fight for and free Ireland from England's tyranny. My generals, Sarrazin and Fontaine, also thank you for your hospitality. We have much to do on this mission and though the English have been pressing us continually, they now lie asleep in the rushes and bogs, exhausted from following me.'

This got a rousing roar of approval from the villagers, which Humbert proudly acknowledged.

'Now I must sit with my generals,' he added, 'and we shall discuss our next move. After that I seek the hospitality of your pastors and men of importance here. Please have them brought to me. Merci. Vive l'Irlandais! Vive la France!'

Another roar went up and James shouted along with gusto. He was impressed with this Frenchman's stomach for the fight. Here, at last, was a man who, had sailed from France with his army and who was prepared to give the English a bloody nose. For the first time, in as long as he could remember, a sense of quiet jubilation swelled through him. At last the people were rising again and, despite all his qualms about this journey, maybe he had made the right decision after all!

As the speech was finishing, another column of bedraggled rebels arrived, led by an officer on horseback. Many of those there recognised him and he too got a resounding cheer. James established it was a Mayo man, General George Blake, who was commander of the

214

Irish insurgent group accompanying the French. Following them a Frenchman, General Sarrazin, made his entrance, with his rear-guard column of exhausted cavalry; some men doubling up on mounts, their own shot from under them.

James was mesmerised at the amount of generals, officers and fighting men on display. Surely the English could not defeat this amount of men and weaponry, could they? And yet it was only yesterday he had heard of the massacre of many rebels at Granard by a small well-armed garrison. His head swan reflecting on the vagaries of war.

Close to where he stood, a large bench had been hastily commandeered from the inn and was dragged into the open street and by torchlight, General Humbert gathered his officers round it. Laurence had yet to return with Ginny and he saw McGovern and some of the others eating scraps from the French leftovers. However James decided to stay close and perhaps he might overhear some of the important talk of these generals. Blake and Teeling were standing near to him and as the discussion began, Teeling translated Humbert and Sarrazin's words into English for the Mayo general.

'So far we have eluded the army of Cornwallis, who are somewhere south-west of here,' Humbert began. 'But Lake has being hounding our rear echelons since we entered this county.' He looked over at one of his generals. 'Sarrazin, present your report please?' The elegant Frenchman bowed slightly.

'I have been commanding our rear-guard defence for two days,' Sarrazin outlined. 'We have managed to contain General Lake's thrusts; we have even counter-attacked on occasion, but have lost many good Frenchmen in doing so. We are greatly outnumbered and this pressure being exerted will surely tell sooner rather than later.'

He deferred back to Humbert, who James noticed was becoming agitated and inattentive. Teeling continued to interpret the talk, only some of which James understood.

'Yes, yes, Sarrazin,' Humbert was saying testily. 'You are carrying out your duties as ordered. It is for me to determine our strategy. The latest intelligence suggests that thousands of Irishmen are mustering in the central divisions called Longford and Westmeath.' Teeling added to the dialogue.

'If I may, general? Only yesterday a messenger informed us that there was much heavy fighting in a town called Granard. However, of the outcome of the engagement, he had no knowledge.'

'That is good news then, is it not?' Humbert said. 'We will march to join them at daybreak. How far is this town?'

James ears pricked up at the mention of Granard. And he knew the outcome of the battle there! Many of the men he had walked with were survivors from the massacre there. Without hesitating he tugged urgently at Captain Teeling's coat.

'Sir, sir, if I may say something, please!'

The captain turned to see a young croppy requesting a hearing. 'Lad, we are busy here. Be on your way.' Teeling tried to dismiss him.

'But sir, I walked here with men who fought at Granard. They were defeated and many of them were killed. Those that escaped said it was a massacre and they were lucky to survive.'

Teeling stared at him, disbelieving.

''Tis the truth sir, I swear. Some of them are over there, taking some food. Ask them.'

Teeling hesitated for a moment then turned and spoke urgently in French to Humbert. A heated discussion quickly ensued. Teeling ordered James to fetch over some of the Granard survivors. When three of them related their experiences to Teeling and Blake, turmoil enveloped the group and James could no longer hear the captain's interpretations. Humbert raised his arms in annoyance. Sarrazin and Fontaine spoke rapidly in their language, and to all intents it looked as if Humbert's plans had been severely disrupted by James' intervention.

James wandered away rapidly, in case blame was apportioned to him. He went looking for Laurence, wondering if he had done wrong or right in speaking up. His last sight of Humbert was of him with two fists on the bench shaking his head in despair. He passed a forge where two blacksmiths, with cavalrymen and rebels gathered round them, were working into the night, busy in front of an open furnace, mending shoes and making as many pike-heads as they could with whatever iron they had. A third man was fixing the iron heads onto long wooden shafts and giving them out to waiting hands. Watching them, James suddenly realised he had no weapon of his own, and here he was preparing to fight against a well-trained army. He hovered near the blacksmith's door and watched the two men, father and son James assumed, manipulating with dexterity the hammer and tongues, doing a mixture of jobs in a very speedy manner. James decided to be brave and spoke to them. 'I am away with the army to fight the English, but I have no weapon. Have you anything you could make for me?'

The older man looked up from his work, his face red, sweat dripping off him. Then he smiled at James.

'Well we can't have a young croppy going to fight and he with no weapon. I have a piece of iron here, not large enough for a pike but I can fashion a long scian for you, like a narrow sword. If you get close to one of the redcoats, jab it into him. You'll get one for me, won't you?'

Working away feverishly, he dipped the length of moulded iron in a barrel of water before running it across a grind stone. He looked carefully at his handiwork and satisfied with the job, presented it to James.

'Put that through your belt, a mhic, and mind how sharp it is. I left the handle rough for you to grip, but it will serve you well at close quarters.'

James thanked him profusely and continued his search for Laurence. Passing the only two-storey house in Cloone, he saw lights inside and made out Humbert and his generals being entertained by some of the local dignitaries. He found it strange that they could turn so easily and quickly from waging war to drinking the health of local officialdom. Roaming through the crowds of men, he finally spotted Laurence beside Ginny and some of the men they had walked with. Laurence was sporting a pike and was practicing poking it into the air and thrusting it before him, testing its unwieldly weight.

'Look what I got, cousin,' he said, seeing James approaching

217

him. 'These pikes must be a formidable sight to the enemy. I am told it will easily take a man and his mount down.'

James, in turn, showed him his sword and Laurence tried to withhold his laughter at the puny weapon.

'Now we take our rest cousin. The men are saying we will march at dawn or else the redcoats will be upon us. They also say there is an army of Gaels waiting for to help us in Longford. English armies are behind us and in front, but everyone believes that General Humbert is clever and lucky enough that we will escape their clutches again.'

James brandished his long dagger at an imaginary foe.

'Let's hope that what they say is right,' he said, thinking that despite the restful atmosphere of the night, a knot of foreboding had developed in his stomach.

\*

By break of dawn the following day, James had had little sleep. Through the night he had tossed and turned on the grass he lay on, his mind filled with bright dreams of home; of his parents, his cousins, working on the land, sitting by the fire, playing with his brothers and sisters. Then the images gradually grew darker and filled with prescient signs of death and bloodshed. He awoke with a start, sweating and disorientated. Moments later Laurence stirred beside him, stretched heartily and made ready for the day ahead.

'This is our day cousin,' he said, gripping his long pike. 'They cannot say that Louth and Meath never sent men to join the French.' James secretly agreed. Then a man beside them shouted, 'Look! The Frenchmen are already preparing for to march off to battle.'

Soon, Irish commanders were on their horses too, cajoling their men to make ready and form columns. All spare mounts, including Ginny, their cob, were sequestered to carry ammunition and the cousins were downcast as she was led away, still hobbling. Word soon spread that Lake's forces were moving in from the north and were nearing Cloone. Further down the street, long rows of blue-coated men, muskets across their shoulders were mustering, their officers on horseback shouting out orders. Close by, the half dozen cannon they had pulled all the way from Castlebar were chained to teams of horses, with their ammunition carriages lined up behind them, General Fontaine organising their departure.

A short time later, with their colours raised and marching in step to the beat of their drummers, over eight hundred French soldiers and their officers filed away from the village on foot and horseback and away into the morning mist. They were followed up by a less impressive but more numerous formations of over a thousand Irish rebels, flying their green flags of liberty. Many were from Mayo, some from Sligo and Leitrim and a few from Longford and Cavan. In the middle of all these, staying close to the men who they had arrived with the previous evening, were James and Laurence; one with his long pike held high, eager for action, to be part of a battle against the hated enemy; the other, a sense of purpose intact, yet unsure where they were headed and what fate ultimately awaited him.

Again, General Sarrazin and his cavalry force of about a hundred men took up the rear-guard position; his men holding back behind the last of the Irish lines, watching for signs of an attack. Half an hour later, the redcoats sallied forth in their first sortie of the day; maybe fifty light cavalry, dashing forward against Sarrazin's rear horsemen. Forming a line, they turned and fired a volley of musket fire, taking down several of the English vanguard. The redcoats retaliated with their own fire and a few French tumbled from their horses. The same scenario played out for the rest of the morning, with Lake's forces repeatedly engaging Humbert's backline, whittling away at their resolve, gradually forcing Humbert into making a decision to keep marching or halt and make a stand.

In the centre James, hearing the encounter behind them, kept his head down, staying in step with the man in front of him. Beside him Laurence picked up the chant of those in their column, 'Erin go bragh, Erin go bragh.' The Irish chanted it up and down the line, trying to keep their spirits and hopes raised. Hundreds of pikes were raised high in the air, the metal heads glinting in the weak morning sun and balanced against the rebel shoulders, akin to a walking forest that marched south through the lanes and bogs of Leitrim.

Some way out from Cloone, James became aware that there were problems with some of the cannon on the narrow boggy ground they travelled on, and with a fear that, if abandoned, they might come into the hands of the English, they were forced to unceremoniously roll them into a small lough.

Above them the sun was a dim orb through the low cloud when Humbert held a brief council of war with Fontaine and it was decided to halt at the small village they had just entered. Teeling was called up and asking a petrified villager the name of the hamlet, they found it was called Ballinamuck. An impressive round hill stood behind it, with low-lying bogland each side. Humbert, seeking height to gain an advantage in the imminent combat, decided he would place his troops on the hill where the enemy would have to ascend to do battle. On this Saturday morning it was the only advantage he held.

Frantic activity ensued with the French and the Irish as they scaled the hill but left a sizeable force with some cavalry and two remaining cannon on the road leading out of the village, to add an extra arc of fire onto the enemy. The Irish contingent climbed the hill for a short distance, where Teeling and his officers had them array before them, line abreast, pikes to the fore. Anyone lucky enough to have a gun stood directly behind them. And behind them again and closer to the summit of the hill, the French infantry lined up and busied themselves loading their muskets. Humbert positioned a cavalry unit to one side to try and interdict and break up the English cavalry charges. In the short time he had to prepare, this was as much as they could do.

James and Laurence stood at the forefront of the Irish line, facing downhill, clumps of furze and poor damp soil covered in reeds, the only obstacle between them and the first waves of redcoats who were already mustering in the village. Further up on the hill, across James shoulder, he could see Humbert and his entourage survey the topography they had chosen to defend. The general kept pointing to where they had marched from and James suddenly wondered where General Sarrazin's rear-guard where? Had they already been overrun and defeated?

General Bake and Captain Teeling rode up and down, along the lines of pikemen, urging them to fight bravely for the cause. 'Liberty or death,' they shouted, encouraging the men to repeat it after them. The time for marching and subterfuge was over. Now it was time to fight.

James couldn't help but feel inadequate with his short sword as his only means of defence, though some round him had little more than scythes and wooden clubs. He turned to his cousin, his teeth chattering with nerves.

'This is it... Laurence! This is Mountainstown all over again, except now there's more of us... but also a lot more of them.'

Laurence face was set in a grimace, steeling himself for the imminent assault. 'Good luck cousin James. You look out for me and I'll look out for you, like we did with the Wexfordmen at Mountainstown.'

# Chapter Nineteen

## Ballinamuck

The initial English cavalry charges were relentless in their intensity. Again and again they threw themselves against the Irish and French lines in a flurry of horses and swords and a pall of musket fire and red-streaked pikes. Despite some drizzle and drifting low cloud, the reserve units placed on a hill south of the battle site had a panoramic view of the engagement. Just as they had reached their vantage point, they saw the French army led by a squadron of their cavalry enter the village below, followed by a large array of French line infantry and Irish rebels, carrying flags and an assortment of weaponry. They were closely followed by General Lake's cavalry and infantry divisions who quickly closed off any escape route from the north and west. It seemed that the French leader, General Humbert, seeing further enemy units before him, to the south and east, and knowing he was all but surrounded, was determined to make a final stand on the hill above the village. The near horizon was soon full of red and blue uniforms, with green and tricolour flags hoisted aloft. The air was soon thick with musket shot and crack of cannon.

The unit beside Rothwell's hailed from Granard and had been chasing remnants of the rebel forces into north Longford until they were ordered into the reserve force. They knew the area and advised Thomas Gettings and the men the names of townlands before them. Looking north-west, from the hill called Creelaghta where they stood, Thomas could just make the blue uniforms of a French unit surrendering on Kiltycreevagh Hill, to the north of the village. And from a brief lend of a spyglass he could make out their colours being lowered and redcoat soldiers moving through them and confiscating their weapons.

Earlier, they had witnessed the arrival of the French into the village below them, the beat of their drums echoing through the low-lying areas, forcing some villagers to flee their homes in panic. They then took up defensive positions close to the brow of Shanmullagh Hill, with long rows of Irish pikemen below them. They had little time to settle before English artillery units were drawn up and the first cannon shots began to explode in their midst. Despite suffering several casualties, the blue line of the French and the green of the Irish held firm as they waited for the English to advance their infantry up the hill.

Thomas watched the spectacle unfold before his eyes, as if they were hundreds of model soldiers and horses spread out on a panoramic green cloth beneath him. The sound of a horse pulling up to their ranks jolted him from his observations. Looking to his side, he saw Captain Rothwell arriving back to his unit. Rothwell had left for the nearby town of St Johnstown the previous evening, just before Thomas had galloped from Delvin and located his unit. With little ceremony he had melted back into their ranks in Rothwell's temporary absence.

Rothwell reined his stallion to a halt and briefly inspected the developing battle in the near distance. Then he immediately signalled for his lieutenants to gather round him. He outlined Lord Cornwallis' instructions, which were that the local militias and yeos were to hold back from the battle proper, allowing the regular units gain the upper hand and only then were the reserve companies to hunt down and dispatch any rebel survivors of the battle. An additional order was that no French soldier who had surrendered was to be harmed in any way. Rothwell asked if they understood his instructions. As they nodded, he locked eyes on Thomas.

'So Gettings, you made it back just in time for the final reckoning below us. You will be glad to know that it is only the Irish you have to kill this morning. As you've just heard, you are to take any French you find into your tender care.'

Thomas gritted his teeth at Rothwell's sarcastic tone. 'I am here to do my duty sir.'

Rothwell looked around at his officers, as if counting them. 'And where is Lieutenant Manning, may I ask? He was due back here with you.'

'Sir, I have sad news to report. Lieutenant Manning lost his life in the line of duty. We were ambushed by a group of rebels in Delvin as we made our way here.'

The captain stared at him, his steel grey eyes boring into his soul. 'I see. Well, that is bad news indeed.' Rothwell conceded acidly. Thomas suspected that he had realised the implication of Manning not succeeding in getting rid of him.

'And on top of this, those Moore rebels, Rothwell said. 'Brennan tells me you let them escape, despite my direct orders?'

Thomas held himself steady on his mare, feeling the hostility in Rothwell's words. 'Well, we were part of a team, sir, searching for them. Through good luck on their part, they did indeed break away from our clutches.'

'You let them get away Gettings, both of them?' he persisted. 'And now you say that Lieutenant Manning lost his life on the way here. Nothing good emanates from you, sir. Nothing!'

His words rang out, cold yet calculating, his tone emitting a venomous quality. Not a word was uttered by the other officers in earshot.

'We shall see about these things Gettings. You have disappointed me greatly. You have continually failed me and I am losing patience with you. I will have to deal with you myself later, seeing as no one else can.'

He gave Thomas a final withering look before steering his horse away, searching for an update on the progress of the battle currently being waged opposite them.

As Thomas composed himself following Rothwell's verbal threats, he settled his gaze on the sight before him and grasped that the encounter was all but over. The early mist had dissipated and the sun was casting its bright rays on the scene below. Outside the village, one enemy cannon continued to fire, but he could see it would soon be overwhelmed by advancing infantry, while over on the hillside the first line of Irish and their long lances had been broken up by dragoon charges, with several waves of Lake's infantry working their way up the incline after them. On the brow of the hill the French were being surrounded from the sides and rear and, from another brief glance through a spyglass, he imagined he saw their helmets being raised on the point of their sabres, signifying their surrender. Thomas felt the familiar ache in his belly return as he realised they would soon be requested to mop up any residual rebel presence.

Rothwell and Corporal Brennan came thundering back up the hill with news and orders.

'I have just been informed the main enemy force has been broken,' Rothwell shouted at them. 'The French under Humbert have formally capitulated and are seeking terms, while the Irish, under some ne'er-do-wells called Teeling and Blake have resisted laying down their weapons. General Lake's regular army units now control the battlefield, so our job as yeomanry officers is to chase down and destroy any surviving rebels. I repeat - we are to chase them down and give them no quarter. Have I made myself perfectly clear?'

Every officer on horseback nodded their assent.

'Right men,' he roared, sword in the air, 'we go down into the valley and sweep up through the large hill yonder, where the enemy forces were positioned. There are bogs in between so careful with the horses. Charge!'

*

The site of the battle was awash with rebel bodies. Many more who had tried to flee the area lay dying or dead in the bogs surrounding it. Thomas and his unit, in tandem with the other reserve yeos, were given freedom to roam the hinterland, chasing down and putting to the sword anyone that hadn't a French officer's jacket on - and that was practically everyone! Rothwell had Corporal Brennan stay in close proximity to Thomas but he was soon drawn away by the challenge of the pursuit, leaving Thomas a solitary rider along the boggy rim; ostensibly searching the area, even using his sword to swing at random bushes or chase after shadows in the distance. He did not want to ride anyone down and take their lives. In the distance he saw various pursuits in motion; red-coated yeos, sabres aloft, bearing down on terrified individuals who, caught in the miasma of the glutinous ground, were unable to gain any traction or create distance. And the distant discordant shrieks of the victims continued to drift across the boggy expanse as the blades chopped into flesh and bone. Then a temporary silence would prevail for a beat or two until the next rebel was up and running.

A little later as his reconnaissance was drawing to a close, Thomas, despite his best efforts, happened upon four fugitives hiding behind a bush on the east side of Shanmullagh Hill. They appeared to have escaped behind a low thorn hedge, which he had inexplicably decided to ride along. They were lying low, their bodies flat on the ground, but their grey muddied forms were easily visible through the sharp foliage. Should he turn and move back along the hedge, pretend he hadn't seen them? No one would know of the pretence. Yet that idea was quickly cast aside when one of them stood up to surrender, his hands above his head and terror in his eyes

What was he to do now? If he were to attack them they could quite probably pull him of his mount. Another stood up beside the first man, he too raising his arms skywards. Swiftly coming to a decision, and with a determined voice, he ordered the other two out of the ditch as well and had them stand in line. Four more miserable specimens of rebels he had not seen since those on the riverbank at Bellevue.

In the distance he noted a few insurgents were now being force-marched down the hill, towards the village. The blood-letting had ceased, some prisoners were being taken. Had Rothwell's orders to kill all on the hill been overridden, or were they just *his* orders? If so, and to be seen to be contributing to the mopping up operation, Thomas ordered the men to proceed in front of him towards a rebel collection area in the valley. The men responded grudgingly but obediently; the fight gone out of them. They certainly looked a beaten, sorry sight; dishevelled, bloodstained, broken men. One of his captives looked back at him, his

226

eyes squinting into the sun, a quizzical look on his face. Thomas waved his sword at him, towards where they were going. The young croppy looked vaguely familiar, although they all looked the same in their bedraggled, vanquished state.

As Thomas ushered them through an open gap and into a field, next to the road to the village, he sighted Captain Rothwell and Corporal Brennan gallop down the hill from his right, heading directly for him. His heart jumped and he pulled the reins back to stop his horse. His four prisoners also stopped, fearful that they were going to be run down. Rothwell drew his horse alongside.

'Lieutenant Gettings, I see you have being gathering a crop of these villains,' Rothwell quipped. 'Perchance, are you bringing them for some tea?'

Thomas would not be drawn but replied, making a simple report. 'I apprehended them, sir, up at the edge of the bog. They are being taken to an assembly point I see being formed at the village.'

'And who may I ask, gave you permission to do such a thing? You heard my explicit orders on the hill less than an hour ago, did you not?'

Thomas remained silent but felt the tension building dramatically. Rothwell was turning this into a personal attack on him; seeking a confrontation, some sort of inevitable conflict. Meanwhile, Brennan sat on his horse, behind Rothwell, surveying Thomas' prisoners.

'Gettings, you have been a thorn in my side for some time now.' Rothwell sat tall in the saddle of his black stallion, looking down on Thomas. His words were like vitriol and full of menace. He raised his gloved finger and flared up in anger.

'And the bane of my life since I had you training school in Kells. It was the sorriest day I took you on as a trainee lieutenant. Do you understand my utter contempt for you?'

Thomas kept his back straight, his head up. Full of nervous energy, he awaited with bated breath Rothwell's next move.

'What you are going to do now Gettings, at my command and

without hesitation, is strike these croppies down with your sword, which is what you should have done in the first place.'

Thomas blinked in shock.

'All of them, Gettings.'

'They are surrendered combatants, sir. That will be cold-blooded murder.'

Rothwell was about to remonstrate further, but Brennan had been looking intently at the beleaguered prisoners.

'Captain, sir,' he said, 'may I intervene? If I'm not mistaken, sir, I believe two of these captives before you are the Moore cousins you have been searching for.'

Rothwell open-mouthed stopped and turned to Brennan, speechless, his verbal attack on Thomas interrupted.

'What are you saying Brennan? That these Moore wretches are part of this batch?'

'Yes sir, the nearest two men there.'

Thomas too, glanced at them for a moment and it was then he recognised the dark-haired lad, blood-streaked, his shirt hanging loose over his gaunt body. He was the boy from the stables at Parsonstown, the one he had let escape on condition he returned home. And now here he was, a captive following the battle. He was stunned by his audacity, his recklessness in continuing this mad foray.

Rothwell sauntered over to them and with sword drawn he separated the Moores from the other two.

'What serendipity this is,' Rothwell smiled, gloating, putting his sword beneath the fair-haired one's chin.

'To chastise an altruistic lieutenant is one thing, but to have him haul in these two rascals for my amusement is something else entirely. Out of your boundless mercy for traitors, Gettings, you have unwittingly saved these two for me to punish personally.'

He tipped the sword closer to the lad's throat. 'And your name, for posterity, is…?'

'Laurence Moore.' Rothwell turned to other. 'And you?

'James Moore.'

The lad he had saved turned and looked squarely at Thomas, a hint of fear in his eyes. Yes, but also a degree of determination to try and hide it. The other Moore spat across Rothwell's sword, shouting out words of hatred and revenge at his captors. Rothwell laughed at him then abruptly withdrew his pistol. Brennan did likewise and aimed at the third captive, firing at close range. The man dropped to the ground without a word. He began to reload, leaving the Moores to Rothwell. The cousins closed their eyes, knowing their turn was next.

'Brennan, dispatch the other too; we will save the Moores for last.'

The corporal aimed and fired at the whimpering man, who was already on his knees. The bullet pierced his brain between his eyes and he too fell dead. Rothwell turned to Thomas.

'Before I deal with you, Gettings, I will give *you* the pleasure of putting these two ruffians out of their misery, while I watch on.'

Thomas withdrew his pistol but hesitated, not moving.

'Use your sword, Gettings, dammit. Have I not taught you anything?'

Thomas slowly withdrew his sword, a weapon in each hand now. But he remained still, sweating, tense, his mind racing madly. This is it, he thought. Now is the time to prove your worth as a man; to be rid of your nemesis.

Not four yards from him, Rothwell sensed something in Gettings stillness, as if he was coiling like a spring, ready to strike. Had this weakling lieutenant reached a mental juncture, which he was about to cross?

Beside Rothwell, Brennan suddenly seemed to grow impatient and decided to take matters into his own hands. He aimed and fired his pistol at the Moores, who were standing stock-still in the grass. One fell backward with the impact, gasping in agony.

'You are wasting time, Gettings. See how easy it's done,' Brennan shouted with glee. 'That will be one less Moore to trouble you.'

Rothwell turned to admonish Brennan, but in the same instant

Thomas had had enough and decided to resolve his destiny. He reacted to Brennan's indiscriminate action by swinging his pistol up to fire at Rothwell. But the captain had begun to slide off his stallion and Thomas' shot flew narrowly by his head, the report unnerving the horses. Brennan's horse reared and in that second Gettings shot took him full in the neck, the close proximity of the discharge exploding through his skin, muscles and bone, into his shoulder. Rothwell, half off his horse, turned to look, horrified, as Brennan's body crumpled to the ground, his final momentum pulling his horse down with him.

Thomas dismounted, seeking further advantage.

Rothwell, incensed that he had been taken by surprise, fired his pistol wildly towards the Moore prisoners. The second one was hit, a red hole blossoming immediately on his shirt. He toppled over, close to his cousin.

It was just Gettings and Rothwell now!

Both of them pushed their horses away and began to circle each other, pistols empty and useless, now only swords, both gleaming in the September sun.

'Gettings, I didn't think you had the mettle to challenge me. Yet you have! But I have been waiting for this moment. I am only sorry that I didn't pursue it earlier. It would have put both of us out of our misery - you permanently.'

Thomas flashed his sword across his adversary. Rothwell arched back.

'Let us hope that you trained me well then,' Thomas responded evenly, finding courage from God knows where 'and that I will be an equal match for you.'

Rothwell let fly with a series of thrusts towards Thomas' body. He managed to side-step them, pulling his torso in before forcing Rothwell's sword sideways. They parried back and forth, the clash of steel on steel, resounding sharply across the lower hillside. Despite Thomas' younger age, Rothwell was more skilful and his swordsmanship soon found openings in Thomas' defence. Thomas backed away, seeking space and nearly stumbled over one of the rebel bodies. Rothwell lunged forward, his sword arm fully stretched, swiping a gash across Thomas' sword arm.

'I have you now, you coward, Gettings. I'm just disappointed you didn't make it more of a spectacle.'

Thomas raised his sword in a final desperate parry. Rothwell dropped his shoulder and struck his sword forward again, then twisted and caught Thomas' shoulder with the pommel. They clinched tightly, shoulder to shoulder, sword atop sword, eyes flaring, inches from each other. Rothwell forced Thomas away. He lost his balance and toppled backwards onto the grass, his sword flying from his hand.

Rothwell paused for a second, as if winded, but preparing for the coup de grace. Thomas, injured, saw movement in the grass behind Rothwell. He looked for his sword and stretched for it, futilely.

'Prepare for your maker, Gettings.'

Rothwell raised his sword. Thomas watched him, transfixed. Behind Rothwell a figure rose. It was the young croppy, the one he had allowed escape! What was he doing? Rothwell arched back for the final stroke, Thomas raised his good arm, waiting for the end...

Rothwell suddenly froze. Grunting in agony, he looked down in horror at his stomach. A knife, a long knife had pierced his back and was sticking out through the fabric of his uniform, with blood on it...his blood! He groaned deeply again and dropped his sword. Thomas watched in disbelief as the man who had been about to kill him fell to his knees, grabbing desperately at the weapon in him with his gloved hands. Thomas reached for his sword, but Rothwell rolled over on the ground, slowly dying.

Behind him one of the young, bloodied croppies was standing still, holding the bloodied knife, his eyes wide in shock as he withdrew the scian from the falling captain.

Rothwell turned onto his back, blood seeping copiously from his wound and looked with shock and surprise at this... this boy who had dared to end his life. Thomas, grabbing his sword, came and stood near, remaining vigilant, looking at Rothwell's eyes as they began to glaze over, staring at his antagonist as his life ebbed away.

231

The croppy crouched on the ground, holding his arm, almost indifferent to his decisive, fateful action while Thomas stood trembling above Rothwell, until there was no more life there. His hands were shaking, hardly believing that he had survived, that he was still alive and that he had somehow been rescued from a certain death. He turned to the young lad.

'You saved my life.'

James looked at his bloodied arm, then at Thomas.

'And back in Lobinstown, you saved mine.'

Thomas regarded him with amazement, then simply said, 'Thank you.'

Despite his injury, James wiped his scian on the grass and placed it through his belt before crawling over to his cousin, lying motionless on the ground. He wept quietly for him, looking at his bloodied face, moving it to see if there was life. But there was none. Laurence Moore was dead! Laurence who had survived the fighting at Mountainstown, who had survived the battle here in Longford, was now dead, killed in some quarrel between two redcoat officers. He stayed with him, listless, uncaring. Then Thomas Gettings grabbed his shoulder.

'We must be away from this place, James Moore. There are five men lying dead here. It will become very awkward for you if troops or cavalry come along, wondering what has happened.' James shook his hand away.

'I am not leaving my cousin here. You go.'

Thomas knelt beside them and checked Laurence's cooling body. 'James, he is gone. Brennan's bullet killed him. Save yourself now. You are still alive.'

Still James would not budge. Thomas was loathe to leave him there to his fate, yet he was reluctant to take him away from mourning his kin.

Across the hedge and down on the road, there was increased activity and Thomas saw militiamen enter the field. James heard them too.

'Come with me James, please. You need to be away from here. If you are caught they will surely hang you. I will leave you up in the bog then. They are no longer searching in it. I have some water and some binding for your wound.'

For what seemed an age, James held Laurence's lifeless body, but he eventually let go and stood up. Taking one last long look at his cousin, he followed Thomas over to his horse.

# Chapter Twenty
## Home

He survived in the bog with no food for two whole days following the battle, lying in a cleft between a narrow opening beneath a stone wall and a swathe of furze bush above. He had stumbled across it on the evening after the battle, just as another general sweep of the area for remaining rebels had begun. He was so cold on the first night there, that he scrambled from his lair and, following a brief search, took the clothes from two croppies lying dead in the next field. Those fragments of cotton and wool barely kept him alive as he shivered through the night. And for the entire length of the second day, he lay huddled in his lair as lines of cavalry raced across the hills and bogs around the place of battle, searching for and rooting out anyone that remained. But he survived somehow. In the quietness of the third morning he picked some sorrel leaves he found beside the furze and a few berries from nearby bushes. And when the water in the bottle was gone, he cupped his hand into a trickle of turbid bog water next to where he lay. It barely satisfied his thirst.

The yeo officer had left him at the edge of the bog with a roll of cotton bandage and a canister of water. He examined his arm wound and found it was superficial and he advised him to keep the bandage on it for several days. Little was said between them despite having so recently saved each other's life. He mentioned a lady friend who he would return to; Emma he called her and was considering his future.

'I have survived this episode in one piece and will be able to return to her. I will retire from the yeomanry and make a life with her and for that I will be forever in your debt.'

James shrugged as the officer shook his hand. Then he asked James why he hadn't gone home when he allowed him go in the stables.

'I have no home to go to,' James had said simply and left it at that. And long after the officer bade him farewell and cantered off to report the deaths of Captain Rothwell and Corporal Brennan on the field of battle, those few words reverberated round in James' head when he closed his eyes in the darkness. And they were still there when he opened them in the daylight. 'I have no home to go to.'

By the morning of the third day, the noise of troops and horses and killing had ceased completely and a quiet tranquil silence took its place, as if nature had finally reclaimed its rights to the area. He was so hungry now, he knew he would have to leave his den and seek some sustenance or he would die where he lay. He forced himself to rifle the bodies of his dead comrades in the nearby fields and bogs, and in these squalid moments of self-preservation he searched through their reeking pockets and found some grains of corn and the odd crust of mouldy bread, just enough to keep him alive.

That evening, a shallow moon rose and, with the meagre energy left in his body, he returned to retrieve the body of Laurence. In the moonlight he saw movement in the distance; people were out on the hill, moving bodies for burial. He had vowed to himself that he would try and give Laurence some semblance of burial, but with no implement, save his scian, he instead dragged his remains to the nearest ditch and rolling him gently into the bottom he placed as much earth and leaves and shrubbery as he could, so the wild animals would find it difficult to consume his remains.

The next evening, he had gone foraging in nearby fields and yards and, reluctant and afraid to ask for food, he stole it instead, anything he could find. That night, in the crevice beneath the furze bush, wrapped in the rags from the fallen rebels and his belly less empty, he slept soundly, dead to the world.

And on the morning of the fifth day, bright and clear and cold, with the greatest of good fortune, he found Ginny! He had heard the stifled sounds of a horse somewhere close and decided to follow them. He found her alive but trapped deep in a thorn hedge in the bog, not far from his bolthole. She was bleeding from the dawks in her skin but had just enough energy to reach tufts of grass close by. He trickled water into her mouth from his flask and rubbed her nose, hardly believing she was still alive. He checked her condition and despite the cuts on her skin, it was her front legs caught in a tangle of branches which held her in place.

Keeping her watered and fed without freeing her, he knew was cruel, but she wasn't struggling and he had to determine whether it was safe enough to extract her and move away from this place. Would a young lad on a pony excite much interest? There was only one way to find out. Gathering his bits of clothes and secreting his scian under his shirt and jacket, he eventually dislodged Ginny from her captivity. She walked stiffly but once out in the open and grazing on some rough grass, he decided she was ready to travel. He carefully climbed on her, waited a little for her to get used to his weight then guided her down the hill to the road leading east, away from Ballinamuck.

Coming off the hill he saw some women and children in a nearby field, picking praties and up on the bog behind the hill, trenches were being dug for the mass burials of those recently slain. But he didn't look back for too long; he kept going at a gentle pace, not wishing to exert too much pressure on the pony.

'I have no home,' he confirmed to himself repeatedly on the road south, away from the battle site but not quite as sombrely as when he lay in the ditch. 'What am I to do, what *can* I do?' he asked himself aloud, but the further away he got from Ballinamuck, the more he felt he might live again and the horse and road would bring him somewhere.

*

Three days later, after many wrong turns and lots of forced rests by Ginny, a germ of an idea had come to him. He knew he had been dwelling too much on the past, of the what ifs and buts and whether he should have stayed in Louth and of all the family he had lost, but half way between Ballyjamesduff and Virginia, as he sat on a roadside mearing, chewing a raw pratie, a plan began to formulate in his head.

Excitement began to course through him; he even stood up and did a little dance in the road, with Ginny looking at him curiously.

With spirits soaring, he continued his journey, at a leisurely pace now, stopping to ask for directions every so often. The September weather was mild enough that he lay out under the cloud and stars each night, with Ginny tied to the nearest tree. He lay with his hands behind his head, looking up at the night sky, at the cloud cover shielding most his view of the myriad pinpricks of light. Instead of morose memories of the past, those of his future scuttled through his mind; first one way, then the other, like a cat chasing a mouse. Was he making the right decision? Perhaps he should be more circumspect about what he intended to do. But the next morning, rising from the dewy grass, hungry again - Ginny was eating more than he was - he knew he would follow his dream; that he would not diverge from his initial plan.

He finally reached Killary townland after four days of travelling the back roads and tracks of Cavan and Meath. He had removed the bandage on his arm and let the air at it to heal naturally. The scar from the shot was still raw and his arm ached, but he had had worst injuries. It was early evening and he had arrived at George Geraghty's cabin to give Ginny back to him. He hadn't intended to look for George but as he took the horse round the back of the house, George, carrying a pail of water in his hand, came upon him. He dropped the bucket in surprise, looking first at Laurence and then at his horse, as if both were ghosts. Blessing himself he came to Ginny and rubbed her head.

'Mr Geraghty, I'm sorry we took your horse. Me and Laurence had to get to meet the French army.' George looked at him as if he were mad.

'So, are ye satisfied now, after all yer travellin?'

James shook his head. 'There was a lot of people killed where we were. Poor Laurence is dead. Will ye tell Henry and Kate for me? I can't bring myself to go to them now.'

George could have said something about the taking of his horse but he said nothing instead. He was delighted to have his horse back. He petted her before tying her to a fence post. James prepared to walk

237

away, but George turned back to him.

'You'll have a bite to eat and a sup to drink?'

Hungry and all as he was, he was still more anxious to be on his way, away to his destination. He shook his head, saying thanks. George told him to wait and he came back a minutes later with a small package in his hands.

'Here's a few slices of fresh bread for you.'

James thanked him again and asked could he fill his water flask too. Then he asked after William, George's son, who had been injured when their house was fired.

'Ah, he's still not right and I don't know if he'll ever be. He can hardly life a fork, the poor lad.' He shook his head sadly.

'Where will ye go now, lad,' he asked, 'what with your uncle gone to John Moore's? I'm wonderin' do ye want to stay with us for a night or two?'

James said no to the old man's thoughtful gesture, saying simply, 'I'm going home.'

And as he walked down the road he saw George watch him from the shed door, scratching his head, pondering on what the lad had meant. Was he going to where his uncle was staying? He waved after him.

The roads he walked, he knew reasonably well and again the weather was kind to him. He reckoned there would be only two more nights that he would have to sleep under the stars. On the second day's travels he stayed under cover as a troop of yeomen cavalry cantered down the road he was on. He didn't want to be hauled out of a ditch and he so close to his objective. But all was soon quiet in the neighbourhood again and he was able to be on his way.

As he drew near his journey's end, his stomach began to heave, his mind in turmoil, yet he kept walking all the same. There was no turning back now. He was nearly there.

Down the lane he walked and he soon arrived at the cottage, and he had no words prepared to say. Arriving at the door, there was no one around, but he heard voices from inside, and someone gently humming a tune, a tune he remembered well. Knocking gently on the half-door, he reached for the ring Sylvie Kavanagh had given him. Carefully wrapped in his pocket, he held it tightly as he knocked on the door again. Inside the familiar tune had stopped and there was a hush. He waited nervously, his feelings somewhere between expectation and panic. Then, as if in a dream, she appeared at the door. He had spent days conjuring up this moment, hoping it would be her he would see first. Surprised only for a second, Mollie smiled up at him with those kind dark eyes he loved.

'You're home?' she said.

'I'm home.'

**Events during the 1798 Rebellion relating to this narrative:**

**6th Aug:** Captain Dwyer retreats with his rebel forces from Glenmalure to the Glen of Imaal in Co Wicklow.

**22nd Aug:** A French army under General Jean Humbert lands at Killala, Co Mayo.

**27th Aug:** The Battle of Castlebar. The Loyalist garrison is defeated by Humbert's forces.

**31st Aug:** The Republic of Connaught is established by Humbert.

**4th Sept:** Humbert's French army, supported by Irish rebels, begin their March west from Mayo into Sligo.

**5th Sept:** United Irish forces set up camps at Mullingar (Wilson's Hospital) and Granard in anticipation of the French arrival into the midlands.

**6th Sept:** The rebel forces at Granard are beaten by local yeomanry and militia units.

**7th Sept:** The camp at Wilson's Hospital is attacked and the rebels dispersed by local yeomanry and militia units.
Humbert's forces reach Cloone in south Leitrim.

**8th Sept:** Battle of Ballinamuck. After a brief battle the French forces surrender while the Irish insurgents are slaughtered. The Rebellion, which begun at the end of May is finally extinguished.